KV-105-445

Last Bus to the Grave

NEATH PORT TALBOT

WITHDRAWN
FROM
CIRCULATION

LIBRARIES

By the same author

Nailed
Bullet for an Encore

Last Bus to the Grave

Michael Litchfield

NEATH PORT TALBOT LIBRARIES

NEATH PORT TALBOT

WITHDRAWN
FROM
CIRCULATION

LIBRARIES

HALE
CRIME

ROBERT HALE · LONDON

© Michael Litchfield 2005
First published in Great Britain 2005

ISBN 0 7090 7864 1

Robert Hale Limited
Clerkenwell House
Clerkenwell Green
London EC1R 0HT

The right of Michael Litchfield to be identified as author
of this work has been asserted by him in accordance with the
Copyright, Designs and Patents Act 1988

2 4 6 8 10 9 7 5 3 1

NEATH PORT TALBOT LIBRARIES	
2000481834	
RES	10.09.05
M	£16.99

Typeset in 10/12½pt Palatino
Printed in Great Britain by St Edmundsbury Press,
Bury St Edmunds, Suffolk.
Bound by Woolnough Bookbinding Ltd.

As always, for the three Princes pivotal to my life –
Michele, Luke and Savannah

Also a special thank-you to my editor, Gill Jackson, for her
commitment to detail and accuracy. Her eagle-eye has again
spared me a lot of blushes.

Murder has a habit of changing lives irrevocably. For the victim, it is the end. For many others, it is only the beginning.

That was a thought Michael Sloane shared with Joanne Lowen over a cosy celebration dinner, though not until after the denouement of what had begun so unexpectedly and brutally on a dark, harrowing Saturday night the previous November.

So, back to the beginning.

CHAPTER 1

The sprightly, little old spinster climbed aboard the last bus of the day from Swanage to the historic village of Corfe Castle, where she lived with her two cats and a parrot.

Emily Dresden was a regular passenger on Saturdays on the 11.25 p.m. service from the Swanage bus depot. Known locally as something of a character and eccentric, Emily was a keen bridge player. Most Saturday evenings, from autumn until early summer, she would make the short journey to the unpretentious seaside resort of Swanage to partner her long-time friend, Hugh Carrington, in games at the bridge club. Although she owned a car and was a confident driver, even at night, she always caught the bus on these occasions because she enjoyed a drink – or two – when socializing. That is not to suggest she was a lush. Her liver was as active and efficient as her brain. Two sherries or a couple of gin and tonics were her limit. Nevertheless, she would not venture behind the wheel of her new generation Mini Cooper even after just one sip of alcohol. Self-discipline was her mantra. Her vehicular mobility was more important to her than to most people of her age. Hence, on Saturday evenings during the bridge season, she would keep her shiny black car locked in the garage, while she made the fourteen-mile round trip by public transport.

Hugh habitually met Emily at the Swanage bus depot at seven o'clock and would see her safely on the last bus of the day home, which was an integral segment of their weekly ritual.

As soon as Emily had decided where she would sit, Hugh waved goodbye, mouthing, 'See you next week, same time.' She nodded, not hearing a word but guessing correctly the substance of the valediction.

There were never many passengers on that late-night boneshaker. Occasionally, Emily and the driver would even have it to themselves. On this particular Saturday, 8 November, there were only two other passengers – a young couple, who occupied the wide back bench-seat, which stretched from side to side. They were going all the way. It would take more than a mere bus-stop to convince them that their trip was over.

Emily smiled nostalgically. She had her own memories of back seats. Happy snapshot memories, vividly preserved; not to be confused with hazy, rose-tinted ones. Her brain was half computer and half camera. She never forgot a face or scene, no matter how fleeting the shot. Her mind was a match for any machine,

Emily sat directly behind the driver, who conspicuously adjusted his inside mirror so that he had an unimpeded view of the aisle and the rear of the bus.

'Don't be a spoil-sport,' Emily berated him good-naturedly.

'If there's any hanky-panky on my bus and it gets reported, I'll be the one for the high jump,' the driver retorted humourlessly.

'Who's going to tell? Not me. Not you, for sure. And those love birds aren't likely to be complaining about themselves, now are they?'

'You never know who might hop on at the next stop,' the driver said dourly. 'Could be an inspector or some self-appointed moral guardian. I'm not taking any chances. I intend to keep a beady eye on the action – and my pension.'

'Voyeur!'

'No, wise owl.'

'No such thing. Owls are the dumbest of all birds of prey.'

'You're too clever for your own good, old girl. It'll get you in trouble one day, you see.'

'Less of the *old girl* if you don't mind; you're more Christmas turkey than spring chicken yourself. I'd feel safer if I could be certain you were going to keep your eyes on the undulations ahead instead of the ups and downs behind.'

They knew one another the way commuters become bonded by familiarity through shared journeys over many years.

'Why must women always have the last word?' the driver grumbled rhetorically and only semi-seriously, simultaneously pressing a button to close the doors. The hydraulics hissed, the primitive colony of natives in need of a missionary. 'He's heading by car for your county headquarters at Winfrith.'

'I'll see that the officer in charge of the investigation is on hand here to greet him.'

'I'm obliged. If there should be any obstacles whatever, just contact my private secretary.'

End of conversation.

This was the first murder inquiry Detective Inspector Joanne Lowen had headed. It was already complicated enough without political interference. She had returned to the crime scene when she was given the unwelcome news on her mobile by Frobisher.

'But just who *is* this bloke Sloane?' she demanded, piqued. 'Is he a politician, civil servant, cop, peeping tom, necrophile, or what?'

Frobisher spluttered. 'He's not one of us; that's all I know.' The chief constable was overtly embarrassed by his own ignorance.

'An outsider! Just great! That's all I need! I don't get it. An elderly woman is spiked a hundred and fifty miles from the political centre of gravity, the case is barely two days old, the trail as cold as the corpse, and already we have the big guns from Westminster aimed at us.'

Lowen, a spirited and confident honey-blonde who had been promoted from detective sergeant only a month ago, was not amused. Her irritation was not lost on her chief.

Frobisher quickly tried to assuage her. 'Inspector, no one's on your back, let me assure you of that. You're not being monitored and I won't allow you to be compromised. You must believe that.'

'Then what *is* going on? I mean, Emily Dresden wasn't exactly the Queen or Prime Minister. Nor indeed Madonna. I accept that her violent death is as appalling as anyone else's, but I fail to see the special case.'

'I agree with you. I'm as much in the dark as you are. Play it by ear. Everything should become transparent in the passage of time. Just do your job. Don't allow this shadow Sloane to spook you. Regard him as a fly on the wall.'

'And swat him!'

Frobisher gulped. 'You *are* joking?'

Lowen was known as a joker, but that side of her nature was being rested at that moment. 'Only time will tell.'

Frobisher sensed gathering storm clouds. 'Be patient and diplomatic,' he pleaded. He was asking a lot of a woman renowned for her impetuosity and bluntness. 'Please be back here before one o'clock to meet Sloane.' This was an order, only thinly veiled as a request, and Lowen was left in no doubt that she was faced with a *fait accompli*.

'I'll be there,' she said miserably.

Lowen had a caricature image in her mind of a snooty chauvinist, aged about fifty, with an imperious demeanour; mean-mouthed, tall, lean, balding and conservatively dressed, his voice tortured with mandarin snobbery. Hence her raised eyebrows on meeting Michael Sloane at security in the front lobby.

'Can we get some lunch around here?' said Sloane, without preamble, as they shook hands perfunctorily, his grip pincer-strong.

'There's the canteen ...'

Sloane sniffed reprovingly. 'I was thinking more of a pub; a decent boozer.'

'There's no shortage of those.'

'How about it, then?'

'Fine, shall I drive?'

'That makes sense to me. You get the stress and I'll buy the cure.'

Sloane was not the uppity slime Lowen had been expecting. He had short, tufty brown hair, an almost permanent self-mocking expression, brown eyes that suggested they could forgive almost any transgression and a face hewn over the years by combative living. Instead of the sober uniform of the city, he wore a black leather jacket, matching ankle boots, jeans and an open-neck, pure silk shirt, all covered by a camel-haired overcoat, fastened by a tie-belt around his trim waist; no sign of the almost mandatory paunch that went with fat cats of high office. Rather than being in his fifties, Lowen guessed that Sloane was nearer thirty-five, her age. And instead of towering over Lowen, he was no taller than average male height.

Lowen was immediately seriously concerned that she was in danger of quite liking the mysterious Mr Sloane, who made it necessary for Lowen to further redraw her stereotypical preconception of him when he ordered a pint of draught beer and a cheese and pickle sandwich. She would have wagered a month's salary that he was a gin and tonic tippler, with a lunchtime appetite for something a little more trendy, a quiche even.

'You don't get many country pubs in London,' said Sloane, the mischief in his eyes confirming that the wry humour was intentional, as they settled into an alcove beside a window with a panoramic view of the rolling landscape.

Lowen returned the smile, feeling illogically guilty for having ordered only an orange juice to drink. 'You're not exactly what I anticipated.'

'What *exactly* did you expect?' Sloane spoke with the hint of a regional accent, the provenance of which eluded Lowen.

'I expected a grey suit, at least.'

'Oh, I have one of those, but I try to keep it mothballed as much as possible.'

'I'm glad to hear it.'

Sloane decided there had been enough fencing. He drank half of his beer with one pulsating intake, then said candidly, 'I'm not here to tread on your toes. If I get in your way, I want you to tell me so. However, for me to fulfil my mission, it's essential we rub along without too much friction. There has to be mutual trust. But why *should you* trust me when you haven't a clue what I'm doing here, right?'

'I'd be lying if I denied that such a thought hadn't crossed my mind,' Lowen conceded equally frankly.

Sloane quaffed some more, but ate little. 'The best I can do at the moment is tell you what I'm *not* doing. How does that sound?'

'It sounds promising for a beginning.'

'OK, I'm not spying on you. Until today, I'd never heard of you, and that's not intended as an insult. It wasn't until I was halfway down the motorway that I learned the officer in charge was a Detective Inspector Lowen. You had your expectations; I had mine.'

'And what were yours?'

'A pot-bellied plodder. Male, of course.'

'So we were both wrong.'

'Proving just how dangerous it is to be presumptuous. A lesson for both of us, Inspector.'

'It's Joanne.'

'And I'm Mike by preference. You know who I am, but not *what I am* and that, I'm afraid, is how it's going to have to remain until ... well, perhaps forever. I think the best approach is to think of us as working along parallel lines, with similar goals but a disparate denouement in mind.'

Lowen shrugged and finished her orange juice. 'I'll do my best to make our co-existence amicable.'

Sloane communicated gratitude from eyes that seemed to swallow up everything within their radar-sweeping range. 'How much progress has been made?'

'We're still building a picture.'

'You mean a profile of the victim?'

'More a picture of the circumstances surrounding her death.'

'I know little more than I've read in the newspapers,' Sloane lied glibly, feigning ignorance to build a bridge towards trust. 'The body was found by the church verger, Harold Parkes, I understand?'

'That's what the papers say,' Lowen replied obliquely.

'And you?'

'The Press got something right for once.'

'So there'd been no attempt to hide the body?'

'Apparently not.' Lowen was more accustomed to being the inquisitor than the interviewee, and it showed.

'It was inside the churchyard?'

'Just inside the lych-gate, on the grass, a few feet from the path leading to the church entrance.'

'Was she killed where she was found?'

'No. She was attacked on the pavement outside, nearby.'

'Who says so?'

'Forensics. There was a frost that night. Drag marks were detected, leading to the spot where the body was left. There was also a bloodstain on the pavement.'

'Matching Emily Dresden's blood group?'

'A perfect DNA match.'

'Only one stab wound?'

'Just the one, yes.'

'Time of death?'

'Around midnight. A few minutes before or after.'

'That's an accurate pinpoint. I suppose it was made easy for you by the evidence of Hugh Carrington and the bus driver?'

Lowen's forehead became creased with curiosity.

'Carrington was interviewed on TV and he was asked about seeing Emily on the last bus of the day from Swanage to Corfe Castle.' Sloane addressed the unasked question.

Lowen mentally noted Sloane's sudden use of the victim's first name. Was that a slip? Did it demonstrate familiarity? Had it any significance, or was she being over-imaginative? Lowen filed her queries for future reference.

'We know all about Miss Dresden's Saturday routine. It has been easy to verify her movements during the last hours of her life. There are more than thirty witnesses to her presence at the bridge club where she partnered Mr Carrington. She was seen leaving the club with Mr Carrington, as usual. The bus driver remembers her vividly because they exchanged banter about a pair of young love birds on the back seat. Throughout the whole brief journey there were only three passengers. There are two stops in Corfe. Miss Dresden alighted at the first. The couple remained on the bus. There's nothing to suggest that Miss Dresden had any reason to make a detour. Assuming she headed directly for her cottage, she would have reached the church in five minutes, meaning that she encountered her killer a little before midnight.'

'No one heard the attack?'

'If they did, they haven't yet come forward.'

'What do you know about the old girl?'

'That's a question I could equally put to you.'

'I asked first.'

Lowen smiled whimsically. 'She seems to have been an open book. She lived alone with her pets – Persian cats Mickey and Mouse, and a parrot named Dodo.'

'Obviously she had a sense of humour.'

'So it seems. She was no fool, either.'

'What makes you say that?'

'She played a mean hand of bridge.'

'According to her partner, Mr Carrington?'

'And opponents at the bridge club. We've spoken to quite a few. They're all agreed: she had a sharp brain and a retentive memory. She could recall every card played and in sequence. She didn't like losing and wasn't coy about giving her partner a roasting if she reckoned he'd misread the hands.'

Sloane's antennae pricked up. 'There was overt friction, then, between Emily and Carrington?'

'No more so than between most addicted card players. Bridge buffs are passionate about the game and take it very seriously, but elderly gents don't go around killing their partners every time they lose or get rebuked. Not in these parts, anyhow.'

'Nor in London, I assure you.'

'At least in that respect, then, civilization finally has reached the capital.'

'That sounds like a chip.'

'No, just an observation; smugness if anything,'

'Do you come from around here?' Sloane seized the opportunity to become personal.

'I was born and raised in the country, but not in Dorset. Cities aren't for me. I was sitting on a pony before I could walk. I still ride; I have my own horse. I wouldn't give up that for anything, not even to be the Metropolitan Police Commissioner. I understand the mores of country folk. Poachers, for example, are often good, upright citizens in every other respect; the salt of the earth.'

'So you preside over a poachers' paradise?' Mischief returned to Sloane's dancing eyes.

'Not so.' They sparred, but without barbs. 'My message was that I understood the way of life here. Poachers see a lot. They trespass. They move with stealth. They keep out of sight as much as possible. They are the unseen, but are privy to goings on away from the public eye and on private land. There's not much that they miss. If I nicked all poachers, it would be tantamount to severing a pipeline, a lifeline to law enforcement even. So I turn a blind eye ...'

'And they reward you with information. Symbiosis.'

'Down here we call it horse-trading. City cops have their own network of underworld informers, mostly petty criminals, the urban equivalent of poachers. It's simply a matter of having an affinity with your turf.'

'I sense you're suggesting a city cop wouldn't have a chance here.'

'Absolutely. Not a chance. Are you offended?'

Sloane laughed heartily. 'I'm not falling for that. I've played poker, too, you know. You'll need to be more machiavellian than that if you really do want to trick me into dropping my mask.'

Now Lowen's smile was fuelled by an inner warmth. 'I'll remember that ... and work on it.'

The pub was filling up fast with lunchtime regulars. 'Hi, Cagney,' several of them greeted Lowen, as they threaded their way purposefully to the bar.

'*Cagney*?' Sloane queried inquisitively, head cocked to one side spaniel-like, his forehead furrowed.

'Silly stuff,' said Lowen, coloured by embarrassment. 'Cagney was the platinum blonde in the TV detective series *Cagney and Lacey*. Remember?'

'Of course I do. It's still re-run as matinee viewing.'

'Well, some local wag came up with the nickname for me and it stuck. No use fighting it. No one has a say in what they're called by others. That's the lesson of christening.'

'You're nothing like Cagney.'

'You mean I have more flesh on the bone.'

'I mean you're not a bottle blonde. You're no fake.'

The double entendre was intentional.

For a few seconds their eyes tangoed before Lowen released her hold. 'Anyway, I'm faintly flattered. Cagney always made a collar; always got her man ... or woman.'

'And how does *your* track-record match up?'

'I'm not *that* far behind. How about you?'

Sloane shook his head. 'You just won't give up, will you?'

'A dog with a bone, that's me. Dogged.'

'That sounds to me like a "Beware of the mutt" warning.'

'Believe it.'

Sloane pushed his way to the bar to have their glasses replenished. The natural hiatus was the cue to return to business as soon as Sloane was back at the table.

'What's known about Carrington?'

Thoughtfully Lowen ran a manicured fingernail around the rim of her glass. 'An ex-military type.'

'Army?'

'SAS, according to local rumour. Reached the rank of major,

but has never used his title, apparently, since leaving the service after his twenty-two years.'

'The SAS are born killers,' Sloane remarked absently.

'They're trained to kill in combat; there's a big difference,' Lowen corrected him. 'They have to be as disciplined, if not more so, than the Royal Marines Commandos, though I've no doubt that's something you're already aware of.'

Sloane had no difficulty retaining his inscrutability, despite Lowen's persistent probing.

'According to everyone at the bridge club, he never went into detail about his service days,' Lowen continued, her West Country accent barely noticeable. 'One of the oldest members of the club is a retired colonel and he says Carrington never mentions the missions he went on. They often talk about their army days in general terms and share anecdotes, but there's a line Carrington will never cross.'

Sloane listened intently, engaging with Lowen's eyes, but he did not make notes. 'Is he married?'

'Was. His wife died more than five years ago. He has grown-up children, all living away from home; out of this area. He's certainly not short of money.'

'What makes you say that?'

'Not only does he own a large house overlooking Swanage's seafront, he employs a resident housekeeper. She has her own quarters, comprising two large rooms – one her bedroom – plus a bathroom.'

'How old is she?'

'Oh, late forties, I guess. A smart dame. Well bred, without a doubt.'

'Like your thoroughbred.'

'I can't afford thoroughbreds. My old fella's a low-life hack, but I wouldn't swap him for a champion stallion.' Loyalty figured high on Lowen's priorities.

'We *are* talking horses now?'

Lowen grinned. 'Even though I'm separated from my husband, I would never rubbish him to a virtual stranger as a low-life hack or an old fella.'

Another unasked question had been answered.

'Is it a strictly business arrangement?' Sloane steered the

conversation back on course and Lowen picked up the thread without missing a beat.

'Hard to say. Has it any relevance?'

'That's your call.'

'Exactly.'

Any tension between them now was mostly fabricated and forced.

'What's the housekeeper's name?'

'Faye Mitchison.'

'Is she a bridge player too?'

'Apparently not. If she does play, she doesn't team up at the club with her employer. She cooks, cleans, polishes and is something of a paid companion to Carrington. In return, she's rewarded with a small wage and rent-free accommodation, with full use of the garden and other facilities, such as the garage.'

'Was she employed there while Carrington's wife was alive?'

'I don't think so.'

'So Mitchison was the replacement?'

Lowen's countenance hardened. 'Only as a chattel, as far as we know. Carrington's a pensioner, sixty-eight years old, and he can afford to hire help, so why shouldn't he?'

Sloane held up his hands in mock surrender. 'I'm not making any judgements. I'm seeking nothing more than clarification.'

'I don't see that any of this can have any bearing on Miss Dresden's murder.'

'You're probably right. Just how much is known about Emily?'

'She moved from London about ten years ago. We're still looking for relatives. We haven't had any luck around here.'

'Had she known Carrington before she came down here to live?'

'Not according to Carrington. He says she replied to his advert in the local newspaper for a bridge partner after his wife's death.'

'Does he drive?'

'He has a two-year-old Rover.'

'Did his housekeeper witness his return from the bridge club on Saturday night?'

'She did, because she always makes a hot chocolate drink for him at midnight on Saturdays. Always. Like clockwork. She took him the drink this Saturday after hearing him come in. They talked for ten minutes, mainly about his night at the bridge club, the rotten hands he'd been dealt, and the hard time his partner had given him. She went to bed leaving him reading.' After a pause for brief mental debate with herself, she continued, suddenly more conspiratorial, 'There *is* something I should tell you that you won't have heard on TV or read in the papers.'

Lowen then told him about the lipstick graffiti on Miss Dresden's forehead. *MOTHER WHORE!*

Sloane suppressed his emotions, asking simply, 'What do you make of that?'

'Some of my officers believe it points to a local Satanist or escaped nutter.'

'And you?'

'I was thinking along similar lines, but not any more. If it was as one-dimensional as that, you wouldn't be here, now, would you?'

Sloane had no answer to that.

CHAPTER 3

Lowen explained that she had to return to Corfe Castle that afternoon. Sloane asked if he could tag along. Lowen replied affably that he was 'welcome' – and almost meant it. So they drove directly from the pub to the village that found itself unwittingly, and most certainly regretfully, in a public goldfish-bowl.

During the drive, Sloane questioned Lowen further about the dead woman's home and her circumstances.

'To be truthful, so far we've been focusing much more on the crime scene than the cottage,' said Lowen, not for a second taking her iridescent eyes off the sinuous road.

Her oval, friendly face – a disarming weapon when interrogating a suspect – was tense with concentration as a swirling sea-mist, as blinding as a desert sandstorm, blew inland from the coast, reducing the temperature by several degrees in a matter of minutes and visibility to no more than fifty yards. Instinctively, Lowen's left hand reached down to the heater to trigger the booster so that more warmth was quickly circulating. Simultaneously, she shuddered, as if to highlight the need for the action she had taken. Despite the damp, bone-penetrating cold, her cheeks remained roseate. Her shoulder-length hair was allowed to go whichever way the wind gusted. As ever, she had used make-up sparingly, but to maximum advantage, accentuating through understatement her outdoor mien. Blood-red lipstick, although discreetly applied, was her badge of honour, advertising generosity of spirit. Whenever her lips parted, Sloane caught sight of teeth worthy of any toothpaste commercial. Her navy-blue trouser-suit somehow underscored how elegant, yet at the same time carefree, she would look astride her hack. Despite an innate inner purity that flowered from deep within her psyche,

Sloane sensed that Lowen's public persona had been assiduously groomed, the way she nursed her horse, and, beneath the surface, decorous and decadent influences tussled for dominance, possibly in equal measure.

'I doubt that there'll be much of interest for us that comes from the cottage,' she continued flatly.

'What makes you say that?'

'Well, for a start, the door keys weren't stolen; they hadn't been removed from her handbag. I know I'm repeating myself, but it's important: she had money, credit cards and car keys on her, none of which was thieved, even though her handbag was open.'

'Any evidence of the killer having rifled through it?'

'No. There was an impression of the contents not having been disturbed. Her door keys were on top of everything. My guess is that she opened her handbag herself and was fishing for her keys when she was attacked. After all, she was very nearly home. It's something we all do automatically as we approach our car or house.'

'Where was the handbag in relation to the body?'

'Beside it.'

'So the killer retrieved the handbag from the pavement? I'm assuming it dropped from her hand when she was stabbed?'

'That's our interpretation of the sequence of events. I've already ruled out robbery as a motive; it just doesn't stand up to the litmus test of logic. She had almost a hundred pounds in cash on her. If the killer knew where she lived, he could have taken the door keys and enjoyed a free run of the cottage.'

'How do you know the keys weren't taken and then returned to the handbag after the killer was finished in the cottage?'

'You have only to step inside the place to know, beyond all doubt, that no burglar has visited. Burglars work fast and inconsiderately.'

'That's because they're afraid of being rumbled, which didn't apply in this case,' Sloane continued to play devil's advocate. 'This one would have known that the owner wouldn't be returning – ever.'

'True,' Lowen conceded reluctantly. 'Even so, burglars don't like hanging about. They're easily spooked. They ransack places. Then run. They don't empty drawers and cupboards, then put back unwanted items the way they find them. In this case, we're talking about someone who'd just committed murder. In those circumstances, he would have wanted to distance himself from the crime as quickly as possible. It's human nature; the instinct of survival. He couldn't be one hundred per cent certain that he hadn't been observed, resulting in the police being alerted.'

Sloane could not argue with Lowen's reasoning and said as much, then changed tack.

'Did the overnight frost help forensics?'

'By the time the scene of crime team arrived, the pavement and gravel path to the church, through the graveyard, were patch-works of footprints. A whole early-morning congregation had planted their hoofs on top of one another along the same strip of path and pavement as used by the killer, whose prints would have been smudged or obliterated completely by the stampeding church-goers. So, the answer to your question is no, the frost didn't work in our favour.'

'What's known about the weapon?'

'Dagger-type implement. Six-inch-long blade, thin, double cutting-edge.'

'Still missing?'

'Still missing. Two hundred officers are currently combing the area, inch by inch, for the knife.'

'Emily hadn't reported being followed, harassed or threatened in the weeks prior to her murder?'

'If she had, she didn't make a complaint to the police. Neither did she mention anything of that sort to Mr Carrington. If she had been troubled by anything of that nature, it seems certain that she would have told him.'

'No leads from village residents? No other scary incidents in recent weeks?'

'Nothing – so far.'

'Are the scientists working on the lipstick-writing on Emily's face?'

'For what it's worth, yes, but I'm not holding my breath. Miss Dresden never wore lipstick, according to neighbours and Mr Carrington. No lipstick was found in her bedroom, bathroom or handbag.'

'So the killer brought it with him.'

'It would appear that way.'

'A rather deliberate, premeditated act, wouldn't you say? Not consistent with a random killing by someone deranged and psychotic.'

Lowen withdrew into reverie. When she resurfaced, her voice was laced with irritation, as if she resented being tested by an outside dilettante. 'There's something in what you say, but I don't think it's conclusive. The killer could have some kind of hang-up, some kink, and he went out with the lipstick, intending to slay anyone fitting the vignette in his addled head. *MOTHER WHORE* makes me think we could be getting into Freudian, back-to-the-womb territory. Maybe the target had to be an elderly woman, around the same age as the killer's mother. At the moment it's all uncrystallized, but I'm hoping a definite shape to the investigation will emerge in the next few hours.'

'Have you brought in a profiler yet?'

Lower shook her head in slow motion.

'Why not?' It was a genuine enquiry, without a hint of criticism.

'Because it's too early. I've already got enough people guessing.'

'Such as me?'

'Yeah, such as you!' Lowen managed a smile, about as insipid as a winter's sunrise.

'Nothing unusual about the lipstick itself?'

'Nothing, except for what it was used for. It was the most common colour – vivid red. Could be the product of any cosmetic company; there's no special distinguishing feature that's obvious. I can't see how identifying the maker would help to give us a fix on the killer.'

The castle was suddenly silhouetted ahead of them, straddling the serrated horizon with menacing symbolism, as if, like a Herculean monster out of ancient mythology, it had just loped from behind hill and headland to block the way ahead. The night-sky awning was already being unfurled above them. Daylight was dying prematurely from sickly anaemia. Shadows had come out to play trick or treat. Lights were popping on across the forest and meadow landscape like enlarged glow-worms. Sloane sank into his seat, a reflex retreat from the engulfing cheerlessness.

In the village, people were huddled in animated little groups on corners and in shop doorways. Clearly there was still only one topic dominating every conversation. Scene of crime officers were toiling in the graveyard under arc lights, many of which had been erected in trees. Yellow tape had been used to rope-off a stretch of the pavement, the epicentre of which represented the spot where, apparently, the attack had occurred.

Lowen drove on another fifty yards or so and pulled up sharply outside a detached, whitewashed thatched cottage – *Rainbow's End*. Some epitaph!

A uniformed woman police officer was posted on the pavement outside the green swing-gate that opened the way to a path of concrete slabs in a sloping descent to the front door.

'I assume, from your questions, you'd like to poke around,' said Lowen unenthusiastically, not waiting for an answer.

The female sentinel switched on a smile of recognition as Lowen prised herself from the driver's seat of her unmarked car. The smile was turned off just as mechanically the moment Lowen, followed by Sloane, had passed into the cottage.

'Mind your head,' Lowen warned, as she stumbled over the low threshold. All lights were burning and a forensic detective, proffering two pairs of surgical gloves, approached from the foot of a spiral timber staircase.

'Put on these before you touch anything,' he said unequivocally. 'We've only been here half an hour. I don't reckon there's anything for us. No sign of a break-in. The whole place has the appearance and feel of normality.'

'I'm sure you're right and it's just the way she left it on Saturday evening,' Lowen agreed affably. 'We'll just have a little sniff around. We might come across correspondence from relatives, giving us a name to contact ... or possibly some written evidence that she was caught up in a long-running feud with someone locally.'

'Like a quarrel with a neighbour over the height of a hedge?' the detective from forensics ventured.

'Something like that,' Lowen humoured him. 'If we're going to be in your way, just say so and we'll wait until you've finished.'

'It's all yours, Inspector. I'll hang around just in case you come across anything you want us to examine. There's only two of us here and we're both itching for a smoke. We'll step outside for a drag.'

Sloane heard creaking footsteps overhead from an attic which he was later to discover had been converted into an office/study.

The front door led straight into the sitting-room, where there were sturdy oak beams, a sagging ceiling and an open fireplace in which a modern electric fire, incorporating mock logs and a South Pacific sunset glow, had been installed. The furniture – armchairs and a sofa – were chintzy; old but well preserved. All the windows had been double-glazed, yet another concession to the march of progress, while an old-fashioned TV set had been abandoned in a corner to gather dust. The armchairs and sofa encircled the stone fireplace. A dining-table dominated the window area of the sitting-room, the bulging walls of which were graced with framed prints of the castle and Jurassic coast-line. A pendulum clock ticked away noisily on the stone mantelpiece, showing the correct time. At the base of one armchair was a low coffee-table, bearing a collection of maga-zines and two newspapers that had been tossed haphazardly. Included were the current issues of *Newsweek*, *The Spectator* and the *New Statesman*. The two newspapers were last Saturday's issues of *The Times* and the *Daily Telegraph*. The autumn-coloured carpet was worn thin in parts, but was not threadbare. Dust hung in the air like pollen.

The kitchen and bathroom, both modernized, yielded nothing, so they moved to Miss Dresden's bedroom, which was at the rear.

The brass-framed bed had been made and was covered by a rose-patterned duvet. The white furniture and pastel décor was designed to compensate for the limited natural light from an undersized window. There were no immediate surprises in the wardrobe and drawers, which were full of the kind of clothes one might expect to find in the home of a pensioner spinster. On a bedside table, and next to a reading-lamp and a collection of John Le Carré paperback spy novels, was a black-and-white framed portrait photograph of a handsome man.

'Mind if I take it from the frame?' Sloane asked out of protocol, rather than in deference.

'Be my guest,' said Lowen, not feeling that Sloane's initiative in such a trivial matter threatened to usurp her authority.

The name Ernst Lergen was written in a right-slanting signature on the back of the print and dated 1970. Above the name and date was the sentiment, *All my love*, followed by three kisses.

'The love of her life,' Sloane surmised poignantly. And then, turning to Lowen, who was peering over his shoulder, 'How old would you say he was when this was taken?'

Lowen took hold of the print, while Sloane retained the frame. 'About thirty. It's not easy to estimate because his old-fashioned hairstyle, with the trench-like parting low down on the left side, probably matures him beyond his years.'

'Still, I reckon thirty is about right. That would make him sixty-three, Emily's age.'

'If he's still alive.'

Sloane handed the frame to Lowen, who took possession of it, along with the photograph, unsure of their significance to the investigation.

'Perhaps we'll come across some correspondence – love letters from her youth, that sort of thing – that might shed more light on the old flame,' Sloane said optimistically.

'Well, there's nothing in here and I'd have thought the bedroom was favourite for romantic trophies,' opined Lowen.

'Perhaps not when you reach Emily's age; a photo, yes, but love letters might well have gone into cold storage years ago.'

'*Cold storage?*'

'How about a basement or attic?'

'There's no basement, but the attic served as an office, so shall we ferret up there?' Lowen said rhetorically.

As they prepared to leave the one and only bedroom, situated on the ground floor, they heard the forensic detectives departing through the front door.

The attic-office comprised a Dell PC, printer, metallic filing cabinets, swivel computer-chair and a diminutive window. High-wattage spotlights had been fitted into the low, pine-panelled ceiling in shell-like sockets. The lights were operated from a dimmer wall-switch just inside the door, while a string-switch was suspended from the ceiling.

Sloane tried to open the filing cabinets, but they were locked. Lowen produced a bunch of keys. 'These were in Miss Dresden's handbag,' she explained. 'One is for the front door. Three of them fit the car – ignition, boot and petrol-cap. There are two more, one of which looks as if it might be for these cabinets.'

'Let's see, shall we?'

'Bingo!' Lowen exclaimed, as the key turned in the central locking system, releasing all the drawers.

The top drawer was filled with three high-tech cameras, plus long-range telescopic lenses and unloaded film in boxes. The second drawer was the refuge for two powerful pairs of binoculars – one bulky and the other the size of opera glasses.

'Either she was a bird-watcher or Peeping Tom,' suggested Lowen, not bothering to remove the binoculars, but instead hastily going to the next drawer, working her way downwards methodically. Now came paperwork; buff folders containing bank statements, copies of accounts submitted to the Inland Revenue, and then a bundle of coloured photographic prints of people, all of whom had clearly been shot from a distance with telescopic equipment. It was also obvious that none of the subjects was aware that they were being photographed. Mostly the subjects were men, though not all. Some were entering buildings or emerging from them. Others were behind the wheel of vehicles. A few were in shopping malls. Their ages spanned the whole gamut, from early twenties to late seventies. Ethnic minorities were included. None of the photographs was identified by name. Instead, on the back of each print, pencilled in capital letters, were identification codes, such as, *Job Lot 14J* and *Job Lot 6A*.

'What do you make of these?' Lowen wondered aloud, face arranged in puzzlement, as she shuffled the pack of pictures, like fanning a hand of playing cards.

'Perhaps she was into blackmail,' murmured Sloane.

'Are you being serious?' Lowen looked into his playful eyes.

'No.'

Sloane began scrutinizing the bank statements and accounts. 'Every month there was a direct transfer of the same amount – two thousand, six hundred pounds – into her current account.'

'Suggesting she was in salaried employment,' remarked Lowen.

'No doubt about it.'

'But what *kind* of employment?' Lowen was not soliciting speculation from Sloane. 'The bank and Inland Revenue should be able to solve that riddle. Who would have thought it?'

'What?'

'That this little old lady was running some kind of lucrative cottage industry from her sleepy rustic nest.'

'Carrington might be able to help you on that score.'

'That's a point. When I interviewed him, I didn't think to ask him about Miss Dresden's career history. It didn't seem important. Whatever she'd done for a living, I assumed she was retired and living off a pension. Maybe all this is still unconnected with her death.' She gesticulated with both arms in bewilderment. 'On the other hand ...'

'It's all very intriguing,' Sloane cut in.

'You can say that again!'

'One more drawer in the filing cabinet,' said Sloane. 'We might as well complete the grand tour.'

Lowen knelt to open the bottom drawer and her awestruck eyes immediately hooked on to the only two entombed items – a .38 revolver and a carton of cartridges.

'Some sweet old-fashioned dame, indeed!' Lowen whistled.

CHAPTER 4

The Smuggler's Inn, where Sloane had booked a sea-facing room, occupied a prime location on the cliffs at Lulworth Cove. In the seventeenth and eighteenth centuries, the inn had been a favourite haunt of cut-throat pirates, who landed their bounty by moonlight on the shingle in the sheltered cove below. The bawdy romance of buccaneers was perpetuated in the preserved architecture and artefacts, the swashbuckling art on the walls and, certainly not least, the roistering tales, most of them unashamedly apocryphal, recounted by the loquacious local fabulists.

Lowen had agreed to dine with Sloane at the inn, though she doubted that she would be there 'much before nine'. While waiting beside a crackling log fire, Sloane nursed a pint of *real* ale – the colour of gravy and almost as thick – and flicked through glossy brochures that beefed-up the tourist hot spots of the region, including a potted history of Corfe Castle, which, despite its modern image of tranquillity, was no stranger to violence. The Saxon boy-king Edward the Martyr was murdered there by his stepmother in 978, according to macabre legend.

Lowen finally showed at nearer 9.30 than 9.00, blowing in like a squall from the choppy ocean, all wet and windswept. She had replaced her trouser-suit with jeans and a jumper, but looked no less smart. Her hair had been tangled by the wind, enhancing the casual, unsophisticated image that suited her so well. She shook the hair and sea-spray from her eyes as she flopped into a chair next to Sloane beside the fire, simultaneously tossing her overcoat carelessly across the tacky table, almost dislodging Sloane's pint of ale. Her face was etched with the strain of a long, bad day.

'I nearly didn't come,' she admitted with ambivalence. 'I tried to connect with you on your mobile, but there was no network ... never is in this godforsaken neck of the woods.'

'Isn't that part of the attraction of bucolic life?' Sloane tested her.

'There's a difference between living in the country and being completely out of touch. I even had to leave my car half a mile away and leg it the rest of the way because vehicles aren't allowed down the only road to this place.'

'Surely police officers investigating a murder aren't bound by bylaws.'

'At this moment, I'm socializing, allegedly.' She turned a simple statement of fact into an insult, without offending.

'You're too honest.'

'It goes with the job. Well, that's what I believe.'

'God bless the incorruptibles! What do you want to drink? Communion wine? The blood of Christ?'

'I'll make do with cider,' said Lowen, unshocked. 'A pint. The strong stuff. Scrumpy. Not the baby's milk they sell for cider in the city.'

'Your complex is showing to the point of indecency.'

Lowen continued to complain when Sloane returned from the bar. 'Not only did I have a half-mile hike, but I then had to climb Everest.'

'Hence the sermon on the mount!'

Lowen pretended not to hear. 'A thick fog is closing in. I can see myself being stranded here for the night.'

'There are worse places to be marooned.'

'What the hell made you choose here to stay?'

'It was recommended to me for its escapist charm.'

'This is exile, not escapism.'

'You could always have called me on a land-line to cry off. This is your world, not mine, that you're rubbishing.'

'I needed to see you,' Lowen said, coming off the boil, though unhappy by such an admission. 'Miss Dresden didn't have a licence for her gun. What was she up to? Why *are you* here? I'm not happy with this situation.'

'What *situation*?'

'Your role. The whole thing stinks. It's obvious now there's much more to this than we originally thought. I had strong reservations at the outset about this arrangement.'

'What *arrangement?*'

'Don't piss me about, Mike. You know exactly what I'm talking about. You know far more about what's going on here than I do, but you're not sharing, and that's intolerable.'

Sloane finished his drink, then wiped away the alcoholic spume from his lips. Positions reversed, he would have been equally brassed off, probably more so. 'I'm working within tight parameters, Joanne,' he said, almost apologetically.

'All of which leaves me wearing blinkers,' said Lowen, relying on an equine analogy to articulate her frustration. 'I'm not going to stand for all this shit. I'm going to make a fuss, starting first thing tomorrow. I shall demand that the chief constable takes me off the case. I'll go public. The Press will want to know what the hell's happening and I'll give them plenty of column inches.'

'That would be tantamount to writing your own professional obituary.'

'So be it. Suicide suits me. It's uncompromising. But I'll take you down with me, I swear – and whatever you're up to.'

'I didn't realize this was personal.'

'It's personal to me. It's personal that I'm being prevented from doing my job.'

'How have I hindered you?' Sloane pressed, pained.

Sidestepping the question, Lowen said, 'Nothing that we uncovered at Rainbow's End cottage surprised you, did it?'

Sloane gave this some eyeball-rolling consideration before replying candidly, 'I suppose not.'

'Not even the gun?'

'Pass.'

'You really are high-fibre shit! Emily Dresden was well known to you, wasn't she? Every time you've mentioned her by name you've referred to her as Emily. Clearly you're *au fait* with things that might boost our chances of nailing her killer. By withholding that information, you're jeopardizing the investigation. That's a point I intend pressing.'

Sloane leaned forward, big-cat fashion, squaring up, unprepared to concede territory but not ready for a showdown, their heads so close that they were inhaling each other's breath. 'It's not my choice that I'm being so secretive.'

'That's not the issue. The reason for your *modus operandi* is immaterial. What counts is the consequence, nothing else.'

'I'm not here to sidetrack you.'

'So you keep saying, *ad nauseam*, but your actions don't match your words.'

Sloane flipped a mental coin, which came down in favour of his taking a calculated gamble with Lowen. 'You're right that Emily Dresden is no stranger to me. She was born in Voss, Norway on 12 May, 1940.'

'Emily Dresden doesn't sound very Norwegian,' Lowen commented sceptically. 'What's the explanation? Were her parents British?'

'Her mother's name was Leila Muller. Emily was originally given the name Yvette. During her early childhood, she was known as Yvette Muller, the name on her birth certificate.'

'What's the family history?'

'Leila Muller was quite a girl.'

'Translate.'

'She got around, as in being socially mobile.'

'*As in being* promiscuous? Is that the word you're looking for?'

Sloane studied Lowen intensely for a full minute, as if conducting some form of clinical evaluation, before replying tentatively, 'You have to consider Leila Muller within context, within her time-capsule and historical footage. She was a ripe teenager during a world war, an *ingénue* growing up in an occupied country. There was a shortage of Norwegian boys her age. There was a shortage of everything, especially food and clothes.'

'Is this an apology for those who fraternized with the enemy?'

'Retrospective judgements are dangerous, that's all I'm saying.'

'It's not Sunday, so spare me the homily.'

'OK, have it your way, Leila Muller was a good-time girl.'

'*My way*, Mike, is to classify her a slag. Now, what's known of Miss Dresden's father? You haven't mentioned him. And please save me from any more social sanitization.'

'Nothing.'

'*Nothing*!' Lowen intoned derisively. 'You mean her dad was an unknown warrior? Or should I say wanderer?'

'He was undoubtedly a German soldier.'

'A Nazi?'

'Well, he would certainly have been serving in Hitler's army. Make of that what you will.'

'Nazi will do for me. Why are you being so picky? Country folk like me don't mince our words. If it's a spade, let's call it one and not try to pretend it's a silver spoon.'

'I'll remember that, but I'm trying to avoid being emotive and prejudiced.'

'Well, don't, city softie! I'm a big girl. I'll do my own editing, thank you.'

Normally, Sloane would have admired a combative woman, but now he was irked because Lowen was making life difficult for him.

'So Yvette Muller, the late Emily Dresden, was conceived out of wedlock by this Nazi toy-girl,' Lowen continued contemptuously. 'Did Leila Muller ever marry?'

'Apparently not.' Sloane was subdued.

'How did she survive; live? Did she have a proper job, or did she rely on the protection of the Nazi umbrella?'

'She was well looked after until the collapse of the Third Reich.'

'She was a kept woman until then?'

'I doubt that she was ever a one-man woman. As far as I know, she was never anyone's mistress.'

'She played the field?'

'That's one way of putting it.'

'Can you do better?'

'Not at such short notice.'

'OK, she was a common whore?'

'We're not going to quarrel over that.'

'So how does Yvette Muller, the bastard daughter of a Norwegian prostitute and an unknown Nazi soldier, end up an archetypal English spinster – apart from the .36 revolver – in a sleepy village with the name Emily Dresden? Have I missed something, such as some amazing feat of genealogical alchemy?'

Sloane leaned towards Lowen again, his elbows dented by the patinated table and his fingers steepled under his pugnacious chin. When he spoke it was in a conspiratorial cadence, with complementary body language. 'After the end of the

Second World War, Leila Muller lived in penury for many months.'

'Comeuppance. Served her right. Good.'

'Not good for her child. Leila was disowned by her parents.'

'Good for them!'

'But, once again, not good for the kid. Where's your heart?'

'Where it should be, so it doesn't impede my brain.'

Sloane gave his head an exasperated shake, releasing some of the frustration knotting his muscles. 'Leila worked the streets. It was the only way she knew of putting food on the table and clothes on their backs.'

'You make it sound as if she should have been canonized.'

'As I said before, there's no mileage in being judgemental.'

'Maybe that's not your call.'

'Nor yours.'

'*Touché*! What became of the child all that time?'

'She was neglected, inevitably. She was left unattended, locked in her bedroom for hours on end, while her mother plied her trade.'

'How do you know all this?'

'It's documented.' Once again fancy mental footwork was called for.

'Where?'

'In files.'

'What files?'

'Confidential archives.'

'How do I access them?'

'You don't.'

Lowen's friendly features faded. 'There must be public records.'

'Scant.'

'So where *does* your information come from?'

'The confidential source I've been talking about.'

'Which you're denying to me?'

'*I'm* not denying you anything.'

'But I have to rely on you as my conduit?'

'Is that a problem?'

'The problem is you're an unknown quantity, so how can I judge the nutritional value of the drip-feed?'

'Talk with your chief constable. Look, I'm doing my best to lay markers. Do you want me to continue with the narrative?'

Lowen was not by nature a shrew, but now she gave a classic imitation of one. 'You might as well,' she said churlishly.

'A British Army captain by the name of Horace Dresden was in Voss two years after the end of the war. He was a historian by profession, specializing in the medieval period; that part's irrelevant, but it gives you a bit of flavour. He was a military conscript and had been posted to Norway to compile an historical record of the Nazi occupation of that country for the British Government. His wife, Karen, an officer in the Women's Royal Air Corps, was also stationed in Voss, so they could be together. It was there that they heard all about Norway's *whore children* and the scandal of the way they were treated.'

'*Whore children*?' Lowen's voice and eyes melted marginally.

'Between ten and twenty thousand children were born to Norwegian women during the Second World War with Nazi soldiers the fathers. After the liberation, many of the women were beaten or stoned. They were permanently ostracized. Most parents were afraid to offer their wayward daughters support or shelter for fear of uncompromising retribution. Those who did and defied the mob were made an example of; some of the revenge was unspeakable. There were countless cases of houses being torched during the night. Graffiti, such as *Whore Lover*, would be daubed on properties where these single mothers were being harboured. This wasn't something that went away with the passage of time. Many of the children were singled out for persecution well into adult life. Yvette was regularly spat upon in the street, by adults as well as by other children. She was bullied at school, where the staff did little – or nothing – to save her. Eventually, she was too scared to attend school, which angered her mother even more.'

'Because it cramped her style?'

'Exactly.'

'Tell me more about the Dresdens.'

'Well, they were so moved by what they saw that they decided to try to adopt one of those tormented children. The military authorities did all they could to deter them, assuming the Dresdens' intention was nothing more than a token gesture.'

'They were probably right.'

'I disagree and I'll rely on analogy for justification. Police officers, such as yourself, will often argue that a certain measure is justified if it saves just one life. That was the Dresdens' line.'

'And it prevailed?'

'Not straight away, but they persisted.'

'But how did Yvette, Emily, get on the adoption market?'

'She never did, officially. Horace Dresden read in the local daily newspaper about Leila Muller being arrested and charged with trying to blackmail a city councillor, who was being granted anonymity by the courts. Leila was released on bail, but it was evident that if she was convicted, she would go to prison for a substantial stretch. The newspaper did not miss the opportunity to highlight the fact that Leila had a daughter by a Nazi officer, who, presumably, was then back in Germany, if he'd survived. This was a none-too-subtle way of loading the case against Leila, whose address was also published, further jeopardizing her safety. Horace and Karen made up their minds to visit Leila, which they did. Leila jumped at the proposition. Getting rid of her daughter would give her a return to the freedom she resented having lost. Of course, she demanded money.'

'Did the Dresdens cough up?'

'Not officially. Whether anything was paid under the counter, who can say.'

'Was it really possible for a foreign couple to arrange an adoption so easily?'

'I'm not sure how easy it was. You have to remember, however, that Norway, like the rest of Europe, was desperately rebuilding her economy. Britain was her great friend and liberator. And the "whore children" were a great embarrassment. So "good riddance to rubbish!" was the philosophy of officialdom to anyone wishing to take any of these children off their hands. Most resistance came from the British military authorities. But they relented, eventually. Horace had quite a pull because of his job. He was more academic and political than soldier. He had clout where it mattered most.'

'When did they return home with their adopted daughter?'

'The end of the 1940s.'

'When the child would have been what? Nine? Ten?'

'Thereabouts. She could already speak fluent English, like most Norwegians. So she had no difficulty blending into English school life and socializing easily with her peers.'

'Were the Dresdens still in the forces?'

'No, they were discharged shortly after being repatriated. Horace became a lecturer in History at Oxford University, while Karen conformed with the mores of the times, busying herself as a full-time mother and housewife. Two years after they adopted, Karen gave birth to a son, Adrian.'

'At what point did they change the name of their adopted daughter?'

'From Muller to Dresden, immediately.'

'How about from Yvette to Emily?'

'Never. That was their daughter's unilateral decision much later, when she was twenty-one. Emily seemed a quintessential English name to her. She loved this country. It was her way of completing the bonding. Yvette was her last reminder of her miserable past, her anguished heritage, which she was eager to jettison. Becoming Emily was her final act of freeing herself from a lurid legacy that had overshadowed so much of her early life.'

'How would she have known about the reality of her roots?'

'Her parents were very honest folk. When she began asking questions, they gave it to her straight.'

'The *whole* truth?'

'More or less; abridged slightly but not distorted. They treated her like an adult from a very early age. Consequently, she responded in grown-up fashion. Her maturity was one of her striking features as a teenager, from all accounts.'

'Not something to which you can testify from personal experience?' Now Lowen was once again searching for more of an insight into Sloane than into the murder victim.

Sloane eschewed flippancy this time. 'I'm being as open with you as I dare. In fact, I'm probably exceeding my authority. Nevertheless, it's not part of my brief to assist a murderer to escape detection. In view of Emily's history and an extraordinary dimension to her death – the lipstick inscription – a connection between the two cannot be excluded, you may well think.'

'I would put it stronger than that, though the slogan, *MOTHER*

WHORE!, baffles me, even given the circumstances of her birth and early years. She never married, did she?'

'Not to my knowledge.'

'Never had children?'

'Once more, not to my knowledge.'

'So *MOTHER WHORE!* doesn't make sense.'

'Most likely it's an allusion to Leila. Slogans cannot tell the whole story. Also, the killer clearly intended for an air of mystery to prevail. It's a riddle.'

'For me to solve?'

'Could be.'

'You mean this is a game for someone?'

'Or a message to the world; or even some form of catharsis or exorcism.'

'You knew from the outset that this wasn't a random hit, didn't you?' Lowen sought to compromise Sloane.

'We had our suspicions,' he confessed guiltlessly. 'We had to find out.'

'*We*?'

'Yes, *we*. I shall feed you as much as I can; as and when it's feasible.'

They had both forgotten about eating. Their hunger now was for something far more sustaining than food.

'Did Emily grow up in Oxford, where you say Horace Dresden lectured?'

'To begin with. They owned a house in the country a few miles north of the city, but within sight of the dreaming spires. Emily went to the village school. Later, they uprooted to London. Horace was commissioned to do more work for the government. He was also by then lecturing at the University of London. Their home was in Islington, long before it became fashionable. It was a Victorian, terraced property; quite large but without a garden and only a city sprawl for a view. Very different from their lifestyle in Oxfordshire. Both children were sent to the same private school.'

'As boarders?'

'No, day pupils.'

'How did they get on?'

'Famously, it would seem.'

'Neither child was treated differently from the other?'

'Karen and Horace Dresden weren't the kind of parents to show favouritism to their biological child. They would have resisted any temptation to dispense preferential treatment.'

'Might not Adrian have resented mere equality?'

'You mean he might have expected to be the favoured one?'

'It's possible, isn't it? You've already said that the Dresdens were frank with Emily about her provenance. It follows they must have been equally frank with Adrian. He had their blood: Emily didn't.'

Sloane ruminated over this like a court judge being asked for a legal ruling by opposing lawyers. 'I'm afraid I can't shed much light on Adrian,' he said finally. 'Shortly after changing her forename, Emily joined the Women's Royal Air Corps, following in her mother's footsteps. Throughout her life, from a teenager, she *adopted* Karen as her *real* mother. Leila was expunged. After being embraced into the Dresden family, she had a wonderful childhood. I can't imagine there was any friction between Emily and Adrian. Karen had been a radio operator in the Air Force during – and after – the war.'

'And Emily?'

'The same. She served only seven years though, after which she became a civilian air-traffic controller, based in the London area.'

'And what became of Horace and Karen?'

'They died in a road accident when Emily was thirty.'

'So who picked up the inheritance? Adrian or Emily? Or was it shared equally?'

Sloane's smile was powered by admiration. 'Good question. I see where you're heading. Unfortunately, I can't provide an answer. I don't even know if there was a will, though I imagine there would have been. Horace, in particular, was very punctilious in everything he undertook. Even with a will ... well, yes, I can see circumstances in which there could have been bad blood between Emily and Adrian.'

'Everything might have gone to Emily in an act of positive discrimination, compensation for her pitiful early years,' Lowen speculated. 'That could have inflamed jealousy in Adrian, especially if he was experiencing hardship by then.'

'I doubt very much that Adrian would have been excluded completely, but it's conceivable he might have felt cheated. However, that was long, long ago.'

'Time doesn't always facilitate healing. It can fan the flames if there's already something smouldering inside someone's soul.'

Sloane had to acknowledge that Lowen had a point. She was no country duffer, he had decided within minutes of their initial meeting. 'The family must have had a solicitor,' he articulated his thoughts.

'But you don't know who that was?'

'I haven't a clue ... and that's the truth.' Something made him underscore the fact that he was not holding back on anything. A guilt-complex was a new experience and it did not sit easily with him.

Lowen's face suggested that the jury was still out on the question of Sloane's credibility. 'I need to locate Miss Dresden's solicitor. He should be in possession of the financial trail.'

'A trail that, in my view, will be cold from the outset.'

'Maybe; maybe not. Checking it out is the only way to find out. You've no idea, I suppose, if Emily and Adrian kept in touch?'

'She never ...' This was Sloane's first slip and although he braked sharply, it achieved no more than damage-limitation.

'I think you were going to say that Miss Dresden never mentioned Adrian to you.'

Sloane leaned back in his chair, massaging his chin with a finger and thumb, appraising the detective inspector like an art collector trying to put a price on a painting. This was becoming a harder hand to play than he had envisaged. He had not fallen into the trap of underestimating *her*, but he feared he had failed to recognize *his* own susceptibility to seduction. Not blatant sexual seduction, but something far more subtle and potent.

'I cannot tell you anything about Adrian. Let's leave it at that. I doubt very much if he figured in Emily's adult life. I could be wrong, but my gut feeling is that you'd be wasting your time if you moseyed in that direction.'

'Did she come to live down here when she retired from air-traffic control?'

'Not directly.'

'God! It must have been easier squeezing goodwill from

Scrooge. Look, although Miss Dresden had retired from her job as an air-traffic controller, she wasn't living here in retirement, as proved by the findings at her cottage. What was she up to?'

Sloane shook his head negatively and with about as much sincerity as a second-hand car salesman. 'She could have been acting in some capacity in the campaign for compensation.'

'*Compensation?*' Lowen queried, the searchlights in her eyes turned on again.

'Legal proceedings for compensation have been initiated in the European Court of Human Rights against the Norwegian Government.'

'By whom?'

'A group of the war *whore children*, who are now all in their sixties. At the dawn of the new millennium, Kjell Magne Bondevik, the Norwegian Prime Minister, made a public apology in his New Year's Day speech.'

'It doesn't add up,' Lowen pronounced starkly.

'What doesn't?'

'The way she died. The lipstick slogan, the background you've outlined … it all points to a crime spawned by hatred.'

'Could be.'

'So, I'd have expected a frenzied attack; desecration. Yet she was stabbed only the once in a very *clean*, clinical killing, as if the murderer knew exactly where to insert the knife.'

'Avoiding overkill.'

'Precisely. Also avoiding emotion.'

By now, dinner had been deleted from their evening's menu.

CHAPTER 5

Next day, Sloane had an early breakfast and then headed for Swanage. He was ringing the front door-bell of Hugh Carrington's home before ten o'clock, without having had to seek directions from Lowen.

The door was opened with guillotine sharpness by a decorous woman whose austere features were more threatening than those of any guard-dog.

'Yes?' she snapped, without baring her teeth.

'Is Mr Carrington at home?'

'Who's asking?'

'Michael Sloane.'

'Are you expected?'

'I'm sure he's expecting me, but if you're asking whether I have an appointment, then the answer's no.' Sloane's nature was dangerously disarming. Like most Taureans, he had a long fuse which could burn away his patience interminably before he finally detonated. Nothing ever fazed him and he was a rock that could withstand all weathers without suffering erosion.

Humans, just like any other animal, instinctively recognize strength, weakness and vacillation. Faye Mitchison's manner had been crafted over many years to be overpowering, but the animal in her counselled against mental arm-wrestling with this stranger. All the signals picked up by her radar warned her to back off.

'Wait there, please, while I find out if he'll see you,' the house-keeper requested, her voice strong and empty of dialect. As she disappeared into the bowels of the building, Sloane took the oppor-tunity to familiarize himself with the surroundings. The exterior of the house was grey stone and grim. The north and south corners were dominated by turrets, projecting a forbidding, fortress appearance. All the windows were small, accounting for the depth of darkness into which the housekeeper had been sucked. There were three storeys, plus windows in the roof. The property, unimaginatively named Hill House, stood alone, encircled by evergreens at the rear, further rationing daylight. Hill House was reached from the shore road by a steep, circuitous climb for more than 200 yards. Below, the sea continued to foam and fume in the bay, targeting everyone and everything within spitting distance. The scampering clouds were so low that the hilltops across the bay were blacked-out and the white cliffs wore dark veils.

When the housekeeper returned, she had softened marginally – from steel to iron. 'Come in.' This was neither retreat nor defeat, merely realignment.

Carrington was waiting for Sloane in his large sitting-room, posturing awkwardly. The two men shook hands the way strangers would.

'Thank you,' Carrington said to his housekeeper, which translated into, *That will do, you may leave us alone now.*

Nothing more was said until the housekeeper's footsteps were heard receding like hammer-blows along the corridor.

'Bad business,' Carrington broke the ice.

'How much have you told the police?'

Despite his age, Carrington still retained a military bearing. As he turned away from Sloane disconsolately and gravitated towards one of the small windows, framed with ivy on the outside, he moved in a slow, mechanical march, the old swagger still evident, his spine ramrod straight and his centurion head held proudly high. Although his hair had been reduced to a few silver slivers, it was combed flat and meticulously parted. He wore slippers, cord trousers and an army sweater with suede lapels and elbows. His eagle nose, bird-of-prey eyes, trimmed eyebrows, pendulous face and waspish mouth all helped to preserve his aura of authority. Without the loose flesh around his neck and the brown spots on his wrinkled hands, he could have passed for middle-aged.

'I answered only asked questions.'

'What *were* those questions?'

Carrington had his back to Sloane now, his hands clasped behind him.

'About the final hours of Emily's life.'

'Surely you were quizzed about your association with her.'

'Of course.' Carrington's voice was clipped and crisp. 'I told the truth.'

'The *whole* truth?'

'Hardly! I explained that we were bridge partners; that we met after I advertised for a playing partner.'

'Detective Inspector Lowen will check that out.'

'Of course she will and that'll confirm the veracity of what I told her.'

'Did Emily sense danger?'

Carrington swivelled, just like a squaddie on the parade-ground doing a snappy about-turn. 'She didn't say anything to me. God, I feel so guilty!' He closed his eyes, then reopened them slowly, as if hoping the world had somehow changed dramatically in the brief interlude. Perhaps it had all been the surreal graphics of a nightmare; unfortunately not.

'What have you to feel guilty about, Hugh, if she had no premonition?'

'I was too remote.'

'That's your role.'

'I didn't give her a chance.'

Sloane did not comprehend and said as much.

'Our Saturday rendezvous became nothing more than a rubber-stamping occasion. A handler should be more than someone with a performing poodle on a leash.'

'You had plenty of opportunity to chat during your walks to and from the bus depot, surely?'

'She'd hand over documents, such as her weekly reports and photographs. We'd discuss progress. I'd listen and advise, yes. But everything was always operationally focused. I never actually asked her if anything was bothering her.'

'I doubt that that was necessary. Emily would always be forthcoming.'

'When was the last time you dealt with her direct, Mike?'

'Oh, ten years ago, when I briefed her originally after she'd been fully screened, just before she came down here. I explained how she'd make contact with you; that she should look out for an advert in the local paper for a bridge partner.'

'A decade is a long time.'

'Are you telling me she changed.'

'We all change.'

Carrington had not finished, so Sloane waited patiently.

'If her cover was blown, I'm not certain she'd have been as forthcoming as you think.'

'What evidence have you for that?'

'None, just a gut feeling. I think she'd have seen it as a personal weakness, personal failure, and would have been afraid of being considered past it; a spent force and a liability. When we played bridge, she could never take the blame for playing a hand badly.'

'That's a character flaw that wasn't identified in the rigorous personality assessments.'

'As I said, we all change.'

'Why didn't you draw my attention to that fact?'

'Because she was doing a good job; because it didn't seem important. I put it down to the ageing process. Insecurity goes with age. No one over sixty is secure; the setting sun and its lengthening shadow over the grave see to that. Also, there was the fact that she wasn't really exposed.'

'Everyone in the field is *exposed* to some extent, you of all people should know that.'

Carrington sighed in the manner of a man waking up too late to see the dawn. 'The only comfort I have is that even if I had been more solicitous, it's doubtful Emily would have been communicative, though that's scant consolation. She was no introvert, but she was a very private person.'

'I guess she had plenty to be private about.'

Carrington knew exactly what Sloane meant. 'I think she was happy … in her own way.'

'I'm sure she was.' And then, with breathtaking change of pace, 'Who *did* kill her, Hugh?'

'God knows!' Carrington swung away from Sloane again and, hands drilling deeply into his trouser pockets, maundered with melancholic absent-mindedness to a glass cabinet, from which he plucked a bottle of malt whisky. He poured himself a large measure into a tumbler and then offered Sloane one.

'Too early in the day for me,' Sloane declined.

'Since the weekend this has become a matter of maintenance

for me,' Carrington admitted, emptying his glass with one backwards jerk of his head.

'What did you make of Detective Inspector Lowen?'

'Bright. Ambitious. No fool.'

'I'm not sure whether that's a good or bad thing for us, but I agree with you.'

'I got the impression that the police think it's a case of Emily being in the wrong place at the wrong time.'

'Not any longer.'

'You've put them in the picture?' Carrington said incredulously.

'Only a portion of the picture.'

'Which portion?'

'Birth, background, adoption and early career details.'

'Nothing about me? Us?'

'Of course not. As far as Lowen's concerned, we've never met.'

'Does she know you're here now?'

'No.'

'Will you tell her you paid me a visit?'

'I won't volunteer the information, but if she asks me the direct question, I won't lie. After all, your housekeeper ...' Sloane allowed the elliptical sentence to trail away.

'She's trustworthy.'

'But would she lie for you?'

'Not if she thought I'd committed a crime.'

'In that case, never take her into your confidence.' And then, 'I want to hear all about your last meeting with Emily.'

Carrington sighed as if weighed down by a load he was unfit to carry. 'First I must get myself another drink. You're sure you won't join me?'

'Sure.'

Carrington's first drink had already flushed his cheeks with a whisky fever. Now he gripped his refill as if it was nectar, which it was for him at that moment, of course.

'Let's sit.'

They faced one another from armchairs on opposite sides of a stone fireplace that in a previous age, long before central heating, would have been the epicentre of all warmth for the room.

'We met as usual at seven,' Carrington began disconsolately.

'She was as chirpy as ever. She handed me a brown-paper package.'

'Did she say anything about it?'

'Only that the prints were good quality. A full report, as usual, was enclosed.'

'She didn't elaborate?'

'No. Emily wasn't one for histrionics. She always under-played her hand, unless she was at the bridge-table. She was a natural watcher, Mike; a professional. She accepted that her role was merely to observe, to capture the moment for posterity whenever possible and appropriate, and to report back. Extrapolation was not her business and that was something she acknowledged, content to leave interpretation to others, like I do. She never aspired to be more than she was. She was a true trouper. It also explained why she was able to play the part so well. We'd chat about the weather and her animals – I hope they're being cared for?'

'I haven't asked. They weren't at the cottage when I was there. The RSPCA would have been called in to find new homes for them; that's the normal procedure.'

Carrington's glass was empty again. He nursed it like a small child caressing a comfort doll or garment. Looking down forlornly into the glass, as if peering hopefully for answers in a crystal-ball, he said, 'Have the contents of her last delivery been analysed?'

'The package was opened on Sunday before we knew that Emily was dead. The pics and her report were on my desk when I arrived first thing yesterday.'

'You must have known by then she'd been murdered.'

'I was apprised of the fact around midnight on Sunday, shortly after your tip-off, for which the hierarchy was most grateful.'

Praise is rarely wasted. Despite a lifetime of risking his neck for crown and country, Carrington still responded to appreciation. Mind you, compliments never went to his head the way whisky did.

'The biker courier picked up on schedule at eight o'clock Sunday morning. It was too early for any news of ... You know, her body had only just been found. I heard on the radio around lunchtime about the discovery of a corpse at Corfe Castle, but the identity wasn't made public until much later. Do you think she got too close?'

Sloane switched into the inscrutable mode. '*Too close* to what? To whom?'

'The latest subjects.'

'I'd have thought you were in a better position than me to answer that.' If there was any chance of tossing back a hand grenade, Sloane would always do so. It was agency technique.

'She always was a bit of a chancer.'

'That wasn't the impression you gave earlier,' Sloane tested him.

'She was never reckless or unprofessional, nor did she ever exceed her brief, but neither would she tacitly accept defeat.'

'*Defeat?*'

Carrington's sightless gaze was aimed towards a motionless spider on the ceiling as he raided his brain for the clarity of explanation that eluded him. 'She would try to make things happen. She wouldn't be passively philosophical and say to herself, OK, nothing's going to happen today. I'll pack up and go home. Perhaps it'll come good tomorrow.'

'So what *exactly* would she do?'

'She'd try to force it. Give it a little push.'

'*Force it?*'

'Yes. I'm finding this difficult, Mike. I can't give you specific examples. It's more a definition of her tenacious character. If she felt that one shot wouldn't be conclusive enough, she'd always endeavour to get closer for another crack at it.'

'So you think she was murdered by someone she'd been watching recently.'

'Don't you?'

Sloane had no intention of mentioning the MOTHER WHORE! lipstick inscription. Lowen would not have revealed it to Carrington as it was something the police were wisely keeping to themselves. If Carrington alluded to it in any way he would be incriminating himself.

'She had been doing very well,' Sloane said evasively.

'Too well for her own good, I'd say. Do you want her surveillance beat to be reallocated?'

'Without a hiatus, yes. The situation's too dangerous to be left.'

'I agree; accentuated by the recent unfortunate event.'

Sloane's mind went back three months to the August Sunday when three men, of Middle East origin and suspected of being involved in international terrorism, slipped into the UK via the Dorset port of Poole. Within a week, MI5, through its network of informants, knew exactly where the men were in hiding. Emily Dresden had immediately been the 'watcher' of choice to monitor their movements because of her inconspicuous little aunty-next-door image.

Emily Dresden, paradoxically, was the archetypal MI5 watcher. As Sloane always told recruits, 'Few people ever look at the face of a nun or a pensioner. They go unnoticed. No one, you see, ever feels threatened by their presence; that's the secret and the trick.'

But had the trick finally backfired and blown up in their face?

'She must have over-reached,' Carrington surmised, jerking Sloane from his reverie. And then, almost absently, 'You know she was moonlighting?'

'No, tell me about it.'

'Not much to tell, really. She did some private work in her spare time.'

'Such as?'

'Matrimonial, the staple diet of private sleuths. I guess you could say she was the local Miss Marple.'

'How did she come by her clients?'

'She advertised in the personal columns, like most PIs.'

'Giving her address?'

'No, just a mobile number.'

Lowen had not mentioned a mobile phone being found on Emily or in her home. Mobiles stored numbers and messages, voice and text. Now Sloane had a new factor to add to the equation.

CHAPTER 6

From a soulless pub on the stormy seafront, Sloane made a series of calls on his cellular. Lowen was first on the list.

Without preamble, he enquired with businesslike economy, 'Have you come across a mobile?'

'Pardon?'

'Did Emily have a mobile on her? Was one found at the scene or the cottage?'

Initial silence gave Sloane his answers. Lowen eventually responded with a question. 'Do you know she had one?'

'No, it was just a thought,' Sloane lied.

'I'll have someone check with all the network providers.'

'I doubt that she did own one—' Sloane tried to deflect her, unsuccessfully.

'I think she did and you're damn sure of that,' Lowen interrupted acidly. 'You don't ask idle questions. I can't trust you.'

'So you say.'

Sloane sipped his first beer of the day, while windows were being washed by the seaspray, the wind howling like noises from a haunted house.

'I'm sorry you still don't trust me,' Sloane heard himself intoning vapidly, with as much conviction as a chain-smoker making a New Year's resolution to kick the habit as he shook a cigarette from the pack.

'I follow your drift about the mobile,' said Lowen, unmoved by Sloane's feigned innocence. 'We've completed our searches. No mobile in her home, the garage, her car or on her.'

'That might be something for you to look into, then.'

'Why do I get the distinct feeling that I'm going places you've already been?'

'Perhaps because you're becoming paranoid.'

'No, I think it's because you have more than a head start on me. Much more. And I intend to find out how and why.'

'That'll be a misuse of your resources.'

'There you go again, pissing me off with your back-seat driver meddling.'

Sloane had to break this negative circuit. 'Any luck tracing Emily's solicitor?'

'I haven't tried looking.'

There was something in her voice, a tone of deceit, interlaced with truth, that gave away the guile in her statement.

'The solicitor has contacted you, is that what you're saying?'

'My, my, you are a clever boy! I bet you're a dab hand at those cryptic crossword clues.'

'Who is he?'

'Who said it's a *he*?'

Sloane sighed melodramatically.

'Find out for yourself, city slicker!'

'Listen Cagney …' But before Sloane had a chance to plead for maturity and professionalism to prevail, Lowen killed the conversation.

Lowen made a request to see Chief Constable James Frobisher. Assistant Chief Constable Helen Cusack said that Frobisher was 'too busy', but Lowen could speak with her.

'Not on the phone,' Lowen beseeched from her desk.

'Come up for a coffee, then,' invited Cusack, whom Lowen had always considered to be the most approachable of all the top brass at headquarters.

'When?'

'No time like the present.'

Cusack was formidable and friendly, in equal conflicting measures. Her smile could be either melting and welcoming or frosty and forbidding. It was not the smile itself that dictated its succinct message but her expressive eyes, which were such an accurate gauge of even the slightest temperature change. There was nothing cool or hostile in her smile as she motioned Lowen to a chair the opposite side of her desk. A female civilian employee appeared like a genie with two cups of coffee. This in itself was a little treat for

Lowen; a pleasant change from the stained mugs of the Criminal Investigation Department (CID). Pure bone china, too. Spode no less. Made in Stoke-on-Trent, the heartland of the Potteries. Expensive stuff. A delight to behold, let alone to drink from.

Cusack was one of the new breed of fast-track officers. Equipped with a top degree in psychology and applied logic, she had joined the Metropolitan Police in London, rocketing through the ranks with a speed that had made her unpopular and envied among the more traditional plodders, especially those men who were still institutionally racist and sexist.

'Well, what's bothering you, Inspector?' The smile had dissolved with the sugar.

Lowen stirred her coffee thoughtfully with a silver crested spoon, while the assistant chief conducted a visual appraisal, her highly developed antennae tuned into the distress signals.

'The situation's intolerable.'

'What *situation*?'

The sparring was almost tantamount to a tribal war-dance.

'Having this London bloke, Michael Sloane, as a pillion passenger.'

Cusack shifted in her leather seat. She slid her cup and saucer to one side across the ice-rink veneer of her desk, as precisely as moving a chess piece. Out of uniform, no one would guess her occupation. She was slight in build with a rather bird-like face. Her mouth was small, without hinting at any meanness of spirit.

'I know very little about the arrangement to which you're alluding,' Cusack finally said starchily.

Lowen did not believe her. The chief and his assistant dovetailed their responsibilities and workload, both operational and administrative.

'It's not working,' Lowen motored on regardless. 'I can't continue like this.'

Cusack averted her eyes, squeezed her pointed chin with a thumb and forefinger, simultaneously fidgeting uncomfortably. 'This isn't something the chief will want to hear.'

'I can't help that; it's the way it is.' Lowen was as uncompromising as ever and prepared for a clash of strong wills. She would never be intimidated by superior rank.

Now their eyes tangled.

'My understanding is that this Mr Sloane is a mere observer,' said Cusack, still retaining plausible denial of intimate knowledge of the extraneous involvement.

'And that's just what he's not!' Lowen fumed. 'He knew the victim – intimately.'

'In what capacity?'

'He won't say.'

'Where does your info come from, then?'

'He admitted as much.'

'So there's no secret.'

'You don't see.'

'What don't I *see*?'

'He's deliberately concealing relevant facts from me.'

'That's a serious allegation.'

'One that's not made lightly, I assure you.'

Cusack steepled her tendril fingers beneath her bony chin. 'Are you complaining that Mr Sloane is impeding your investigation?'

Lowen refrained from a reflex reply. The blood-rush to her brain was over, a fact embodied in her answer.

'He's not *impeding*, no, but he has a lot of relevant material that he's not passing on.'

'Such as?'

'*Such as* what Emily Dresden was really doing down here. Little old spinsters in our part of the world don't carry guns.'

'How do you know Miss Dresden carried a gun? I thought the firearm was found in her cottage.'

'Let's not split hairs.'

'Fair enough, but at least let's be factual. What else is Mr Sloane keeping from you?'

'Everything.'

'*Everything* is rather a lot!'

Lowen was in no mood for levity. 'It's obvious to me that Miss Dresden was not the one-dimensional character that her friends and neighbours were kidded into believing.'

'With due respect, Inspector, I should have thought that was self-evident from the interest shown in the case in London, regardless of Mr Sloane's behaviour.'

'But who is he?'

'Even I don't know the answer to that question.'

Lowen was fired up. 'I want the case reassigned. I really do.'

'I'd advise against doing anything hasty. After all, this is your first big one.'

'I've worked murder investigations before.' Lowen made a mulish stand.

'Not as the lead officer. This is your test case; the chance to really prove yourself; your window of opportunity, as the cliché goes.'

'Exactly! So I can do without added complications.'

'Do yourself a favour, Inspector: sleep on it,' Cusack advised wearily.

'That's what I did last night, except I didn't sleep. On the contrary, it kept me awake. Sleeping on things is a sure way to insomnia.'

'So you won't take my advice?'

'No.' Lowen could sense that her heartbeat was commensurate to the raised stakes.

'Very well, I'll see that the chief constable hears of your request, but I think you're being very silly,' Cusack warned, unenthusiastically.

Lowen was puzzled. The assistant chief constable usually presided over operational business. True, Emily Dresden's murder had touched a national nerve. Even so ... 'Surely *you* can reassign?'

Cusack hesitated. Vacillation was not within her nature, so what followed lacked credibility. 'I think this should go right to the top for arbitration. In the meantime, I'll rely on you to carry on with the enthusiasm we've come to expect from you.'

'How long shall I have to wait?'

'As long as it takes.'

'Thanks.'

The sarcasm was wasted.

'Don't mention it,' said Cusack dryly.

Every time the entrance to the pub opened, so the smell of seaweed rushed in, propelled by the gusts of wind. The salty pungency went straight to Sloane's head, stirring sleeping memories of an earlier beachcombing existence in the Caribbean, after his wife had killed herself and their young daughter all because of his boorish, self-indulgent behaviour. Immaturity, like other deficiencies, can be a killer, and that was the baggage he would never be able to shed. It was while beach-bumming that he was recruited by the CIA and later transferred to British Intelligence.

CHAPTER 7

Sloane punched out a Whitehall number on his mobile pugnaciously as he slouched in his car, parked on the stormy seafront, not far from the pub in Swanage where he had just indulged in a liquid lunch. Hugh Monkton, Sir Richard Finlayson's Private Secretary at the Home Office, took the call on his direct line.

'Monkton,' the private secretary identified himself in the officious tone of his haughty breed.

'Sloane here.'

'Yes, Sloane, what can I do for you?' He had been fully briefed about Sloane's assignment.

'I'm down in Dorset.'

'I know full well where you are, Sloane,' Monkton manufactured boredom.

'There's a detective inspector here by the name of Joanne Lowen.'

'So?'

'I want access to her personal file.' Sloane had been instructed to deal direct with the Home Office on sensitive police matters.

'I'll need clearance for that.'

'It won't be a problem,' Sloane predicted confidently.

'You'll excuse me for not accepting your word for that, won't you, Sloane?' Yet another poison dart was helped in its flight by a tailwind of sarcasm.

It took less than an hour for Sloane's request to be approved. Chief Constable Frobisher had no objections and was prepared to co-operate fully. If Sloane drove straight to county police headquarters, Lowen's file would already have been pulled for his inspection.

'Tell Frobisher I'm on my way,' Sloane told Monkton.

'No, you tell him yourself,' Monkton retorted disdainfully. Sloane did.

'I hope this doesn't mean you're having trouble with my detective inspector,' Frobisher said, as Sloane was shown into the chief constable's office. Frobisher was holding up Lowen's file, as if waving a stick, farmer-fashion.

'She's certainly spunky,' Sloane answered obliquely.

'This chance for a chat couldn't be more opportune,' Frobisher remarked solemnly, flopping the file on his desk and running his fingers around the edges. With his head still bowed, he continued dourly, 'Inspector Lowen has asked to be taken off the case.' Only then did he lift his head, enabling their eyes to lock.

'I'm not altogether surprised,' Sloane said candidly, sighing deeply and pulling a disgruntled face. 'She gave me advance warning. I thought she might be bluffing.'

'Inspector Lowen never bluffs. I anticipated there'd be some discord between you, but, well, I hoped she'd be professionally mature enough to handle any resentment.'

'I can't tell you how to run your force, but I should be grateful if you allow me the chance to sway your decision.'

'Feel free,' Frobisher agreed generously. 'There's her file, as requested. Have a seat. Browse at leisure. I'm popping next door for a pre-arranged meeting with my deputy. I'll have a coffee sent in for you. If you've finished before I am, just leave the file on my desk. I shouldn't be long.'

'I'm obliged.'

Sloane was an expert at speed-reading. It was something he had perfected during his series of investigations in the Caribbean, when often he had to be able to memorize the bullet-points of a long, convoluted document in a matter of minutes. He read without making notes, confident that he would not forget anything of consequence.

- Born Joanna Lowen 1st May, 1970 in the cathedral town of Wells in Somerset. Mother, Margaret, a teacher, father, Paul, a captain in the Military Police.
- Family moved to the Somerset village of East Harptree, on the slopes of the Mendips, when Joanne was four.

- Joanne had a younger sister, Laura, who was born the year they moved to East Harptree.
- Both girls loved riding. When they were young, they shared a pony. Later, they each had their own. They competed in gymkhanas, regularly winning rosettes.
- Captain Lowen was killed when Joanne was fourteen, shot dead in Port Elizabeth, South Africa, only minutes after having given evidence in court against two white supremacists accused of multiple murders. Captain Lowen had been one of three British military policemen helping South Africa's army.
- A year later, Laura Lowen, Joanne's sister, broke her neck in a fall from her pony and died two days later in hospital.
- Joanne passed all GCSE exams with As and Bs and later obtained good grades in A levels, but did not apply to any university. Instead, she applied to join the military police, but was turned down. No reason given. The next year, after leaving school, she explored India and the Far East as a lone backpacker, before making a second bid for a place in the military police. Again she was unsuccessful. After that, she became a civilian police officer.
- At the age of twenty-five, she married Len Findon, a farmer, who also trained a small string of jump racehorses. Four years into the marriage, her husband was investigated for alleged race-fixing, uncovered by Joanne. He was charged and went on trial at Bristol Crown Court, where the jury failed to reach a verdict. A retrial was ordered; by the time that started, in London at the Old Bailey, Joanne had abandoned him. Again the jury could not agree and, after the collapse of the second trial, the Crown Prosecution Service announced that the case would be discontinued. The Jockey Club, however, refused to renew Findon's trainer's licence and his days in racing were over.
- The farm and stabled were sold, the proceeds divided equally between husband and wife. With her share, Joanne bought a small house in Dorset, the county to which she had been transferred when promoted to sergeant.
- Although the marriage was dead, neither Joanne nor her husband bothered to bury it in divorce.
- Fiercely independent, Joanne retained her maiden name, Lowen, throughout her police career and marriage.
- Commended twice for bravery: once for inching along a six-inch-

wide ledge, five floors up a building, to cajole a man into handing over a baby. The deranged father was threatening to jump with the child in his arms because his wife was leaving him for a woman. The second commendation was awarded for disarming a gunman in a domestic stand-off in which the wife was being held hostage. Joanne had volunteered to swap places with the wife. This was accepted and after a couple of hours, Joanne seized an opportunity to tackle the gunman and wrestle the weapon from him. 'All in a day's work,' she said.

Sloane's demeanour was brooding and contemplative when Frobisher bounded back into his office. Sloane had closed the file and slithered it across the desk towards the chief constable's chair.

'Finished?' Frobisher enquired courteously, circumnavigating his desk to his sumptuous leather throne.

Sloane was still in reverie. 'Very detailed,' he murmured, almost hypnotized. 'Unusually so, I'd say.'

'The selection process has to be multi-dimensional these days,' Frobisher said, enigmatically.

'I'd have thought with her background she was an archetypal candidate.'

'She was rejected by the military police – twice,' Frobisher pointed out icily. 'We had to discover why. When I say we, I mean the recruitment screening panel.'

'Why was she unacceptable to the military?'

'They were uneasy about her motives.'

Sloane now shook off any lingering remains of his trance. 'Are you saying there were fears that she might be a security risk?'

'No, no, nothing like that,' Frobisher assured, his body-language as emphatic as his speech. 'You will just have read about the tragic death of her father. Well, the feeling was that Joanne wanted to join the military police because she had a score to settle.'

'With the military? Did she blame the army for her dad's death?'

'The South African police believed they had identified Captain Lowen's killer, but a decision was taken not to prosecute.'

'Why was that?'

Frobisher shrugged and pulled a face that said, *Who really knows?* 'Someone high up pulled the plug.'

'And the military suspected Joanne wanted to follow in her father's footsteps just to learn who had shot her dad and to reap revenge? To take the law into her own hands?'

'Something implausible like that.'

'Rather far-fetched, don't you think?'

'I just used the word *implausible*, but in their defence it has to be remembered that we live in surreal times, with events often more unbelievable than merely *far-fetched*.'

'What's your take on it?'

'They made a bad call. Their loss was our gain, as you've seen from her police record.'

'Her husband certainly seems to have been the proverbial bad lot. It must have been very embarrassing for her.' This was an iceberg question; most of it lurked dangerously under the surface.

Frobisher shifted uncomfortably. Sloane's blind pitch into the dark had hit something.

'No dirt got anywhere near Joanne.'

Sloane waited, correctly anticipating that there was more to come.

'Joanne started the ball rolling.'

'You mean she fingered her own husband?'

'Joanne overheard certain incriminating and sinister phone conversations. After that, she bugged her husband's office at the stables.'

'Shit!'

'Joanne's a zealot. She expects a lot from people, but no more than she demands of herself. She produced the tapes to prove her husband's guilt on condition that they weren't used against him in court, and that her part in his downfall was never made public. The tapes demonstrated what was going on ... and by whom. The investigating team was led to water. The rest was down to them.'

'But Findon walked.'

Frobisher gesticulated. 'It was a difficult case to prosecute. A key prosecution witness had a dodgy past and was less than convincing in the box. As you well know, we can't choose our witnesses. We have to work with what we've got.'

'Has Len Findon any notion of the role Joanne played in his downfall?'

'He calls her Lady Macbeth; I believe that answers your question.'

Sloane stroked his chin as he regressed into reverie. Finally, he said, absently, 'You could help me in two ways. Joanne has been contacted by Miss Dresden's solicitor. I require his name.'

'I'll get that for you.'

'With discretion, please.'

'Is Inspector Lowen withholding that information from you?'

'Let's just say it's a sore point between us, but I want to avoid it becoming a damaging issue.'

'What is the second matter I can help you with?'

'Do me a favour and disallow her application to be reassigned.'

'But—'

'I know, you were beginning to think we were as incompatible as snake and mongoose.'

'Good analogy, I'd say, Mr Sloane.'

'Except it's inaccurate. *You* need her on this case. And, paradoxically, so do *I*'.

'Well, I am—'

'Surprised?'

'No, *confounded*. Do I get an explanation?'

'You have it already. It's in *there*.' Sloane stabbed a finger towards the folder on Frobisher's desk.

'Lowen won't thank me.'

'Neither will Miss Dresden's killer …'

Within an hour, the name of Emily Dresden's solicitor had been officially leaked to Sloane, who wasted no time calling Henrietta Rolling at her office in Bournemouth. Firstly, however, he prepared the ground by mustering covering fire from the Home Office. Consequently, when he called the solicitor, she had been primed to the importance of collaborating with Sloane.

'I've cleared my diary for the rest of the day,' Rolling said briskly, her voice pleasant, if a shade unctuous.

'I'm on my way,' advised Sloane, equally decisively. 'I should be with you in about forty minutes, depending on your ability to navigate me by remote control.'

'I'll do my best,' she promised prosaically. After giving succinct directions, she added, 'You'll see the brass plate: Rolling, Rolling and Sedgewick.'

'And which Rolling are you?'

'The second, though I make more money for the firm than the first, but it's not something I make a habit of bragging about – except when there's no one to see my blushes.'

Sloane had not expected the skittish touch, but he embraced it with a certain relief.

The offices of Rolling, Rolling and Sedgewick were typical for a provincial law firm specializing in conveyancing, commercial contracts, litigation and wills; bread-and-butter fodder of the legal jungle.

The receptionist was as officious as Sloane had come to expect from frontline deterrents in medical surgeries and legal practices.

'Henrietta Rolling is expecting me,' he said, pre-empting the customary inquisition and muting the matron.

After the mandatory check call, Sloane was escorted – only just minus handcuffs – up uncarpeted, wooden stairs to the first floor, as if he could not be trusted alone with the woodworm and cobwebs. The truncated corridor had three doors leading to the separate offices of James Rolling, Henrietta Rolling and Paul Sedgewick, the name of each solicitor embossed in chipped black paint on the frosted pane of the upper half of each door.

Henrietta Rolling was as handsome as she was decorous, with hair prematurely white for a woman still the flip side of fifty. She wore a generously cut tweed suit, flat shoes and only a modicum of make-up. Sloane suspected that her friendly face was a trick of nature, a mask hiding the dragon, though he had no evidence for such a belief, the provenance of which was empirical prejudice. Her handshake had the pincer-grip of a university Boat Race rower gripping his oar in tideway combat.

As soon as the preliminaries were dispensed with and they were alone, the solicitor said, almost numbly, 'I still find it hard to believe that you're here to talk about Emily Dresden in the past tense.' Despite her state of denial, there was a cathedral resonance to her voice.

'How well did you know her?' Sloane always took the direct route if it was available to him, believing that detours merely delayed or, even worse, helped him to lose his way.

Rolling leaned back in her executive chair and folded her arms across her bosomy chest. 'Not at all well, really. She was no more than a client to me. I don't mean that to sound cold and heartless.'

'It doesn't,' Sloane assured her.

They were getting the measure of one another, sniffing each other's scent.

'You must be aware that I've already given a statement to Inspector Lowen?' she said rhetorically.

'*You* contacted *her*, I believe?' Other questions were mirrored in his eyes.

'She was such a lovely lady; I'm talking about Miss Dresden now,' she began explaining in the manner of a résumé. 'Very bright. No one's fool, you can take my word for that. I had no contact with her socially, you understand. We only ever met here, in my office. I suppose over a period of ten years, we hardly met more than a handful of times, but that was enough.'

'*Enough*?'

'To have an opinion – about her; about her character, the kind of person she was.'

'How did she come to you – in the first place?'

'On recommendation, word of mouth, the very best – and cheapest – form of advertising.'

'Did she come to *you* personally, or the company collectively?'

'I should like to be able to say that she demanded to see me or no one at all.'

'But that wouldn't be true?'

'It would be a downright lie. I got her because I was the only one with nothing else to do.'

Sloane smiled appreciatively. 'Did she name the person who pointed her your way?'

'Is that relevant?' Her carefully manicured eyebrows lifted expressively.

Sloane gestured with his slumped shoulders. 'Probably not.'

'Well, if she did say, I really can't remember; it was of no consequence to me. Business is business, whoever feeds it.'

'What was the purpose of her first appointment?'

'Twofold,' the solicitor stated, suddenly more businesslike. 'Firstly, she was buying property. My speciality is conveyancing; all sorts of contracts really. Secondly, she wanted to make a will, which is probably the most common reason for people of a certain age going to a solicitor.'

'Have you shown Inspector Lowen the will?'

'I faxed her a copy.'

'Have you any objection to making the will accessible to me?'

'Not at all. In fact, I have a copy all ready here for you.'

She reached into a lower drawer of her desk and extracted a buff folder. Sloane noticed Emily Dresden's name on the cover. Many of the documents inside were frayed at the edges and yellow with age, but not the topsoil of the paperwork.

'Here you are,' she said, dealing the will from the deck of documents in the folder and proffering it across her desk. 'You may keep it.'

'If you have the time, I'll skip through it while I'm here, just in case I have some questions.'

'Be my guest,' she said agreeably.

Sloane's eyes worked methodically, like a metal-detector sweeping suspect surfaces for explosive material. He noted the date. It had been signed and witnessed exactly three months prior to the murder. The name of the witness intrigued him; Harry Parkes, the verger, who had found the body.

'I see that this invalidates all previous will and codicils,' remarked Sloane ponderously, without looking up. 'Are you in possession of her earlier will – or wills?'

'I am. There was just one, as far as I'm aware. If there were any before that, they weren't lodged here and, in any case, they've been superseded.'

'How different is this definitive document from the original?' he asked thoughtfully.

'Very.' Rolling answered, in the economic manner of a well-tutored witness in a courtroom trial.

'In what respect was it so different?' Ferreting was Sloane's forté.

'The first will was drawn up just after she purchased her delightful cottage and in it she bequeathed everything – property, bonds, stocks, shares and money – to an Ernst Lergen.' She imparted this information without the need to refer to Emily Dresden's file.

Sloane was instantly reminded of the signed portrait he and Lowen had unearthed at the cottage. 'And the last one?'

'As you will see, everything goes to charity.'

'*Charity!* The lot? Don't tell me, please, that her whole estate is going to a cat's home? I know she kept a couple of moggies, but—'

'Not that sort of charity,' Rolling, amused, broke in, her smile sympathetic. 'The sole beneficiary is the fighting fund in Norway, to help finance the marathon litigation by the Second World War whore children. Are you abreast of that legal long-runner?'

'I am. I know far less about Ernst Lergen. In fact, I know *nothing* about him.'

Their eyes met and parted almost simultaneously.

'When she made the first will, did she make any comment, any aside, about the man to whom, at that time, she planned to bequeath all her worldly goods?' Sloane pressed.

'That was a decade ago,' she balked.

'I realize that,' Sloane rallied, then tried to jolly her along with,

'But it's not every day one of your clients makes a will in favour of someone in Norway.'

'Who said Mr Lergen lives in Norway – or, indeed, is a Norwegian? I didn't.'

'The name ... and other clues ...'

'You're right, he is Norwegian, as the name indicates, but—'

'He doesn't live in Norway?' Sloane followed the flow.

'It would seem that he and his family have been living in this country for a couple of years. He contacted me as soon as he read about Miss Dresden's death.'

'Have you met him?'

'No need, now he's no longer a beneficiary.'

The solicitor batted Sloane's next questions before they were bowled.

'Apparently, Miss Dresden had sent him a copy of her first will. My name, the address of my company and phone number are stamped on the last page, under the signatures, as in the copy of the last will, which you have.'

Sloane still had more questions. 'Did he say when he received his copy?'

'No. Why should he? The call was more about his seeking information.'

'*Information?*'

'He thought I might have some news about the circumstances of Miss Dresden's death and the investigation; something more than has been in general circulation. Of course, I couldn't tell him anything new. I knew nothing more than I'd garnered from the newspapers; still don't.'

'How did he sound?'

'Very well spoken. Very English. Not at all Norwegian. Sorry, please excuse me, that was a very stupid thing to say because most Norwegians speak better English than the majority of people born and bred here.'

Sloane steered clear of the diversion. 'Did he introduce the subject of the will?'

'Only to clarify how he came to have my name. He hadn't called to ask, 'How soon do I get my hands on the money? Is there a cheque in the post yet?' He came across as the perfect gentleman.'

'Did you enlighten him?'

The solicitor tilted her head to one side inquisitively, seeking elaboration.

'Did you tell the poor guy that he'd been written out of Emily's inheritance?'

'I did. It was my duty.'

'And how did he take it?'

'Nonchalantly. As if it didn't matter to him.'

'You believe that?'

'Totally.'

'How much is he missing out on?'

'Not enough to kill for.'

'Some people kill for peanuts. For less, in fact.'

'Not the Lergens of this world.'

'That's quite an assumption to make from one phone call.'

'One word can be enough to communicate a complete narrative sometimes. You should go to court more often, Mr Sloane, and listen to some *real* trials, static with high-voltage cross-questioning, rather than that stultifying, synthetic dross on TV. Fiction can never compete with real life for drama.'

'You're preaching to the converted.'

'I'm glad to hear it, Mr Sloane. Anyhow, back to Mr Lergen: it would appear that he is a man of considerable means. He gave me his address – Bergen Manor, Riverside Walk, Henley-on-Thames. Know it?'

'No, but it has a fat wallet ring to it.'

'I have quite a nice little business here, Mr Sloane, but I couldn't afford to sneeze in Mr Lergen's leafy territory.'

'Did he talk at all about himself?'

'Only to mention that he was retired; that he had been some kind of publisher in his own country; that he had moved here, with his wife, on his retirement.'

'Why would he give you his address after you'd informed him that he was out of the financial frame?'

'So I could keep in touch if I heard of any developments.'

'Rather strange, don't you think?'

'On the contrary, *rather natural*, I'd say. They must have been pretty close at some stage in their lives. In those circumstances, wouldn't you want to be kept up-to-date about any progress in the investigation?'

'Maybe,' Sloane muttered dubiously. Then, 'You don't think he could have known about the change of will before you apprised him?'

'I'd swear he didn't.'

'So when Emily was murdered, this Mr Lergen would have still believed everything of hers was destined for him?'

'You have a suspicious mind, Mr Sloane.'

'Hewn out of rugged experience.'

'I fear on this occasion it's leading you astray.'

'Only one way to find out.'

'I wish you luck.'

Sloane believed her.

'Oh, one last thing that I almost forgot: did Emily ever mention a brother, Adrian?'

Rolling was shaking her head even before Sloane had completed his question.

'The name Adrian never came up. The reason I can be so positive about that is because she made the point that she had no living family. Nobody whatsoever.'

So, Sloane was thinking as he filtered into the flow of pedestrian traffic, Adrian either died relatively young or was simply dead as far as Emily was concerned. If the latter was the case, what had Adrian done to deserve such exclusion?

What, indeed!

CHAPTER 9

Sloane decided to stay out of Lowen's way for a couple of days. He hoped that by the weekend she would have come off the boil, having accepted the chief constable's ruling that the Dresden murder case was hers for the duration.

Sloane had plenty to keep himself occupied, without the need to liaise with Lowen. Harry Parkes, the verger, interested him immensely. At the outset, Sloane had not seen any point in a separate interview with Parkes, whose involvement seemed one-dimensional and detached. The verger had simply stumbled on the body while on the way to open the church and prepare it for the first service of that Sunday. There was no suggestion that he had been anywhere near the murder scene at the time of the crime. In fact, as far as Sloane knew, Parkes had not been tested about his movements in the hours immediately preceding and following the crime. Why should he have been? There had been nothing to implicate him; nothing to indicate even a tenuous relationship between him and the victim.

Initially, the police had readily subscribed to the theory that Miss Dresden's death was the result of a motiveless knife-attack. No criticism could be levelled against such an acceptance early on, but since then the picture had become further blurred by the revelation that Miss Dresden's will had been witnessed by Parkes: the explanation for this could well prove to be innocuous, with his participation nothing more than a matter of convenience, but why had she not asked, say, Carrington to do the honours? Perhaps she wanted to keep her private life distanced from her handler and The Firm; natural enough, Sloane reasoned as, deep in debate with himself, he headed like a hunting-hound at the head of the chase for Corfe Castle and his quarry.

Parkes was at home and Sloane was immediately struck by the close proximity of his stone terrace house to the bus-stop at which Emily Dresden would have alighted at the end of her near-last journey on this earth. Her final ride would be an even lonelier one, the date of which could not be arranged until the murder investigation had reached the stage at which her body could be released from the coroner's jurisdiction for burial.

Parkes opened the front door cautiously after a single ring of the strident bell. He was in his mid-fifties, Sloane estimated, and his sartorial taste was old-fashioned. He wore a white shirt, the collar so severely starched that it cut into his bull-neck, chafing his red skin into an angry-looking weal. Although he was only pottering around the house, he was dressed in a formal, dark suit, including jacket and matching waistcoat. His tie was mourning-black and his black lace-up shoes had a shine that would have passed any military parade-ground inspection with flying colours. He was slightly below average height for a man and portly, with hair reduced to a few strands, greased down, like flowers flattened by a cyclone. There was a depressing dullness to his evasive eyes that helped nurture his overall melancholic mien, an extension of the mood of his home. His fleshy face was roundish, like a ripe apple, scarred by a few brown blemishes. The redolence of aftershave hung heavily in the air.

'Yes?' There was nothing challenging in Parkes's manner. In fact, he was completely sapped of vigour. Sloane noticed immediately the blue cushions beneath his eyes, which even the wiry spectacles failed to camouflage.

Sloane introduced himself as an old acquaintance of Emily Dresden, acting as the emissary of her family.

'Oh, you'd better come in, then,' said Parkes, unenthusiastically, quickly adding, 'I didn't think Emily had any remaining family. That was the impression she gave.'

'Only very distant relatives,' Sloane said, not wishing to become bogged down with the minutiae of genealogy, which would present him with problems. 'I knew Emily well from her days as an air-traffic controller.'

'You don't look old enough to have worked with her back then.'

'I'll take that as a compliment, but if you have any doubts

about my legitimacy, please call Detective Inspector Lowen or even the chief constable of the county.'

'That won't be necessary.' Parkes waved away the notion that he was doubting Sloane's authenticity. 'It makes no difference,' he continued vapidly, 'there's not much I can tell anybody.' He closed the door behind them with a gentle click, as if afraid of disturbing someone. 'I was in the kitchen. I've just made myself a cup of tea. Would you care for one?'

Sloane said 'No thank you'. He would have said yes to a coffee, but no alternative offer was forthcoming.

'You don't look like one of those newspaper reporter rascals. I reckon I must have had every one of the tribe on my doorstep looking for a story. I gave them all short shrift.'

The kitchen, situated at the rear of the house, was as dated as its occupant. Parkes pulled up a chair for Sloane at a wooden table against a wall and then sat opposite him at the other end. A flowery teapot and milk jug were between the two men on a stained white table-cloth. Through a window behind Parkes, Sloane could see a small, but tidy, garden; there was a wooden shed at the bottom, against which was parked an upright, solid-framed bicycle. Although there was plenty of sunshine, very little of it penetrated the house. It was one of those sharp, sunny, wintry mornings that previewed spring. A wall-clock, with a hanging pendulum, ticked every second intrusively.

'Did Emily worship at your church?' Sloane began harmlessly.

'Occasionally. She wasn't a regular. Perhaps once a month on average. Always at Christmas and Easter.' Parkes spoke like someone who had been trained to be precise and pernickety. His voice was soaked in regional dialect.

'It must have been a shock for you.' It was not necessary for Sloane to qualify this observation.

'*Shock!* I still haven't slept properly since that morning. It's something I'm never going to forget; the most horrible moment in my entire life. And to think it should happen virtually on the doorstep of God's house! That somehow makes it so much worse. It has upset and unsettled the whole village. It'll be a long, long time before we get back to normal in these parts.'

'When did you last see Emily alive?'

Parkes put down his cup into his saucer, spilling some tea, his hairy fingers tremulous. He massaged his smooth, raw chin, still smarting from a recent wet shave, and dropped his rheumy eyes into the puffiness that offered them a soft landing. 'One day last week, it would have been.'

'Which day?'

'I'm trying to work it out,' Parkes said, but not impatiently. 'It must have been either Tuesday or Wednesday.'

'Where?' Sloane did his best not to appear pushy.

'Oh, in the village.'

'Did you speak?'

'We chatted for a couple of minutes, that's all. The weather was none too good; not the sort of day for hanging about. She'd just come out of the butcher's shop in the High Street and I was passing. I'd been to a cash-machine to draw out some money. It must have been about noon.'

'How did she seem?'

'Fine; absolutely fine. I asked her how she was. She said she'd seldom felt better. I said something to the effect, "Well, in that case, you've no excuse for not coming to church more". It was only a light-hearted remark, not a real admonition and she didn't take offence.'

A light-hearted Harry Parkes was beyond Sloane's imagination.

'She retorted to the effect that she didn't require an excuse for being a fair-weather church-goer,' Parkes continued hesitantly. 'She pointed out that she lived near enough to the church to be able to follow services and join in the hymns from her bed, if she had a window open.'

'And after that brief encounter in the village, you went your separate ways?'

'She was going home, I believe. Certainly she was heading in that direction.'

Sloane prepared for his next question carefully. 'There's a bus-stop almost directly outside your house: are the buses a nuisance?'

'A *nuisance*?' Parkes intoned, looking up from his teacup quizzically.

'Noise-wise, that sort of thing.' Sloane was struggling.

'No more so than from lorries that trundle through the village, bringing earthquake shakes to houses day and night. After a while, though, you become immune to the racket, just like camping on an airport's apron. There comes a time when you're awakened by silence, not noise.'

'Emily must have alighted from the bus outside here on the way to her murder.'

Sloane's questions were beginning to fall into a recognizable shape. Still alarm-bells did not appear to be tolling for the verger.

'I've thought about that quite a lot. The police told me that she got off the bus here. They wondered if I'd seen anything suspicious.'

'Such as?'

'Well, *such as* someone following her.'

'Did you?'

'No, I was already in bed. I sleep in a rear bedroom, for the quiet. I have to be up early on Sundays ... my big day of the week. So I'm early to bed on Saturdays, early to rise on Sundays. Clockwork routine; week in, week out; year in, year out.' And then, in the same breath, 'It's frightening to think that there's someone living around here who could do such a thing. It makes you shudder. If Rita was still alive – Rita was my wife – I'd be terrified every time she went out alone after dark.'

'Why are you so convinced that the killer's a local?'

A mask of certitude came down over Parkes's hangdog face. 'It had to be. I mean ... no stranger would be wandering around the village at that time of night. It's not as if the church is on the main thoroughfare. You could accept that an outsider, driving through, might have followed a young thing in a mini-skirt if he'd seen her getting off the bus, but not Emily, not someone her age.'

'I gather, in view of what you've been saying, that you and Emily weren't close friends.'

Parkes considered this for several seconds, as if faced with a tricky multiple-choice examination question.

'We were always friendly to one another, without there being a friendship.'

'Yet you witnessed the signing of Emily's will for her.'

Parkes did not miss a beat.

'It was a favour.'

'A personal favour. A *very* personal favour. How did it come about?'

Unruffled, Parkes explained, 'She came up to me after the family service one Sunday morning and asked if I was going to be in Bournemouth on the Monday. She knew that it was a ritual of mine to go into Bournemouth most Mondays to visit my daughter and grandchildren. She's a teacher there. When I told Emily that I would be in Bournemouth on the Monday, she mentioned the business of her will. All I had to do was witness her signature; the contents of it were no concern of mine. The whole thing, for me, took only ten minutes. It was no skin off my nose. She was a lovely old girl; it was the least I could do for her. She didn't have anyone close. She must have been very lonely.'

'That's quite a statement, Mr Parkes. How much do you actually know about her private life?'

'Nothing really.'

'What of her friends?'

'She doesn't appear to have had any; well, not in the village. There's been a lot of speculation, as you'd expect. She was very active – always shooting off in her Mini Cooper, but no one seems to have seen her with anyone, except those people she stopped to chat with in the street. It's only since Emily's death that people have really begun to pool their knowledge of her.'

'And?'

'We've come to realize she was a mystery woman, a complete enigma.'

'What about her Saturday evening trips?'

Parkes's face reflected confusion. '*Saturday evening trips?*' he repeated, returning the question to sender.

'Every Saturday evening, from autumn until spring, she travelled by bus into Swanage. She'd have caught the bus from the stop opposite your house, on the other side of the road.'

Parkes now understood and nodded his head to demonstrate as much. 'I do recall seeing her waiting at the bus-stop on a number of occasions. I wasn't aware of any routine, though. It didn't register with me that it was always a Saturday. Did she have family in Swanage?'

'No, she went to play bridge.'

'*Bridge!* Well, well.'

'You're surprised?'

'Only that she went all the way to Swanage for that, especially in winter, when we have quite an active bridge circle here in the village. She must have had some kind of affinity there.'

Sloane refrained from being drawn into disclosure.

'Do you get troubled by vandals in these parts?'

'Less than most places, I'd say.'

'No desecration of the church or graveyard?'

'A couple of years ago one grave was partially dug up and a few days later a dead cat was found with its throat cut.'

'In the graveyard?'

'I'm afraid so; the cat's body was next to the defiled grave.'

'Nothing since?'

'Not around the church. There's always funny goings on up the mound, mind you; by the ruins. Said to be Satanists devil-worshipping. Nothing has ever been proved, though. Stories become embellished and take on a life-form of their own; you know how it is. Plenty of talk of sacrifices, but it's never been substantiated. I take it with a pinch of salt.'

'You don't think there was anything like black magic involved in Emily's murder, then?'

'I've heard all the rumours to that effect, but they're rubbish, in my opinion.'

'How can you be so sure?

'I found Emily, remember. At first I thought she must have suffered a heart-attack. There was only a small amount of blood about, which could easily have come from hitting herself on the ground when she fell. Unless the police are holding something back, she was stabbed just the once. That's not consistent with a ritual, sacrificial killing. If it had been anything to do with Satanism, she'd have been butchered. Sorry, I hope I'm not distressing you, but you get my point.'

'Oh, I do, indeed. So, who *did* kill her? And why?'

'Search me. I doubt that she was worth robbing, but you never know these days. The newspapers are always running stories of eccentric recluses who turn out to be multi-millionaires.'

'Talking of newspapers, Mr Parkes, they reported that you were on your way to unlock the church when you came across Emily.'

'That's one thing they got right.'

'And it was still dark?'

'Miserably so.'

'What's the lighting like in the vicinity of the church?'

'Non-existent, unless you count what comes from the moon. That's why I always have a torch with me in the evening when I'm locking up and first thing in the morning when I'm unlocking.'

'You shone your torch on Emily, did you?'

'Of course!' Parkes was momentarily startled.

'Without the torch, you wouldn't have seen the blood, would you? Especially, as you say, there wasn't a great deal of it.'

Parkes sank into a distant, deep-thought mode. 'I suppose that's right. I was shaken. I reacted instinctively. I'm not, therefore, certain about the order of things.'

'Did you happen to observe a trail of blood?'

'*Trail*? No. It was just on her. On her clothes.'

'She must have been wearing an overcoat in such cold weather.'

'Yes, she was.'

'What colour coat?'

'I couldn't tell you. As I've said, it was still dark.'

'Could you distinguish anything about the overcoat's colour?'

'Only that it must have been green, blue, brown or black, I'd say.'

'You couldn't see the colour of the overcoat, yet you identified dried bloodstains.'

Now Parkes was sweating. Despite his obvious discomfort, he continued to participate in the catechism, the tempo of which was being raised ratchet-style by Sloane by the minute.

'I felt for a heart-beat. I opened up her overcoat. I pressed my fingers on her neck, then her chest, to see if there was any sign of respiration. That's when I saw a stain on her white blouse. I also tried her wrist for a pulse. I was certain she was dead. She was Arctic-cold. Rigid.'

'Face up?'

'Pardon?'

'Was she lying face up?'

'Oh, yes, more or less.'

'Did anything else strike you when you flashed the torchlight on her?'

'How do you mean?' Puzzlement flared.

'Was there anything else to see? Anything out of the ordinary?'

'Finding a body, especially of someone I knew, was extraordinary enough!'

Sloane extended him a few more seconds to reconsider his answer, but Parkes had nothing to add or amend.

Sloane departed the verger's house with plenty to ponder, none more so than the fact that Parkes had made no mention of the lipstick graffiti, *MOTHER WHORE!* on the forehead of the corpse.

Some omission! Some explaining due!

CHAPTER 10

On the Sunday, Sloane drove to Lowen's house on the fringe of Wareham, the gateway town to the Purbeck hills and cliff-face coastline. Lowen was returning home with a batch of newspapers rolled under an arm, raindrops dripping from her face and anorak. The combination of an hostile westerly and a persistent drizzle had washed all shape and lustre from her honey-blonde hair.

Head bowed against the wind, Lowen was about twenty paces from the gate to her small front garden when Sloane pulled up. She broke her stride only momentarily as she squinted through the sprinkling rain to identify the driver. Meanwhile, Sloane was having difficulty forcing open his door against the robust wind.

'What are *you* doing here?' Lowen demanded of Sloane, as he loped towards her, dodging puddles and deploying his hands as shields to protect him from the rain.

'Looking for a friend.'

'Then you've come to the wrong place.'

Sloane chortled. 'I could have made money betting on that riposte.'

'Clever bastard, aren't you?'

'You're about the only person who thinks so.' Self-effacement had merit. 'Look, we could irritate one another just as well indoors, in the dry.'

'Who told you where I live?' She confronted him pugnaciously, eyes ablaze, burning through the rain.

'The Most High.'

'He had no right.'

'Don't knock him, he's on your side.'

'Wrong again, Sloane, he's captain of the arseholes.'

'I've gone from Mr Sloane to Mike and now to stark Sloane with you. That's retrogression by any standard.'

'Bright boy! You're learning, albeit painfully slowly.'

By now they were both drenched. Lowen felt her soggy newspapers and swore. 'Look what you've done, they've turned to pulp.'

'Pulp fiction!'

'Not funny.'

Humour, however banal, can serve as a salve. Sloane was in.

'I won't invite you to sit down because you'll only ruin my furniture with your sodden clothes and, in any case, you won't be stopping.'

Two hours later, they were still talking. Lowen had changed into a floppy fawn jumper, faded jeans and rawhide cowboy boots. The little make-up she had applied earlier had been washed away and she had not bothered with a re-application. She had towel-dried her hair while sitting cross-legged on the thick-pile white rug in front of a crackling log fire.

Sloane had begun by hoisting his handkerchief and declaring it his white flag of surrender.

'You'll have to do better than gimmicks,' she had warned warily.

Still standing, still soaked, Sloane had explained everything to her; well, nearly.

Now, as they sat facing one another on the floor, steam rising from Sloane's clothes like Red Indian smoke signals, Lowen said sarcastically, 'So I have you to thank for the fact that my request to be removed from the case wasn't granted.'

'I was gambling on your having a change of heart when you knew the truth.'

'What *truth*?'

'What I've related to you during the last couple of hours. It's essential that you continue.'

'Why? What difference does it make to you?'

'The killer has to be caught. You'll catch him, I've no doubt of that. As soon as I was satisfied that Emily's murder was unconnected with me and The Firm, I made up my mind to bring you in from the cold, to show my hand.'

'You've taken a chance.'

'A calculated risk. You're good; no bullshit. If you had been allowed to walk away from it ...'

'I still might.'

'I don't think so. You want it. You *need* it. You wanted out only because you believed you were being screwed. The more I got to know everything about you—'

'*Everything*?'

'Your background, your motivation, your psyche, I was sure it would be a mistake for you to be replaced.'

'You're still using me.'

'Of course I am, but much more honestly than before. If my judgement is wrong, I'll be thrown to the wolves, quite possibly by you.'

Doubt darkened Lowen's face. 'You're sure you haven't eliminated too soon the possibility of the killer coming from Emily's *other* life?'

'The motive lies within her roots, make no mistake. I want a deal, a pact.'

'What sort of *pact*?' Lowen asked with distrust.

'We pool everything.'

'You don't need a special relationship with me; you can always go over my head to get everything you want. That's exactly what you've been doing all along. Why change?'

'Because it's not working. I don't want to have to keep kicking the fountain of knowledge to make it flow because it will always keep back something. There'll always be residue.'

'Very astute.'

'Not *astute*, just demonstrating a basic understanding of human nature. After everything I've told you today, you now know why I couldn't be more transparent with you before. Even now I'm breaching all the rules of engagement. I'm at your mercy.'

'Which begs the question *why*?'

'I owe you, but that's not the only reason.'

'You're damn right, it isn't! What do you take me for?' Her flared nostrils did most of the talking.

'Not a fool. All loose ends have to be tied. Together, we can achieve that. If someone else was brought in, it could be a whole lot worse, not an improvement.'

'Better the devil you know, eh?'

'Something like that.'

'Thanks!'

'I'm doing my best to be complimentary.'

'Whatever your talents, a way with words isn't one of them.'

'But do we have a deal?'

That sardonic, self-mocking, half-grin of Lowen's returned. 'How could a girl possibly refuse such a generous offer?'

Sloane proffered a hand. Lowen took it tentatively.

'I have a feeling I'm going to regret this,' she said. 'What you're doing is tethering me. Anything that I dig up that you deem to be sensitive will be decreed a no-go area of investigation for me.'

'Too late for second thoughts,' Sloane said blithely. 'A handshake is tantamount to a signed contract.'

Lowen slipped Sloane's jacket solicitously from his shoulders and hooked it over the back of a chair near to the fire, before fetching him a blanket to wrap around himself Then she went to the kitchen to make coffee, adding whisky to each mug.

Most turning points are recognized only in retrospect. Climatic changes are usually very gradual, creeping up on us without any great fanfare. Lowen was not conscious of a marked warming towards Sloane. Only a third party, a fly on the wall, would have immediately sensed the sudden compatibility of the chemistry in that steamy room. A switch had been flicked. A light had come on. Yet the two players remained blind to it, kept in the dark by the time-lag that delayed the recognition of emotional metamorphosis.

They talked easily now, without the insulation of flippancy for protection.

'I've been following you around, Joanne, trying to keep up.'

'So I hear.'

They caressed their hot mugs for supplementary heat.

A telepathic shorthand was developing between them.

'What did you make of the will?'

This was more than a question from Sloane; it was also a statement that he was up with the pace and was not bluffing when he intimated that wherever Lowen went, he was not far behind.

'I think there is one very disappointed Norwegian.'

'Henrietta Rolling got the impression that Ernst Lergen took the news very stoically that he was out in the cold as regards Emily's will.'

'Do you believe that?'

'I've no reason to doubt her judgement. Have you spoken with Lergen?'

'Not yet. He's out of the country on business.'

Sloane squinted shrewdly, like a poker player appraising a call that did not ring true. 'I thought he'd retired.'

'So he has. He was a publisher in Norway. His two sons are now running the business in Oslo. Ernst is a major shareholder. In fact, he owns the majority stock. He acts as the company adviser, part-time, as a hobby, keeping himself from boredom. Every month he flies to Oslo for a couple of days, while his wife, Greta, stays in Henley-on-Thames. He'll be home tomorrow.'

'Did you speak with his wife?'

'Uhhuh. On the phone. It was quite an awkward call.'

'I can imagine. How much did you have to give away?'

'Not much. Of course she wanted to know what it was all about.'

'How big was your lie?'

'No lie. Truncated truth. I hoped he'd be able to help me solve a rather serious crime against someone he might have known many years ago.'

'Very tactful.'

'That's my style.'

The smiles they exchanged now were almost intimate.

'Anything else catch your eye about the will?'

Their mind games had become drained of enmity.

'You know damn well something did.'

'Have you followed it up?'

'Have you?'

'Yes. I've talked with Parkes. What do you make of it, Joanne; his witnessing the signing of the will, yet claiming to hardly know Emily, and then finding her body? A coincidence or something else?'

'We're trained not to believe in coincidences.'

'So what's your game-plan?'

'We continue with the excavation and see what old bones we dig up.'

'That sounds as if you've already come across some cupboard skeletons. Does he still work, apart from serving the church as verger, which can't be a full-time job?'

'We didn't really start to evaluate him in depth until I saw his signature on the will. He has some history.'

Sloane's daydreaming-eyes widened, like flowers opening in sunshine after a downpour.

'Criminal?'

Lowen ran her tapered fingers around the rim of her empty mug, which she balanced on her knee with the kind of aplomb that comes with practice. Her head stayed dipped as she laboured over her reply.

'Parkes's father was a butler in one of the big houses, now a stately home in mid-Dorset and in the stewardship of the National Trust. Harry Parkes grew up witnessing at close quarters all the repellent excesses of the louche rich. His mother was a cook in the same household and his parents worked a sixteen-hour day for a pittance and even less appreciation. He saw the great disparity between the lifestyles of the servant class, the domestic chattels, and their lords and masters, while his parents accepted their serfdom stoically, gracious losers in the lottery of the womb.'

'Who's told you all this?'

'I'll come to that. Let me tell it chronologically.'

Sloane was silenced.

'The upstairs kids of the household were packed off to Eton and various other high-charging private schools for their education. Harry ended up at the local bog standard comprehensive, but he was academically quite bright, particularly at maths. When it came to figures and algebra, in particular, he was a wizard. His parents were bookish and read a lot – God knows how they found the time! But they did and they encouraged their only child to better himself. They were over the moon when he won a place at Oxford University's Lincoln College. Finance was the big obstacle, of course. The Parkes couldn't afford to send him, but they were determined not to squander this opportunity of a lifetime for their son. So Parkes Snr. went cap in hand to his employer, begging for a loan. Lord and Lady Pemberton played big benefactors, saying that a loan was out of the question; they would sponsor young Parkes and wouldn't accept a penny in return. This was their great egalitarian gesture. But for Harry it was charity he didn't want and refused to thank the Pembertons for their generosity if, indeed, that's what it was.'

'But he took the money?'

'His parents took the money.'

'And Harry spent it?'

'Without guilt. He was outstanding at maths, as I've said, but he didn't do as well at Oxford as had been predicted and his tutors were a little disappointed.'

'Did he under-achieve because of the chip on his shoulder?'

'No, he got sidetracked – by politics.'

'Ah! The great seducer.'

'At Oxford, he came across more class discrimination than he'd even encountered in his childhood. It wasn't long before he was beguiled by the cabal of radical hotheads who looked to revolution, if only financial, to efface capitalism. Most of these pinkies weren't from the working-class, like Harry; they had come from the most expensive public schools. Their parents were affluent intellectuals, the sort of people who populate Islington and north Oxford. Harry was bewitched. In winter he'd go to their clandestine meetings in back rooms of city pubs, and in summer under weeping willows on the banks of the River Cherwell, armed with bottles of wine to fuel their subversive pow-wows.'

'Nothing too unusual about that. Students are supposed to challenge traditional values. Rebellion is the mantra of everyone's student years.'

'Spare me the sermon, Mike, we're not at odds over that.'

'Are you saying our humble Mr Parkes is a raging Trotskyite?'

'It would appear that he *was* something like that. He left Oxford with a reasonable second-class degree and got a job at GCHQ.'

GCHQ is the British Government's communications headquarters in Cheltenham, operating globally and working closely with the intelligence networks of the USA, Canada and Australia.

'Good old British Intelligence! We sure know how to pick 'em.'

'He underwent the mandatory vetting.'

'A safety-net so porous it would have let Stalin slip through.'

'He worked there for fifteen years.'

'Until?'

'He came under suspicion after the Falklands War and again in 1988, following the air disaster in the Arabian Gulf when the Americans shot down an Iranian civilian airliner with the loss of two hundred and ninety lives. GCHQ had picked up communications between the US cruiser that fired the missiles and the flight-deck crew of the Iranian airbus.'

'And information was leaked?'

'Information certainly got out. There was an internal inquiry, led by *your* lot.'

'I know nothing of that. Was Parkes nailed?'

'Only partially. It appears that he had a loose tongue, but there was no evidence that he was selling secrets. He'd been targeted by people who'd no doubt done their homework and decided he was a soft touch.'

'And so they befriended him?'

'You know the drill far better than I do. They'd bump into him in a pub, as if by chance, ply him with booze, and after a couple of jars he was an open encyclopaedia; a garrulous canary.'

'But he wasn't prosecuted, even though he was in clear breach of the Official Secrets Act?'

'No, he was just fired.'

'How did you come by all of this?'

'We ran his name through the system.'

'But, according to your narrative, he hasn't a criminal record.'

'No, but he's listed for reference to the Special Branch as a security risk and not to be considered for any "sensitive" employment. I'm not allowed access to his case-file, but I expect *you* can explain to *me* why he was never prosecuted.'

'How about more coffee?'

'Of course.'

By the time Lowen returned from the kitchen with the refills, Sloane had assembled a plausible explanation.

'I can only theorize. A prosecution of that nature attracts extensive publicity. It's messy. There are no winners. We get our man, but equally we expose our own holes. We also alert the enemy, which, today, is a global network, rather than one nation or one creed, that one of their allies has been taken out. They proceed to fill the gap and we have to start from scratch to identify their new conduit. It's like dealing with a chain circle. A chink is removed and is almost immediately replaced. The chain continues. From what you've told me, any charge against Parkes wouldn't have been too serious. Sounds to me that he was more a loose-lipped gossip than a traitor. A prosecution would have lost more than it gained. What did he do for a living after being kicked out of Cheltenham?'

'He opened a little florist's shop with his wife.'

'Down here?'

'Just off the High Street. It made sense for him to get away from Cheltenham, where he was disgraced, and to start afresh.'

'Yet you said he was brought up in Dorset, so why return to the county where he could have been remembered?'

'Corfe Castle is a very different part of Dorset from where he was reared. He'd be very unfortunate to meet anyone from his past in Corfe. But, bear in mind, it would have been from Cheltenham and his life there that he was escaping. No one in Dorset would have been privy to his treachery in Cheltenham.'

'Unless, of course, Emily had independently uncovered something new about him by accident and was on the brink of unfrocking him.'

Lowen's face froze and framed the moment.

CHAPTER 11

Monday dawned fridge-cold but Caribbean-blue. The sky had emptied its bladder overnight and had stopped urinating on the south coast. The sea was still bullish, though, with froth on the lips of the waves. A few slothful clouds loitered, left behind by the herd that had stampeded northwards.

Sloane was having a lonely breakfast in the restaurant of his smuggler's cove hotel when Lowen gatecrashed by courtesy of the satellite link. Mobiles have become the new fast-food scourge of the digestive system.

'I've had Parkes on the brain all night,' Lowen began, like someone with a compulsion to unload; not exactly breathless, but tight in the chest and vocal cords.

'He would be flattered. Bad demons?' Sloane managed with a full mouth. He was the sole punter in the restaurant. Business continued to be slack during the traditional lull before the Christmas storm.

'No, just thoughts that wouldn't let go, attention-seeking, keeping me awake. Suppose Dresden had come across Parkes's involvement in new, dubious activities, wouldn't she have consulted you?'

'She was on the payroll as a watcher, nothing more. She never instigated assignments, she was allocated them. She was given a brief. She had disciplines to follow. There were strict demarcation lines that could never be crossed.'

'Never ever?'

'Never.'

'So she wasn't at liberty to use her discretion?'

'Oh, but she was, provided she kept within the tramlines.'

'And you laid the tracks?'

'Always.'

'Never anyone else?'

'As I told you yesterday, Carrington was her handler, so the protocol established him as the go-between. The brief would originate from me, conveyed to Emily by Carrington.'

'So if she had discovered something untoward about Parkes, purely by chance, she'd have primed Carrington, not you?'

Sloane stopped eating, having lost his appetite for what was left of his sad-looking fried egg and bacon. His toast was cold and brittle, while his coffee was already on the wrong side of tepid. Through the bay window he could see pools of rainwater resembling an invasion of giant turtles crossing the saturated lawn of the beer-garden. Natural waterfalls, cascading down the cliffs, had started during the night, accelerating the long-term erosion that was eating away the coastline inexorably. A waitress, as starchy as her dated black and white uniform, fluttered into the dining-room to see if Sloane could be tempted into more coffee or toast, but he waved her away. Determined not to retreat empty-handed, she swiped the plate from under Sloane's nose with the alacrity of a sleight-of-hand card trickster. Sloane made no protest; she was welcome to the greasy debris. Breakfast was over and out for Sloane.

'I would have heard from Carrington, yes.'

Exaggerated pause. 'I'm calling from my office. I was at my desk by six. Since then, I've been through all the photos we plundered from Dresden's place. There's not one of Parkes.'

'Suggesting she wasn't doing a job on him.'

'Unless the prints and negatives were passed on but never reached you.'

Now the slow-burn pause was Sloane's. 'Just what are you getting at?'

'Just kicking things around, turning over stones.'

'Carrington's beyond reproach.'

'Everyone is until exposed otherwise. All the best crooks are the respectable ones. The gun-toting thugs are easy to catch. The church-going, God-fearing gangsters who blend into the wallpaper of decent society and rob with their gold Parker pens and silver tongues are the ones who are most elusive.'

'Point taken, but if Emily was doing a number on Parkes, it's more likely that it was a private commission.'

'You have only Carrington's word that she was moonlighting.'

'And the photo files. There'll also be a bank trail.'

'So far the photos are inconclusive,' Lowen argued. 'They're numbered and coded, but they could quite easily relate to investigations she was undertaking for you folk.'

'Except that she wouldn't have held on to them. Never be caught in possession; that's the creed of the sly fox and greedy hounds.'

'She *shouldn't* have kept them, but that doesn't mean she didn't. We all break rules, for varying reasons.'

Sloane's irritation festered. 'Carrington's sacrosanct; leave it at that.'

'Have it your way, but I'm not bound by your judgement.'

'Meaning?'

'I'm keeping a *very* open mind.'

'That's your privilege.' Petulance peaked.

They were both becoming prickly and the silences were no longer soothing.

'Something I didn't mention to you yesterday …' Lowen now sounded as if she was in the confessional, but without contrition. No sins to admit. No penance.

'About Carrington?' Sloane's response was delivered like a snappy bite.

'No, about Parkes.'

Sloane waited. Lowen sensed his gnawing curiosity.

'We've been inundated with hot gossip.'

'What sort of hot gossip?'

'Bad stuff.'

'How *bad*?'

'Not the sort for phone conversations.'

'What's the strength of it?'

'Still to be tested.'

'Do I get to sample?'

'Only on my terms.'

'I thought we had a partnership.'

'No, we struck a deal; not the same thing.'

'OK, where do *we* go from here?'

'*I* go to Parkes's home to arrest him.'

'On what charge?'

'No *charge*. For further questioning. Depending on how it goes, I might be applying to magistrates for a search-warrant; in fact, it's a copper-bottom certainty.'

'Looking for *the* weapon?'

'That would be too much to hope for.'

'What then?'

'Patience is a virtue; let's see how virtuous you can be.'

'Do I get to sit-in on the interview?'

'Only if you promise to be a good boy and behave yourself throughout.'

'What are the conditions?'

'You sit quietly at the back and keep your mouth buttoned.'

'You have my word.'

'Let's hope that's enough.'

'What time's kick-off?'

'Eleven a.m. prompt.'

'Reserve me a seat in the gallery.'

'Bring your own chair; resources are stretched.'

Sloane assumed she was joking.

Lowen was outside the interview-room with her junior colleague, Detective Constable Peter Leonard, when joined by Sloane. Lowen peeled away from Leonard to greet Sloane with businesslike briskness.

'*He's* in there, so keep your voice down,' she said peremptorily, directing Sloane with her eyes to a metal, cell-like door to her left.

'Is he alone?'

Lowen nodded. 'We've been letting him sweat.'

'No request for a solicitor to hold his hand?'

'Not so far. We've kept him in the dark – not literally – as much as possible, hoping the surprise element of our tactics will give us an edge.' Then, to Leonard, a fresh-faced, clean-cut, grey-suited ex-college boy-type with blow-dried hair, 'OK, let's go to it.'

Seeing Sloane was Parkes's first surprise. Instant recognition creased the suspect's hangdog face.

'What's *he* doing here?' Parkes pointed accusingly at Sloane from his chair at an oblong, wooden table in the middle of a small, spartan room. Sloane positioned himself sentry-fashion, legs crossed at the ankles, just inside the solid door, where an upright, hard timber chair had been deposited for him, though he chose to stand. The only other furniture in the chilly, square-shaped room was a pair of chairs for Lowen and Leonard the opposite side of the table from Parkes, backs to Sloane. A round, luminescent, high-powered electric light was embedded in the concrete ceiling. The harsh, white pools of light seemed to illuminate and exemplify the coldness of the occasion. The walls were white-tiled; the floor as cold and unyielding as the ceiling. It was a room without a view, designed purposely for people without much of a future. No window had been included in the design, in order that the entire focus was inwards, as if the outside world was no longer obtainable. It was a room rather than a cell in name only.

Sloane kept to the bargain and left it to Lowen to respond to Parkes's question.

'You've already met Mr Sloane, I believe.'

'He came to my house yesterday, claiming to have been a friend of Miss Dresden's.'

'That was no lie.'

'So what's he doing here, with you people?'

'He's a part of the investigation team, but he's at this interview only as an observer.'

Parkes continued to look confused and Lowen figured that this extra dimension of disorientation would work in her favour. She took the chair directly opposite Parkes, while Leonard sat on her left, next to the tape-recorder, which he would operate. She introduced Leonard, but there was no handshaking.

Lowen opened a buff folder and twiddled a ballpoint pen. She was dressed in a dreary brown trouser-suit that was altogether the wrong colour for her and it did nothing for her confidence.

'We've invited you here this morning, Mr Parkes, so that we can extend your statement concerning Miss Dresden,' Lowen began disarmingly.

'You didn't *invite* me here, you arrested me and brought me against my will and I want that recorded,' Parkes retorted. As he spoke plaintively, so he stared bitterly at the tape-recorder, which Leonard had switched on, at the same time naming everyone in the room, giving the date and time that the interview commenced.

Lowen ignored the correction and proceeded in a monotone, her soul squeezed dry of emotion, a professional requirement in these situations and something that was perfected only when a certain mileage on the clock was reached.

'We've heard all about how you came to find the body.'

'What more can I tell you?' Parkes looked from Lowen to Leonard, then through the gap between the pair of them to Sloane, who met and held his gaze. Parkes broke the eye-lock.

'Let's turn back the clock into your past ...' Lowen allowed the unfinished sentence to tail off, like vapour leaving behind its nasty odour long after it had been blown away. She had stopped playing with her pen. Her eyes, like those of a predatory big cat of the jungle, sabred her quarry.

'Why have you been snooping on me?' Parkes fumed, thumping the table with a podgy fist, his anger spontaneous. He was as neatly dressed as if he was conducting his duties at church on a Sunday. 'What happened in Cheltenham was over and done with years ago. No criminal charges were ever levelled against me. I was foolish and I made a few mistakes, amounting to misdemeanours, for which I paid; that's all.'

'How did you know that was the period of your life I was preparing to tackle you about?'

'It was obvious from the build up, from the moment you mentioned my *past*, as if I'd served time for armed robbery or rape. I don't know who told you about it, but they had no right. I wish I'd not been the one to find Emily. It's been a nightmare ever since. You do your public duty, call the emergency services, act as quickly and responsibly as you can, then find yourself the one in the stocks being pilloried. No wonder people are reluctant to give evidence in court these days. There's no incentive. The innocent are treated as if they're the ones in the dock.'

Leonard yawned extravagantly, bored by the sermon. Lowen pressed on implacably, her eyes as fixed as an alligator's.

'We've had lots of calls and correspondence about you since Miss Dresden was stabbed to death.'

'What sort of *calls* and *correspondence*?'

'Not nice. Summarized, it would appear that you have a reputation for being something of a lecher, a peeping Tom.'

Parkes mustered outrage. 'Who are these people?'

'Anonymous.'

'Exactly! Craven cowards. Sick people hiding behind the apron of anonymity. Getting a kick out of throwing mud without showing their faces. The scandal is that you listen to such people. What evidence have they produced?'

'None.'

'There you are, then!' Parkes was triumphal and bellicose. 'It's disgusting that people should be wasting police time like this, particularly when you've got so much on your plate. What can they possibly get out of it? You'd think they'd better things to do. What sad people!'

Lowen slowed the tempo. She had kicked off her flat shoes and was fidgeting with her stockinged feet involuntarily, an indication to Sloane that she was more tense and self-pressured than the rest of her body-language telegraphed.

'So you deny being a peeping Tom?'

'I'm incensed.'

'Is that a denial?'

'It's an indignant denial. Just where am I supposed to have been doing all this peeping?'

'Have you ever been to Shell Bay beach? It's not many miles from here.'

Parkes changed colour as quickly as a chameleon, though not to his advantage.

'I might have,' he replied cautiously, his wet eyes turning sly.

'You must know. Which is it, yes or no?' Lowen was uncompromising. Shell Bay had been the late Princess Diana's favourite beach, where she would go for secret midnight bathing at the height of the summer, unknown to her husband, Prince Charles.

After some dithering, Parkes hedged his bets. 'I've been to most of the Dorset beaches at various times. Shell Bay is one of them.'

'And you're familiar with the nudist colony there?'

Sloane counted the beats. One, two, three, four, five, then, 'If you live in Dorset, it's impossible not to be aware of such places. The local Press is always featuring the contentious issue.'

'What's your view on naturism?'

Parkes's unease was overt. 'I don't have a view. I mean, I believe in live and let live.'

'You like to think of yourself as something of a liberal, is that it?'

'A free-thinker and enlightened, I'd say, though I must confess I'm not very tolerant when it comes to hooliganism. But this is ridiculous. You're not entitled to arrest people just so you can hold a debate on social issues. Whatever next!'

Lowen ignored the smokescreen.

'You're not a naturist, then?'

'Dead right, I'm not!'

'Would it be fair to describe you as an *habitué* of the Shell Bay beach zone of Studland, in winter as well as in summer?'

'No, it would not be *fair!*'

'I'm not implying that you go there to romp naked in public.'

'Then what are you *implying*?'

'That you're a voyeur.'

'You've a nerve!'

'You deny hiding behind the sand dunes, watching the nudists through binoculars?'

'This has gone too far.' His outrage, however, had lost most of its steam.

'People have been telling us that they've seen you up to your tricks. Not once. Not twice. But frequently.'

'Anonymous people again?'

'Yes.'

'Well, they're liars. Taking notice of them is like listening to Saddam Hussein bleating about being denied his human rights. They're the ones who were up to no good, more than likely.'

'Do you own a pair of binoculars?'

Parkes was flustered by the question and stammered his answer. 'As a matter of fact, I do. I'm a bird-watcher.'

Leonard sniggered irreverently.

'You're a keen hornithologist, huh?'

Parkes missed the cryptology.

'I am, but I doubted that such a big word was within your vocabulary.'

Gloves were off.

'You're also aware that the Shell Bay coastline is something of a paedophiles' paradise?'

'The police are always making arrests there. Have I ever been arrested by your special beach patrols? I'll answer that for you: no, never. Your own records will confirm that. All of which supports what I've been telling you, that you've had your time squandered by mischief-making, malicious liars.'

Lowen filled her lungs before moving in for the kill.

'Do you own a PC?'

A fog came down over Parkes's eyes, hiding the windmills of panic whirling in his head. 'I do, like most people these days.' His apparent composure was worn like a garment that did not fit. 'What's so unusual about that?'

'Nothing. Absolutely nothing. As you say, it's absolutely normal.'

'How much longer is this going on for?' Parkes was suddenly less secure within himself.

'Quite a while yet.'

'In that case, I could do with a glass of water.'

The recorder was stopped while Leonard acted as water-carrier, fetching a jug and three glasses. The same ritual as at the beginning was recited when the machine was restarted.

'Are you connected to the Internet, Mr Parkes?'

'I am. Are you? Is anyone in this room without access to the 'Net?'

'Are you a regular surfer?'

'I don't surf. I have a definite destination. I take the direct route. I'm a regular user; a few minutes every day.'

Lowen steepled her fingers to her chin. 'Your name has been supplied to us by the FBI.'

Parkes's face turned tombstone-bleak. Sloane did his best to disguise his own astonishment. Having dropped the pebble in the pond, Lowen now waited impassively for the ripples of reaction.

'The FBI?' was all that Parkes could muster feebly.

'Your name and address were given to Scotland Yard a few weeks ago and went into a queue pending action. When your name popped up in the Press, an observant officer in London made the connection. I was the recipient of an e-mail within minutes. And here we all are. The world revolves faster by the day.'

Parkes was sliding in his chair, his sinking-feeling very real.

'The FBI, the FBI, but ...' he recited, desperate to make sense of what he was hearing. The jigsaw pieces in his head refused to slot into place. Too many bits and no picture to work with.

'For some years now the FBI has been waging war globally against paedophile networks. There is an army of agents doing nothing else but tracking subscribers to paedophile websites, whether they live in Wareham or Winnipeg. Your name was scooped up in the net.'

'There must be a mistake.' Parkes saw a glimmer of hope; a crack of daylight through which he might squeeze.

'A mistake is always possible.' Lowen offered him a half-open door through which to escape, then slammed it shut in his face with, 'I'm sure you'll have no objection to our taking a look around your home just to satisfy ourselves that you haven't been downloading obscene material.'

'I don't really see ...' he vacillated, squirming.

'You either invite us in or we get a search-warrant. Either way, it's going to happen. You choose.'

'I want to speak with my solicitor,' he blurted out, the way it is done in the movies and on TV.

'No problem. Make the arrangements, Peter. Interview over.'

Lowen stood up in the manner of a didactic Victorian school ma'am ending a lesson, kicked back her chair, wheeled and stomped out, winking at Sloane as she brushed past him.

Sloane followed her out, while Leonard remained with Parkes, explaining to the shaken suspect the procedures that would inevitably follow.

Lowen kept walking briskly until she was satisfied that anything said between herself and Sloane would not be overheard in the interview-room.

'Well, what do you think?' she asked, turning to face Sloane.

'Good work. What a turn-up! I really am impressed. Suppose you find downloaded child porn at Parkes's place?'

'What do you mean *suppose*? We will!'

'Yes, but where does it take us?'

'I don't follow.'

'How could Parkes be linked to Emily's conception, birth and childhood? How can he be reconciled with the MOTHER WHORE slogan on Emily's forehead, whatever his depraved instincts?'

'Have you always been a party-pooper?'

'Sorry, but that's what the Devil expects from his advocate. It comes with the horns.'

CHAPTER 12

Parkes's house was a sewer of child pornography. Images of children in lewd poses or being sexually molested by men – sometimes women as well – had been downloaded from his PC. The photos, in their hundreds, were stashed in his bedroom-wardrobe, attic, garden-shed and a spare bedroom used as a study.

The search, enforced by a warrant, was conducted by Lowen and Leonard during the afternoon following Parkes's arrest and the interview with him. Parkes accompanied the detectives, but Sloane was not included in the search-party.

By the time he was driven to Swanage police station to be formally charged, Parkes was a broken man.

'I'm sorry, I'm so dreadfully sorry and ashamed,' he lamented in endless repetition, almost wailing and braying, as he wept in the rear seat of the car *en route* to Swanage, drowning in floods of self-pity.

Leonard was driving, with Lowen sitting beside Parkes, though throughout the fifteen-minute drive she did not look at him once, preferring to stare sightlessly out of the side window to more attractive scenery. The detectives pointedly ignored every comment and question put to them. Leonard was gripping the steering-wheel as if he had his hands on Parkes's throat. Lowen made a mental note to ensure that Leonard was not left alone at any time with this prisoner. She had seen the danger signals many times before, not with Leonard, but in the enraged eyes of numerous other detectives. Neither was she immune from the urge to throttle someone like Parkes; the desire was very strong and took considerable resistance.

Before being charged at Swanage police station with offences in relation to child pornography, Parkes said tearfully, 'This is going to ruin me, more so than if I'd killed Emily, which I didn't. I swear to you I didn't harm her. I shall plead guilty to everything else, but I had no reason to hurt Emily and I didn't. You *must* believe that.'

After Parkes had been charged and bailed, Lowen called an impromptu briefing for her troops at county headquarters. Parkes's house was to be revisited. This time the searchers would be looking solely for the murder weapon. Floorboards would be ripped up, drains and drainpipes flushed out, gutterings swept and inside walls tested for secret hiding places. Other officers would be assigned to door-knocking, trying to find any of Parkes's neighbours who saw him out and about on the Saturday night that Emily Dresden was stabbed to death. Something tangible was now required to tie him to the crime.

Lergen was always pleased to be home. That is not to say he was unsettled by his regular trips to Oslo. After all, Norway was the country of his birth. He grew up there among the fjords and on pollution-free mountain slopes, where they had owned a Swiss-style chalet. He was married there, founded a flourishing business there and raised his wonderful children there. Norway was his homeland, but no longer his home. For Ernst, home was the place where his slippers waited for him, where the aromas of his wife's cooking greeted him, and where the contours of the bed had been shaped by his own nocturnal restlessness. Despite having lived, worked and played in Norway for sixty-plus years, Henley-on-Thames, England was now his home.

Greta gave him a wifely peck on the cheek as they embraced unemotionally on the threshold of their magnificent residence that was perfumed with affluence from top to bottom.

'How are the boys?' was her first question; always her first question when Ernst returned from his monthly flying visit to Oslo.

'Fine, just fine; they send their love,' he replied, which was as much a repetitive answer as the repetitive question.

'Good flight?'

'All flights that land safely are good ones.' Another off-the-shelf reply.

'I've poured you a glass of your favourite pre-dinner wine. I saw you driving up. Dinner will be rather late this evening ...'

'I'm glad. I ate on the plane. I won't be hungry for a couple of hours ... at least.'

'The wine is in the lounge.'

'I'll change into something casual first.'

Ernst could read his wife's mind – or so he liked to kid himself – as easily as he could the giant advertisements on the roadside hoardings on the way to and from Heathrow Airport. Without glasses. Without insight. Without any doubt over the message. And as he made his lethargic way upstairs to the bedroom, while Greta headed for the kitchen, he was convinced that his wife was bothered by something. Whatever it was, it would emerge during the course of the evening, of that he was confident. There had been something esoteric mirrored in her pained eyes, like mystic telepathy or a Masonic sign; nothing that anyone else would have noticed, of course: a certain smile that was not really a smile at all; a nervous quiver of the mouth; an out-of-place flutter of the eyelids. You needed to have lived a lifetime together to be able to read the smoke signals before even the fire was lit.

The Lergens' marriage had been a long and undulating one, without extreme highs or lows; typifying urbane sociability and born out of calculations of the head rather than romantic expectations of the heart. Conceived in the boardroom, not the bedroom, theirs had been a sound and sensible marriage, a rare union that had met with the infinite approval of both sets of in-laws.

Ernst had inherited his entrepreneurial blood from his father, an orphanage boy who became the Artful Dodger of Oslo as a teenager, picking pockets to survive, yet by the age of forty he was a feted magazine magnate. Greta's father was a bank manager and her mother taught economics at university. 'Ah! A lady with a head for money – just the wife for our Ernst!' was Claude Lergen's enthusiastic exclamation when he first heard of Greta's credentials. If it had been an arranged marriage, it could not have been arranged better.

Ernst had been a good provider and Greta had proved a pillar of support, not to mention a stabilizing influence. Greta, whose education had been rounded off at a Swiss finishing school, possessed all the social graces that helped to open the doors for Ernst that led to the upper echelons of European society. She also brought her organizational flair to motherhood. No depression, panic-attacks or debilitating feelings of inadequacy for her. Bringing up children had been enacted with military precision. Ernst and Greta's marriage had been cemented in a bed of respect, with only a thin overlay of passion. That is not to say the marriage was completely loveless. Respect had been the seed from which a certain kind of love had grown. But it had always been practical and mature love, without the reckless blaze of physical desire. And their partnership had worked, as a business, as Ernst and Greta Lergen plc.

It was not until dinner was almost over and their wine glasses were virtually empty that Greta proved her husband right about his ability to read his wife's mind.

'You're not in any kind of trouble are you, Ernst?' she began tentatively and awkwardly.

'What makes you ask that?'

'I had a phone call while you were away, from a police officer, a detective inspector.'

'And what did he want?'

'It was a *she*. She didn't give away much. All she'd say was that she thought you might have known someone in a case she was investigating and perhaps you could help her; something like that. To be truthful, I didn't like the sound of it. I explained that you were out of the country.'

'And what did she say to that?'

'She'd call again, when you were home.' Then, frowning and intense, 'What can it possibly be about, Ernst? Have you any idea?'

'None whatsoever,' he lied competently. Eyes and expression radiated candour. But a lie-detector would have registered the tell-tale fluttering pulse and the sudden blood-rush to his head.

'Am I being silly to be worried, Ernst?'

'Very silly,' he purred, looping an arm around her trim waist in a touching gesture of supportive togetherness. 'I am absolutely positive it's nothing of consequence.'

He was lying again, of course. But still it did not show.

CHAPTER 13

Ernst Lergen slept well; Greta Lergen did not. She was up and about by four o'clock, making coffee, pacing, and trying to read, but she could not concentrate, not even on household chores. Once, for more than half an hour, she posed at the French windows of their capacious lounge, just staring into space. Vast pools of cold-hearted moonlight shimmered with metallic glint on the River Thames that stretched like a curled python at the foot of the gently sloping lawn, but she saw nothing of this. Her eyes were inclined inwards.

Unknown to the Lergens as they discussed Greta's sleepless night over a breakfast of croissants, freshly squeezed orange juice and coffee, Sloane and Lowen were on the road, on the warpath even, making good headway northwards along the A34 towards the turn-off for Henley-on-Thames. When they were no further than a quarter of a mile from the Lergens' sumptuous residence, Lowen parked in a lay-by and phoned. The time was exactly 8.00 a.m.

A trawl during the past couple of days of all network providers revealed that Miss Dresden had a business account with Orange and had been supplied with a Motorola handset, the model having been updated six months ago to include Internet, email and photographic facilities. A print-out of all calls made from her cell phone, during the four-week period up to her death, had been assiduously followed up by the worker bees of Lowen's hive. The one item that leapt from the pages above all others was the last of all the calls, a mobile-to-mobile operation lasting barely twenty seconds and made at nineteen minutes after midnight on the Sunday morning of 9 November. In other words, if all else was to be believed, Miss Dresden had made a call on her mobile some twenty minutes after she was killed. Some woman! Even more intriguing for Lowen and Sloane, was the call's destination – Ernst Lergen's mobile. Lowen personally reexamined Miss Dresden's phone and address book. No Lergen was listed. Nor was Ernst's mobile number listed against a code name.

She must have kept the number in her head or in her mobile's memory, Lowen had deduced, a view later expressed by Sloane, when they had a chance to evaluate the implications.

During the drive that morning, they had discussed that *impossible* phone call from the grave.

'The time of the call is beyond question, so what was she doing taking so long to walk that short distance from the bus-stop to her cottage?' Lowen asked herself as much as seeking an explanation from Sloane.

'Maybe she did detour, after all.'

'Why? It doesn't make sense.'

'Perhaps if we knew the answer to that the entire mystery would be solved,' Sloane suggested.

'Why would she have been calling Lergen at that time of night from the silent village streets?'

'For help?'

'When he was more than a hundred miles away,' Lowen said dismissively.

'Perhaps he wasn't; perhaps she was expecting him; perhaps they had planned a secret rendezvous. If she'd been aware of being in trouble and had time to make a call, it would have been to Carrington or the local police. The mobile is missing, so presumably she had it on her and it was taken by the killer.'

'If Lergen was the perpetrator, he'd hardly be calling himself with his victim's phone.'

'Unless he wanted to point us in the wrong direction. It could always have been a hired knifeman who was reporting, "Job done".'

'Which all makes for a fascinating conversation to come,' remarked Lowen, then added, 'Early bird catches the worm,' as she punched the numbers on her dinky Nokia.

Greta answered, immediately alarmed. In the old days, when Ernst ran his business empire like an emperor, the phone would be ringing all hours of the day and night, but not since he stood down to make way for his sons. Only bad news nowadays came between the hours of 10.00 p.m. and 9.00 a.m. So she was already on her guard.

'May I speak with Mr Lergen, please?' Lowen kicked-off sweetly.

Greta wavered, then, 'Whom shall I say is calling?' The stilted question was superfluous. Greta knew.

'Detective Inspector Lowen.'

Greta's sudden asthmatic intake of breath was clearly audible to Lowen. When finally Greta responded reticently, it was with a tight chest and knotted throat. 'I'll see if he's available.'

It was only a few seconds before Ernst Lergen breezed on the line.

'Good morning,' he said cheerfully. 'What can I do for you?'

'I have a few questions to put to you.'

'Fine, fire away.'

'I'd rather do it face to face.'

'As you wish. When have you in mind? I'll fetch my diary.'

'I have to see you now,' said Lowen, not giving him any room in which to manoeuvre.

'Now!' Ernst was surprised, but not disconcerted.

'I'm already in Henley,' Lowen continued quickly, finalizing the fait accompli.

'Well, you'd better come for breakfast,' Ernst said affably, with a hint of a chuckle. 'Tell me where you are and I'll give you directions.'

Five minutes later, Ernst was greeting them at the door with a firm and friendly handshake.

Lowen introduced Sloane as her 'colleague' and left it at that when the Lergens showed no interest in his rank or position, something Lowen had banked on.

'Come on, let me take your coats,' Ernst fussed, playing the grand host, as if his visitors were guests at a dinner party.

Greta, anxious to keep herself busy, volunteered to hang the overcoats in a closet, while Ernst showed the way into the lounge.

If Lowen had been asked to describe Ernst Lergen in one word, she would have said 'distinguished'. Despite the passage of time and the grey hair, she would have recognized him instantly from the autographed photograph, taken so long ago, that had been removed by her and Sloane from Dresden's cottage. The years had aged him sympathetically. The skin around his jowls was still taut and one needed to be close up to be aware of the crepe-wrinkling around his neck. There was something distinctly centurian about his features and his eyes were as penetrating as an X-ray machine. His green golfing slacks, white loafers and yellow designer sweater, bearing a pair of golf clubs motif, portrayed him as exactly what he was – a recently retired executive with money to burn and time at his disposal to keep the bonfire of pleasure blazing.

'Now, how about some tea or coffee?' Ernst rubbed his hands vigorously, not because he was cold but as an allusion to the temperature outside and underscoring the reason why the visitors might be tempted by the offer of a hot drink. More likely, however, thought Lowen, it would give him the opportunity to pack off his wife to the kitchen without making it too obvious that he was not keen for her to hear the questions – and most certainly not the answers.

Both Sloane and Lowen agreed on coffee, believing that it was in their interest to have Greta otherwise occupied.

'Is it all right if I trot off to the kitchen, or do you want to speak with me as well?' said Greta, with a plea for release in her jumpy eyes.

'It really would be best for us to have a few words in private with your husband,' said Lowen pleasantly, not missing Greta's ambivalence.

'Very well,' agreed Greta looking strained. 'If that's all right with you, dear?' She looked to her husband for his approval, not wishing to leave him alone with the jackals (her thoughts), if he had any reservations.

'That's all right, you skip along and do the business,' he said blithely. 'I think I'll be safe left alone. They don't look the sort that will subject me to the third degree.'

As Greta exited the room with the deportment of a model and the grace of a socialite, Lowen was thinking what a handsome couple they made. Greta had a strong face and a resolute chin that suggested in normal circumstances she would be neither compromised nor intimidated. Her eyes were as steely as the colour of her hair, which she controlled the way she did most things in her life. Although still in her silk housecoat and fluffy slippers, she was as smart as if in an evening gown.

'Of course I know why you're here,' said Ernst, the moment his wife had closed the door behind her and they were all seated.

Shrewd, thought Lowen. Taking the initiative, just what I'd expect from someone of his standing. Let's just see how good he is at the game.

'Do you?'

'I read about poor Emily in the papers. Why would anyone want to do a thing like that? I called her solicitor. After that, I guessed you'd come calling, sooner or later. And here you are. Welcome!'

'Didn't it occur to you to get in touch with us?'

He looked perplexed. 'What for? How could I help?'

Now it was Lowen's turn to stick on a puzzled face. 'In that case, why were you so sure we'd come to you?'

'Because you'd stumble across certain things. Only I could know they wouldn't lead you anywhere but down a dead end.'

'You could have saved us time ... and a trip.'

'Nonsense! You'd still have come. You'd still have wanted to ... what is it you say? ... bottom it out.'

He was right, of course; something that Lowen acknowledged, but only to herself.

'You obviously knew that you would benefit from Miss Dresden's original will.'

'I was sent a copy years ago, yes, when we, my family, were still living in Norway. Of course, as you're aware, that document is obsolete, null and void; a document as dead as its originator.'

'But you didn't know that until after the murder?'

'True, very true.' He paused as a charitable smile washed his suntanned face. 'I don't mean this to sound ungracious, but I had no need for Emily's money or property. I have been fortunate and life has been kind to me. I can honestly say there's nothing I want for. Emily's estate would be wasted on me. I would have sold her home and pocketed the proceeds, making zero impact on my lifestyle. It would have amounted to pocket-money, small change.'

'Her cottage might fetch half a million these days.'

'I know the value of property.'

This was a statement that said half a million pounds was nothing to him.

'Did you make Miss Dresden aware of your feelings?'

'Certainly not; that would have been churlish and hurtful.'

'Why should she be leaving you everything of hers, in the first place?' Lowen probed. 'What were you to her?'

'We were lovers.' He glanced furtively towards the door, as if to assure himself that his wife was not about to enter. 'Not lately, you understand, but a long, long time ago, when we were young and idealistic, carefree and unrealistic.' There was something wistful and regretful about him as he travelled back down the rocky road of time, reminiscence proving a chafing experience.

'Who ended it?'

'We were going to be married,' he said, not immediately answering the question. 'We were very much in love. It was a serious thing. We hadn't got as far as fixing a wedding date. I called it off. I don't think she ever got over it.'

'How would you know that?'

'We kept in touch for many years.'

'How?'

'We wrote to one another.'

'Love letters?'

Ernst grimaced. 'Affectionate letters.'

'Mutually so?'

Ernst was becoming increasingly unhappy with this line of questioning. 'These are very personal matters, Inspector.'

'A woman you once loved has been brutally murdered, Mr Lergen,' said Lowen, as a salutary, though rather unnecessary, reminder.

'Who said I ever—' Ernst cut himself off, suddenly regretting almost articulating what he was thinking.

Lowen made a guess and finished the sentence for him. 'I think you were going to say that you never stopped loving her?'

'This is a pointless conversation.' Ernst struggled clumsily, shaking his head.

'Did the letter-writing continue after your marriage?'

'On and off. Not frequently. I had to be discreet.'

'Because of your wife?'

'But of course!'

'Did Miss Dresden write to you at your home address?'

'Heavens no!'

'To your office?'

'Yes, always.' He desperately wanted out of this.

'Earlier you used the word *lovers* to describe your relationship: were you ever officially engaged to be married?'

'Yes, for about three months.'

'Who broke it off?'

'I did.'

'Why, if you still loved her?'

He swung away and wrung his hands as if indulging in a self-cleansing process. Self-loathing suddenly disfigured his face.

'Let's just say there was parental pressure.'

'Your parents didn't approve of her?'

'Afraid not.'

'Why was that?'

'We're talking about difficult times, Inspector. Europe after the war. Deep prejudices and old hatreds.'

'I'm a good and patient listener, Mr Lergen.'

'My parents were obsessed with pedigrees and appearances. My father was what over here you'd term a self-made man. He had created a little business empire and he was determined that I should develop it into a dynasty. He looked on marriage the way equine people think of stud farms. Put bluntly, he wanted me wed and bed with a classic filly.'

'And Emily wasn't a *classic*?'

'Not in his eyes. In mine, yes. A winner all the way.'

'Why didn't you stand up to your father?'

'Does that matter now?'

'You don't strike me as feckless.'

'Fathers and sons, mothers and daughters – the chemistry is strange and can be potent, unpredictable, dangerous even.'

'Are you intimating that your father threatened to wash his hands of you if you disobeyed him and went ahead with your plans to marry Miss Dresden?'

'Something like that, yes.' Shame did not suit him.

Lowen manufactured an impish grin. 'I always thought the young were ruled by their hearts.'

'I almost gave up everything for Emily.'

'So what was the deciding factor?'

'I suppose it was the fear of insecurity.'

'*Fear*? *Insecurity*?' Lowen could not visualize this debonair man, with such an air of confidence, ever being plagued by a crisis of self-belief.

'I doubted whether I could make it on my own.'

'But you wouldn't have been alone; you'd have been with Emily.'

Lergen shifted uncomfortably. 'I didn't really have a career, not in the sense of being qualified professionally for something. In those days, I was my father's factotum; hardly an eye-grabber for my c.v. I was a bit devious, too.'

Lowen waited for the explanation without spoiling the flow. She was also becoming aware of the time that had elapsed since Mrs Lergen had gone to make coffee, a thought that had equally occurred to Sloane. Surely she must be eavesdropping at the door? Surely Mr Lergen must also realize that by now, yet he continued, apparently uninhibited.

'I thought I could cheat and have it all.'

'You mean you planned to continue seeing Emily after telling your father that it was all over?'

'I even considered marrying Emily secretly, embarking on a closet marriage.'

'Why didn't you?'

A world-weary sigh told the story far more succinctly than his eventual words.

'Emily wouldn't have it that way. She wanted a proper wedding and to be accepted; that was very important to her and always has been.'

The door opened; almost flew open. Greta entered, head held imperiously high, carrying cups of coffee on a silver tray. Her cheeks were no longer porcelain white, but the hue of an angry, allergic rash, yet her eyes were as cold as ice-cubes.

What timing! thought Lowen.

'Sorry I took so long,' said Greta, her apology shallow. 'I was delayed by a call on my mobile. I'll leave everything here on the coffee-table and you can all fight over the milk, sugar and biscuits. Shall I leave you to it, then?'

The question was fired, like a poisoned arrow, at her husband.

'If you wouldn't mind, dear. I don't think we'll be too much longer.'

'I'll say goodbye, then,' Mrs Lergen addressed Lowen and Sloane, shaking hands in the manner of a queen warily touching the flesh of her commoner subjects.

'Now where were we?' Ernst asked, knowing full well.

Lowen did not mind playing games. 'You were saying how Emily demanded a proper wedding and nothing less would do.'

'Ah! yes, so I was. Well, things just drifted. I was introduced to Greta by my parents. They were friends of her folk. They invited her to one of our dinner parties. She was seated strategically next to me. We got along. No great spark that ignited a flame, but we dated and our relationship matured. It would be indecent and disloyal of me to elaborate, suffice it to say we married, had children, and have lived *reasonably* happily ever after, which is more than most couples can claim, wouldn't you say?'

'I don't think I'm qualified to comment,' said Lowen, which Sloane accepted as an obscure message for him. 'You have spoken, Mr Lergen, about keeping in touch by letter with Emily, but did you continue to meet?'

'Quite often to begin with. I'd call her and say I had to see her. She felt the same way.'

'Is that what she *said*, or was it your assessment of her feelings?'

'It was articulated.'

'What about after the wedding?'

'We'd still rendezvous, but the trysts became less and less.'

'When did you last see her?'

'Oh ...' – he gazed at the lofty ceiling as if seeking celestial input and, after a few seconds of pretence, went on – 'it must have been about five years ago.'

'While you were still living in Norway?'

'Yes, but I was flying around the world on business in those days. I came to London a lot. I drove down to Corfe Castle in a hired car and took her out to dinner.'

'By appointment?'

'No, as a surprise.'

'How were you received?'

'As friendly as ever. She'd forgiven me years ago. "Life's too short" was one of her pet sayings. Emily didn't hold grudges. She was a sweet human being, but didn't live in the clouds; very practical and philosophical.'

'Did you speak with her again after you took her to dinner in Dorset about five years ago?'

'No.'

'Did you continue to communicate by letter?'

'No.'

'So that last meeting was something of a watershed?'

'I don't follow.'

'Oh, I'm sure you do, Mr Lergen. You were lovers; you became engaged to be married; you ended that engagement to marry someone else; you stayed in touch over several decades, behind your wife's back; then you turned up unexpectedly one day to take her out for a meal and you never talked or corresponded with her again. It was a defining moment. A door closed. It was closure.'

'Put that way, I understand what you're getting at.'

'So what's the answer?'

'There was no falling out, if that's what you're thinking. No recriminations. No blood-letting. It was a convivial evening, but Emily thought it best that we had no further contact with each other.'

'Why after all that time?'

'She considered it futile to go on meeting, even very occasionally. She told me she'd been sustained most of her adult life by a belief that one day we'd get together again, properly, legitimately, but she had finally accepted that it was not to be.'

'And that's when she told you she was writing you out of her will?'

'Not true. Her will was never mentioned. Emily wasn't a spiteful person, as I've already said. She was also fully aware of my financial circumstances. As I made clear to you earlier, her assets were meaningless to me.'

'Did she threaten to tell your wife about all your deceit over so many years?'

'That wasn't Emily's style.'

'A simple yes or no will do.'

'No.'

'What do you know about Miss Dresden's early life; her childhood?'

'Everything.'

'What do you mean by *everything*?'

'Exactly what *you* mean by it. I know all about how she came into this world and what happened thereafter.'

'Did this information come from her or from a third party?'

'From her; early in our relationship.'

'And was that the reason for your parents' hostility towards her?'

Lergen's sigh was inflated, though not artificially. 'I'm afraid so. Wars breed hatred, prejudices and persecutions. Just look at the situation in the Middle East, Eastern Europe and numerous African states. Genocide is with us as much today as in Nazi Europe during the Second World War. Little changes for the better. Most *progress* is retrogressive. All wars to end war are the opening shots of the sequel. My father loathed the Nazis for their bigotry, yet couldn't see that he was just as bigoted as they were, demonstrated by his contempt for Emily and her unfortunate kind. Emily was a victim. How she survived with such dignity I shall never know. Despite everything, she really made something of her life.'

'And you feel ashamed of how shabbily you treated her?'

'Of course I do.'

'At your last supper with her, you're absolutely sure there was no warning from her, however thinly veiled, that she might make it known to your wife and family that you'd been unfaithful, at least spiritually, for your entire marriage?'

'I've already answered that.' Petulance simmered beneath the surface.

'And you have nothing to add nor change?'

'Nothing whatsoever.'

'Why do *you* suppose she was killed?'

'I can't believe there was a rational motive, other than she was in the wrong place at the wrong time; destroyed by someone deranged.'

'You know of no one who might have wanted, wished, her dead?'

'Good God, no!'

'And yet she provoked hostile emotions in your family and with others in your homeland who were under the influence of mob, witch-hunt mentality.'

'She was safe from all that here.'

'Apparently *not*, Mr Lergen!'

'I think when you find her killer you'll discover that he had no knowledge of his victim.'

'Perhaps you're right, Mr Lergen. Perhaps you're not ...'

Their eyes sparred.

'Well, Mr Lergen, I think we're finished, for now.'

'I can't say it's been painless. I've had better days at the dentist.'

Lowen smiled politely, but without warmth. 'Before I leave, there is one more thing I must put to you as a matter of routine – and nothing more, you understand.'

Not disarmed, Lergen braced himself in anticipation of the most important question of the morning.

'Were you in the UK on the Saturday night Miss Dresden died?'

'I was.'

'Perhaps you could tell me your whereabouts that day.'

'At what time?'

'Let's say from eighth o'clock onwards.'

Lergen was not unprepared. His brain had already processed the answers.

'I was at home.'

'With your wife?'

'No, she'd gone into town, into London, to a show in the West End.'

'And you're not a theatre-lover?'

'Shakespeare or modern drama, yes; musicals, no. I had a do in the afternoon at my local golf club. I wasn't playing, but a friend of mine, Jack Fairweather, was having a sixty-fifth birthday bash. It went on a bit, as those do's tend to. I'd had far too much to drink by the time I left the club – by taxi, of course! I knew well in advance that it was going to be a pretty hefty thrash and that was one of the reasons why I didn't even consider going with Greta to London to the theatre. I was home by seven-thirty. I'd eaten at the golf club, so I snoozed for a while in front of the TV, then went to bed early.'

'What do you call *early*?'

'Oh, by ten.'

'And that's where you stayed until the morning?'

'I don't recall anything after that until Greta brought me a coffee around eight o'clock on Sunday morning. I shan't forget the hangover in a hurry, either.'

'Weren't you even woken by the call on your mobile?'

Lowen had left the blow below the belt until very late.

'What call?' Innocence creased his face.

'The call from Miss Dresden.'

'What are you talking about, woman?' He was agitated now and pricked.

'Phone company records indicate that she called you at nineteen minutes past midnight, around the time of her murder.'

'I didn't take any call. I was asleep, as I've told you. I didn't even know she had my mobile number. I never gave it to her. My number was changed after I gave up full-time work and I shifted from a business tariff to a private one.'

'Do you switch off your mobile when you go to bed?'

'Always. I put it on recharge.'

'But messages can still be left, by voicemail or text?'

'Of course, but I can assure you there was no message from Emily waiting for me next morning.'

'So how do you explain it?'

'I don't. That's your job. Someone somewhere has cocked up, that's certain.'

Lowen decided that any more pushing might close more doors than it would force open.

'Thank you very much, Mr Lergen. However, to round off our visit, in view of your answers, I think I'll have to get some corroboration from your wife.'

'If you must,' he said slowly.

'It won't take a minute. There's no need to bring her back in here. I can speak to her on the way out.'

When they were in the hall, grouped at the front door, Ernst called to his wife, who appeared, more agitated than ever, as she rejoined them from upstairs.

'Your husband has been telling us you went to the theatre in London a week last Saturday evening, Mrs Lergen.'

'That's correct,' she replied, without hesitation, but flashing her husband a grim look that seemed to be demanding: *What the hell is this all about?*

'What time did you return?'

'Oh, it was quite late.'

'How late?'

'Gone midnight.'

'How long after midnight?'

'Oh ...' She gazed to the gods for guidance. 'It must have been about twelve-thirty.'

'Could it have been later?'

'Yes, but only by a few minutes.'

'You're certain of that?'

'Within a few minutes either way, yes.'

'How did you travel to London?'

'By car.'

'Alone?'

'Yes, alone; there and back.'

'You didn't go to the theatre with anyone?'

'No. Ernst was going to a stag celebration at the golf club, so it was an ideal opportunity for me to pop up to town to see *Les Miserables*, at the Queen's. I love musicals; Ernst loathes them.'

'So there's no one to testify to the time of your return?'

'I suppose not, because Ernst was asleep in bed.'

'And that would have been approximately twelve-thirty?'

'Twelve forty-five at the very latest.'

'Did you phone home at any point during that evening?'

'No. I had no reason to.'

'Did you handle your husband's cell phone when you got back, before going to bed?'

Perplexed, her eyes toured the ring of faces, before answering, 'No. It would have been on recharge, but why the question? What's the inference?'

'It's probably unimportant, Mrs Lergen.' Lowen jettisoned the subject.

'Finished?' Ernst butted in, a little too smugly for Lowen's liking.

'For today. Thank you both for being so frank with me.' The sarcasm was hardly masked.

Lowen believed she recognized a flicker of apology in Greta Lergen's pensive eyes just before the front door came between them heavily. The drawbridge had been pulled up; the Lergen fortress was refortified; the invaders repelled.

Not a word passed between Lowen and Sloane as they ambled to their car. Neither of them glanced over their shoulders, even though they were conscious of eyes drilling into their necks from the corner of curtains.

They drove half a mile before Sloane punctured the tense silence.

'Well, what did you make of that?'

'Confusing. Especially his answers to questions about the call from Miss Dresden's mobile.'

'Even so, if his alibi holds up, there's no way he could have done it. A Formula One champion Grand Prix daredevil couldn't have driven one hundred and fifty miles in forty-five minutes.'

'I'll have to get someone to check with the golf club; see how the timescale really stacks up. How did it play with you?'

'Phoney. And not just because he's been a two-timing, morally bereft shit.'

'Did you see the size of that house! It's palatial! Yet there wasn't sight nor sound of a servant. Didn't you find that strange? If you had all that dosh, wouldn't you surround yourself with domestic lackeys?'

'Maybe Greta's the kind of woman who likes to do everything herself, a sort of hands-on control freak. Everything we've seen virtually excludes Lergen as a suspect. He was the last person in the world who needed Emily's money.'

'Who says moolah was the motive? Or if it was money, perhaps it was to protect what he has already.'

'You're not *really* thinking Emily may have been blackmailing him?'

'Why not? She was doing other things you didn't know about, like moonlighting. Most certainly she was no one-dimensional little old spinster.'

Sloane could not argue with that.

CHAPTER 14

The news was out that Harry Parkes had been charged with offences involving child pornography.

The Dorset police press office was besieged with crime reporters, representing national newspapers as well as local publications, seeking a briefing, even if only off-the-record, from lead investigator Joanne Lowen. They all had the same breathless questions on their tabloid lips. Were these just holding charges? Was Parkes now the prime suspect for the Emily Dresden killing? Would he be charged with murder within the next few days? What was the breakthrough? Had the knife turned up? Had he made a confession? Was it possible that he had killed before? What was the score? What was the big picture?

Lowen knew exactly what they were after and had no intention of feeding the frenzy. It was equally imperative, however, not to try to impose a complete news blackout. Firstly, it would not work. The Press would only be pricked into being even more provocative; taking chances with 'flyers' and ending up way off target; maybe even cocking up the entire operation. Secondly, the public's co-operation was still vital in the continuing search for the murder weapon and this could be kept on the boil only through Press coverage. So Lowen's instructions to the press-office team were to dish up frequent light meals of information to the hacks but to save the feast for later, which was tantamount to keeping sharks hungry and expecting them not to swim deep in murky waters hunting for a juicy catch.

Simon Rowlands, the vicar of St Mark's Church in Corfe Castle, had been interviewed by a junior detective on the same Sunday that Parkes had 'discovered' the body. Now he became pivotal to the media's renewed focus on the case. How long had he known Harry Parkes? Did he feel that his trust in him had been betrayed? Had there been any complaints by his flock over the years about Parkes's behaviour? Did he believe Parkes could have slain Emily Dresden, and if so, why?

His statement to the *Daily Echo*, Bournemouth, was a template for everything he was ever to say on the subject.

'Harry has been a faithful servant to the church for many years. I have come to regard him as a friend and someone in whom I have had implicit trust; a stalwart, a pillar.

'To say that I am shocked to the core by these developments is a gross understatement. It is all too much for me to absorb and I am just hoping in the fullness of time it will be sorted out satisfactorily. By that I mean I am praying for Harry to be exonerated.

'As you might imagine, my prayers have been rather emotional these past few days. I have been praying for the soul of dear Emily. Now I am praying just as hard for Harry, who, presumably, will have to face the judgement of his peers before the judgement of his Maker.

'However, it would be wrong of me to make any comment that might be prejudicial. I pray as much for the sinner who robbed Emily of her life as I do for Emily herself. We are all sinners – some more so than others, of course. And we are all – the good and the bad – God's children. The parable of the Prodigal Son is as relevant today as in Biblical times. There has always been a place reserved in God's kingdom for the black sheep that returns to the flock.'

When quizzed by the reporter about the night of the murder, he had explained, 'The vicarage is no longer next to the church, as it was for more than a hundred and fifty years. I live in a relatively modern house on the outskirts of the village. I was indoors all that Saturday evening, preparing my sermon for the Sunday morning family service. I don't suppose I got to bed before one o'clock. The theme of my homily was to be about compassion, humility and respect for each other, and that's what I'd have been composing at the very moment someone was taking away Emily's precious life. She was a lovely lady; a real sweetheart; very spirited, not particularly spiritual, but vibrant and bristling with tireless energy; a *grande dame* without a hint of vainglory. I loved her. *Loved* as in admiring and respecting someone, although she'd always been something of an enigma, you know. Some people considered her eccentric and reclusive, but that's not my memory of her. I saw her as a self-possessed, self-sufficient loner; someone perfectly content with her own company, and that's a very different thing altogether.'

The newspaper article concluded with the stark factual details that the Reverend Rowlands had a wife, Sandra, and two children, Matthew and Sarah, aged fourteen and twelve respectively. He was forty-two, the same age as his wife. Before moving to Corfe Castle, he had been an army chaplain, but had been discharged in circumstances not worthy of being included in his c.v. – and not worth mentioning to the reporter. Rowlands had not volunteered the information. The journalist had failed to ask the question that might have landed him a front page story instead of an inside feature.

Faye Mitchison, Carrington's housekeeper, dodged the puddles between her Vauxhall Astra and the Carlton Hotel, which she entered through the rear entrance from the car-park. As soon as she was out of the rain, she lowered her compact, black umbrella. Unlike most women of her acquaintance in south Dorset, Faye Mitchison was not one for those rainbow-hued, tent-sized umbrellas that she regarded scornfully as garish, fit only for fish-and-chip holidaymakers. Her preference was for all things conservative, even, or especially, when it came to men. She hated snobs and had never seen one in any of her mirrors. She had lived with self-delusion a long time and it was unlikely that they would be parted this side of the grave.

No man came more conservative than Dr Sefton Cameron, who was waiting for Faye in Fredrick's restaurant-bar, characterized by its masculine, clubby ambience; squeaky leather chairs and bench wall-seats, dark-wood panelling, graced with framed caricatures of notable politicians through the ages; the perfect setting for this dated couple. And, despite their stuffy appearance and outward restraint, they were undoubtedly a *couple*; there was no mistaking that, not even to the casual observer, such as a waiter.

'Hello, Faye, I took the liberty of ordering you a dry martini,' the doctor greeted her, unfurling stiffly from his chair at a table beneath a portrait of Sir Winston Churchill and his famous victory salute.

'Just what I need.' Her haughtiness was worn like protective clothing, her bullet-proof vest that would prevent her from being hurt. She allowed the doctor to peck her on the cheek with a kiss that was only a shade less formal than a handshake. As she sat, she crossed her legs elegantly and removed her elbow-length white gloves as if peeling bananas.

'Bad morning?'

'Yes, but what's new in that. The old codger still behaves as if he's in the army. Handles of all teacups have to face the same way. Every time he passes wooden furniture, he can't resist running a finger over the surface, testing for dust. Each time we pass, he gives me a reproving look, as if admonishing me for not slinging him a salute. He's fast driving me to drink.'

'Drink up, then!'

Faye Mitchison, svelte and decorous, did as entreated. 'That's better!' she purred, instantly gratified.

She uncrossed her legs and recrossed them in the opposite direction. Cameron's perceptive eyes followed to an evanescent glimpse of black suspender, which disappeared from view as suddenly as the silky movement, following the sheen of stocking beyond the knee and almost to the plimsoll line, where nylon surrendered to the flesh. He swallowed on something hard as the peep-show was eclipsed, as if a bedroom curtain had been drawn over the window of opportunity. Mitchison adjusted the hem of her classical navy-blue skirt primly.

Cameron flicked his fingers for attention in the autocratic manner of a nineteen thirties colonial in Singapore's Raffles Hotel. A waiter duly appeared at the table with the speed and diligence of a genie.

'Refills, please. Another dry martini for the lady and a large gin and tonic for myself.' Cameron spoke with the authority and pomposity of his passé class. He waited until the waiter had gone about his business before continuing his conversation with his companion.

'Let's hope it's not for too much longer.' He reached across the table to touch her hand just the once in a gesture of camaraderie. Although he now spoke in semi-code, his meaning was transparent to Faye.

'So you keep saying.' Uncharacteristic tiredness seeped into her voice.

'It's essential we keep Margaret on side a little longer.'

'How long is *little*? How long is *longer*?'

'A few months.'

'Two, three, six ... twelve?'

'Please don't turn the screw, Faye. I'm under enormous pressure as it is, without your adding to it. If I'm going to be able to tough-out this crisis, I'll need all the cover I can get from Margaret. If I walked out on her now, she'd release the trapdoor and I'd swing. So would our future together.'

'I'll stand by you.'

'I know you will, Faye.' This time he took her hand across the table firmly and did not let go. 'You're a brick.'

'Bricks are hard, Sefton.'

'They're also made to withstand stormy weather.'

Faye smiled wistfully, her spirits warming, but not melting completely.

'You're an old flatterer.'

'Less of the *old*.'

They drank some more. The nectar took the short, rather than scenic, route to the brain. The slight tremble at Cameron's fingertips vanished. The waiter reappeared with menus and departed again, saying, 'I'll come back to take your orders.'

'There's no hurry,' said Cameron, meaning, *Give us a few minutes alone.*

Now they had the bar to themselves.

'Is it going to blow over without a public showdown?' Faye asked earnestly, the trenches of her frown running deep.

Cameron closed his eyes, but it did not help to shut out his troubles. 'Evidence is still being gathered.'

'Have the police become involved?'

'Probably. The fly in the ointment is the Hayter family; Pauline and Reginald Hayter to be specific. They won't let go; they're dogs with bones, trying to chew me to pieces.'

'Vindictive!' Faye wanted to say *vindictive bastards*, but that would have exposed a side to her nature that she tried to prevent penetrating her public persona.

'You know what the problem is.'

'Yes, I do; they're after the old girl's money.'

'There's more to it than that. Pauline Hayter was a nurse. She thinks she has more medical knowledge than she does. I also think there's a guilt-complex. Subconsciously, she believes she failed her mother.'

'You're far too generous, Sefton. I think she's an out-and-out gold-digger; nothing more nor less. And in the process of trying to get her grubby hands on it, she's prepared to jettison your career, if necessary.'

'Without the Hayters, I'm convinced the whole tasteless affair would have been dropped weeks ago.'

'What have the Hayters got in the way of evidence? I'll rephrase; what do they *think* they have?'

Cameron took a blue silk handkerchief from the breast pocket of his grey jacket and dabbed his forehead, where beads of sweat had formed like blisters. It was not overly warm, but he had started to overheat.

'I wish I knew. The whole thing has become complicated by the death of the snoop.'

'The bridge pal of my employer?'

'Does he ever discuss her with you?'

'Incessantly, but without ever mentioning what she was up to; her business. All they had in common, so it seems, was bridge. Bridge mad, the pair of them. I've tried to steer him round discreetly to her business affairs, but he's a canny old so and so. He never bites. He always manages to swim around the bait.'

'What's certain is that the Hayters employed her to dig up the dirt on me, if any existed.'

'Or invent it, just as likely.'

'I've no proof of that.'

'This worsens your position; you *do* see that, don't you?'

'Frankly, no.'

'*That* woman, Pauline Hayter, is bound to go to the police now, if she hasn't already. She'll start intimating that you had a better reason than anyone to wish the Dresden woman out of the way.'

'That's nonsense!'

'You know that, I know that, but just look how it will seem to those vultures with suspicious minds.'

'That Dresden woman must have been snooping on loads of individuals and companies, all with due cause to nominate her their enemy number one.'

'True, but—'

'Listen, I've enough to worry about without adding *her* to the equation. People have to accept that old folk do die. We all die. There's only so much a GP – any doctor – can do for his patients. We're nothing more than mechanics of medicine. You can repair a vehicle only so many times. When my patients approach the end of the road, I try to make the last few miles as painless and comfortable as possible. I've never been guilty of what the secular world calls mercy killing; I don't assist people to die: I assist them to cope with whatever they have to face, including death. I help them to retain their dignity as their life draws to a close.'

'But what will you say if you're questioned about terminally ill patients changing their wills, leaving everything to you?'

'I'll tell the truth. I have never in all my life pressured any patient of mine to make me a beneficiary in his or her will. In fact, I've never even discussed a will with a patient. I've been embarrassed when I've learned I've been left money or property by a patient. When a solicitor has contacted me, it's usually been the first I've known about the legacy. I don't go touting on my house visits.'

'Of course you don't, but it's what people will think that worries me.'

'I can't go around worrying about the workings of other people's dirty little minds.'

Faye pondered a moment, then, 'What's your answer should anyone ask why you didn't give back any of the bequests?'

'I'll simply say that it would be an insult to the departed person who had wanted to make some kind of statement, either thanking me or punishing relatives who had been neglectful and yet still expected to cash in.'

'Is Mrs Hayter attempting to have her mother's medical records released?'

'Who knows what she's doing behind the scenes.'

'If it should happen, what will they show?'

'That she died of natural causes; pneumonia. Bone cancer was a secondary cause.'

'But you were prescribing morphine for her?'

'I was, but within the recommended dosage.'

'So there's nothing really to be anxious about?'

'The problem is, Faye, you never know what people are going to make of *nothing*. Now, let's change the subject, order our lunch and enjoy the meal and good wine.'

As soon as the detective's car was out of sight, Greta Lergen said to her husband, 'Well, what was that all about?'

He replied tersely, his expression sardonic, 'As if you don't know! You heard every word.'

Greta's face flared. 'And I heard nothing that was new to me. You never could leave that tramp alone, could you?'

'And you've never been able to change the poisoned blood you inherited from your parents.'

'*She* cast a shadow over our entire marriage. The only reason for moving to England, was so you could be near her.'

'That's ridiculous!'

'Says you!'

'She was old. I was older. She didn't want me.'

'But you *wanted* her!'

'You're sick.'

'*Sick* of your ways, your lies, your deceit.'

'You've never wanted for anything.'

'Other than fidelity!'

'Now that Emily's dead, for God's sake let her rest in peace, please.'

'But what about you, Ernst, can you rest in peace?'

'What are you getting at now?' He squinted through metallic eyes.

'Did you see her on *that* Saturday?'

'You know damn well I didn't.'

'I know no such thing.'

'You know exactly where I was.'

'I know where you *said* you were.'

'There are at least thirty witnesses to my presence at the golf club.'

'But what about afterwards? You could easily have driven to Dorset.'

'I was drunk. I came home by taxi. That's on record, too. The taxi company will have it logged. Neither would the driver forget coming here.'

'You could still have driven from here.'

'Not in the state I was in.'

'You could have been faking.'

'And Father Christmas could be real, after all!'

'You had the opportunity, Ernst.' Greta had gone from seething virago to forensic ice maiden.

'For what?'

'Think about it.'

'You have an evil mind, as well as an illogical one. Emily was killed around midnight. You were home by twelve thirty, twelve forty-five.'

'You need that alibi, Ernst, and don't you forget it.'

As Harry Parkes made his way to the shops, so everyone who knew him crossed the road to the opposite pavement.

Three shop assistants in succession refused to serve him. The grapevine had always been the speediest news network. Mothers pulled their toddlers close to them the moment they saw him approaching. The less inhibited of the women hissed. 'Why don't you drop dead, you filthy beast!' implored one in supplication, rather than asking a question.

Feeling wretched, he headed for home, abandoning the rest of his shopping. When he arrived at his house, he was shocked to discover hate messages in chalk all over the front brickwork: 'Scum!' and 'Dirty Kid-Buggering Bastard!' and 'Let's Castrate the Fucker!'

He had only just locked the front door behind him when a brick crashed through a front window. He called the police. A rather desultory officer said someone would be around when 'he or she could be spared'. It would probably not be until the following day, though.

When Lowen and Sloane heard about the call, they went to Parkes's address immediately.

'He won't come to the door unless he knows who it is,' said Sloane, after they had been ringing the doorbell continuously for a couple of minutes.

Lowen stepped back on to the pavement to use her mobile. Parkes did not answer. One of the downstairs windows was completely shattered. There had been no attempt to affect temporary repairs. Further hate graffiti had been added to the initial contributions.

'I'll do it,' Sloane volunteered.

'Thank you,' said Lowen.

Everything else was telegraphed by telepathy.

Sloane went through the door on the third shoulder-charge.

Parkes was in the kitchen, sitting at the table, staring blankly at two bottles of paracetamol tablets. The bottlers were empty, of course.

CHAPTER 15

The first question from the senior of the two paramedics at the scene was how many tablets had there been in the bottles. The second question was how long since they had been taken. Harry Parkes, the only person with the answers, was not forthcoming.

Lowen and Sloane trailed the ambulance at speeds of up to eighty miles per hour to the hospital in Poole, where Parkes was more co-operative with the female registrar on duty in over-worked Accident and Emergency. The bottles had each contained sixteen paracetamol when bought about a fortnight ago at separate chemists. Parkes had taken about six for headaches, at intervals, since buying the bottle.

'That means you swallowed about twenty-six all at once today, then?' Dr Prudence Carlisle said, her mental arithmetic sound.

'About that,' Parkes replied vacantly, unconcerned with numbers. 'It seems a lot, but I wasn't counting. I didn't think I was going to get them all down, but I was determined.'

'When did you take them?'

Parkes looked up at the doctor as if having difficulty computing the input.

'What time is it now?'

'Just after four o'clock … in the afternoon.'

Parkes's milky eyes were becoming increasingly unfocused.

'It must have been about noon, then.'

'Four hours,' Carlisle announced loudly, which to the young doctor and two nurses in the cubicle with her translated into, *We can save him. We're inside the time-frame. Let's go to it*!

Lowen and Sloane were kept waiting in a corridor for half an hour before Dr Carlisle emerged to tell them, 'It looks like we got to him in time. As you know, with paracetamol the chances deteriorate by the hour. After eight hours, when there has been a heavy overdose, the prognosis is grim. A big paracetamol overdose results in liver failure, although it may be thirty-six hours or longer before the patient collapses into a coma. Right now, we're pumping his stomach; it's a pretty unpleasant procedure. We've also set up a saline drip; all routine stuff.'

'But he *will* live?' Lowen pressed.

'Unless there are complications, I think it's safe to say he should make a complete recovery.'

'Has he said why he did it?'

'No. With respect, they're questions for you, not me. In A&E we treat life-threatening conditions, not the cause. If someone's brought in from a road accident, we're not concerned with who was to blame. We stitch, plaster, plug holes and kick-start faltering life.'

'But if someone was brought in unconscious, the cause could be a brain tumour; surely you couldn't separate cause from result?' Lowen reasoned, irritated by the lecture. 'You'd need to tackle the cause in order to eliminate the effect.'

'In that scenario, the patient would be admitted and transferred to the appropriate specialist team.'

'You pass the buck?'

'No, we pass the body.'

'When shall we be able to speak with Mr Parkes?'

'Not for thirty-six hours.'

'Not even for five minutes?'

'Not even for five seconds.'

Lowen knew a brick wall when she ran into one.

That evening, Lowen and Sloane went together for a meal in a family run Italian restaurant beside the river in Wareham. They drank a bottle of red wine with their food. Then ordered another bottle to keep the conversation oiled.

'Just five minutes with Parkes this afternoon and he could well have been ready to confess,' said Lowen, fingering the rim of her glass, everything about her mellowed by the grapes of cordiality.

'To what, though?'

Now Lowen sipped her drink as tentatively as if she might be holding a poisoned chalice.

'What would it take for you, Mr Sloane, to ever consider

Parkes as our man?' There was no mistaking the skittish tone as she rolled out the *Mr Sloane*

'A lot more than a confession,' he replied, provocatively.

Smoky eyes, dancing with amusement, partnered Sloane across the table.

'Wouldn't it depend on the content of the confession?' she both teased and tested him.

'Nothing short of the knife with Parkes's name all over it would persuade me.'

'His *name all over it*! That level of proof would even give Judas a chance of being cleared.'

'I'm talking about fingerprints; being named and damned by dabs. I honestly don't see a chance of getting anywhere without the weapon.'

'Might not a confession lead to the knife?' Lowen drank some more to lubricate her desiccated throat. Red wine always made her husky. Men found it an attractive feature. To her, however, it was bothersome, an impediment. But pouring more red wine on to the problem was tantamount to watering a plant with acid rain.

'I think you know as well as I do why Parkes tried to end it all.'

'I do?' she mocked him mercilessly.

Sloane parried the taunts. 'If he killed someone, I think he could justify it, at least to himself. It would be jealousy, a moment of madness, a drunken act, revenge for a perceived injustice, a crime of passion. He might well regret committing murder, especially when caught, but at least there would be a degree of daring, even courage, about it; certainly logic, with which some people would identify and even have an empathy.'

'Pardon? What's brave about jumping an elderly woman, late at night, spiking her in the heart, then fleeing? Surely that's the embodiment of abject cowardice?'

'OK, perhaps *courage* and *daring* are inappropriate, but the odds are that this was an honour killing.'

'*Honour killing*?' Lowen gasped. 'Come on!'

'Whoever killed Emily did so because of events many decades ago,' Sloane explained himself. 'A hatred had been harboured all that time until it could be contained no longer, or it was triggered by a single incident.'

'You're really hooked on the *Mother Whore* clue, aren't you?'

'And you're not?'

'Not to the same extent that you are; not to the exclusion of all other possibilities. You see, I don't think it's *that* cut and dried.'

Sloane downed some more wine and tossed back his head in thought.

'The killer must have known about Emily's childhood; that's pivotal, the cornerstone, the starting-point.'

'It would seem that way,' Lowen conceded partially, 'but I don't believe we should saddle ourselves with tunnel vision. She could have confided in Parkes, for example, about her early days, about being victimized in Norway.'

'They weren't *that* close,' Sloane pointed out doggedly.

'They were close enough for her to get Parkes to witness her will,' said Lowen, holding her ground steadfastly. 'They may have become much closer than Parkes would have us believe. After all, Emily's not around to dispute anything he says, now is she? Another thing, *Mother Whore* doesn't really make sense, does it? Emily was neither whore nor mother … as far as we know.'

'Not in reality, but in the addled head of the killer, who knows?' Sloane continued to press his case.

'She could have been *anything* to her killer and that's why we mustn't be blinkered.'

'You're the one who's sold big-time on Parkes.' There was no petulance in this point-scoring contest.

'Wrong. I'm *sold* on not eliminating him just because we're stuck for a motive. Your theory has its problems.'

'I'm sure you'll tell me why.'

'You talk of *harboured hatred*, building and festering over many, many years. For consistency, the stabbing would have been an outpouring of all that pent-up resentment. One would have expected mutilation on a grisly scale. Yet, no. What do we have? One neat puncture to the heart. Cold and clinical. No overkill. Inconsistent, right?'

Sloane threw up his hands in mock surrender.

'I really fear you're in danger of falling into the trap that bedevilled the Yorkshire Ripper inquiry.' Lowen sprinkled salt liberally on the scratches she had just inflicted. 'Do you recall the "I'm Jack" tape?'

'How could anyone forget?'

'The alleged serial killer, purporting to be a contemporary Jack the Ripper, sent a taped recording to West Yorkshire Police, amounting to a boastful monologue of how he would defy detection and continue with his killing spree. And for poor old George Oldfield, the late Assistant Chief Constable of West Yorkshire, it became personal, a one-to-one duel, a virility test and obsession. He was so seduced by the tape that he was beyond questioning its validity and provenance. Not for one moment did he pause to say, "Hey, wait a minute, how can we be one hundred per cent certain that this really is the Yorkshire Ripper and not just a clever hoaxer?" At a stroke, he discounted anyone as a suspect who didn't have a Wearside accent. That's why Peter Sutcliffe was able to stay free for so long. Just think how many women's lives might have been saved if Oldfield hadn't been so easily duped. He was surrounded by officers cautioning him against closing his eyes and ears to alternatives, but from the arrival of that tape he was strapped to one wheel. He couldn't help himself. He was on a treadmill. OK, eventually he got his man, by sheer luck, but he lost the duel. Oldfield died of a heart-attack, a broken man. Broken by the taunting voice of the bogus Jack; broken by his own stubborn folly; broken by his own conscience.'

'I'm not the one hung up,' Sloane protested. 'I was simply making the point that, in my opinion, Parkes most likely tried to do himself in out of shame over his sexual perversion, because society would be less tolerant over his being a paedophile – the ultimate taboo and rightly so – than being a murderer.'

'He could be both. Perverts do murder, you know.'

'He could indeed, but I reckon it was the porno exposure that drove him to overdose.'

'Let's change the subject,' said Lowen, as if putting a full-stop to the end of a chapter.

'I bet you're hell to live with. How's that for a new line in chat?'

'At least it's different.'

The smiles had made a comeback.

'Original?'

'I wouldn't go that far.'

'You're a real ball-breaker.'

'That's what my husband said … just before he was taken away in handcuffs.'

Sloane showed no shock.

'Now I've just learned something else,' said Lowen, her smile wry.

'I know, I should have feigned incredulity, right?'

'Only if you wanted to be dishonest with me. Who marked your card on – how shall I put it? – my rather colourful and eventful marriage? Old Froby?'

'I've seen your file.'

'That's more than I have.'

'Your reputation is well deserved.'

'That could mean almost anything.'

'I'm talking about your detective cred.'

'I do my job,' she said dismissively, almost embarrassed.

'Better than most.'

'Is that a compliment?'

'Doesn't it sound like one?'

'You could be hinting that I don't have much competition.'

'Listen, Joanne, why don't we stop tiptoeing around the edges.'

'Of what?'

'The dividing line that separates professional from personal.'

'Because to cross that line would be unprofessional.'

'No, it would be human.'

'I don't know anything about you, Mike; not *really*. No one's given me *your* personal file to read. For all I know, you could have a wife and six kids back home – wherever *home* might be.'

'That was an unkind kick in the teeth, but you weren't to know.'

And that was the moment when some mysterious, invisible chemistry bonded them.

'So you have a sob story, too, eh?'

'I thought I'd stopped crying a long time ago, but when I saw those downloaded photos of sexually abused kids ...' A lump of emotion prevented him from finishing.

'Sounds like we're two emotionally damaged people. Any relationship between us is likely to be built on quicksand. I don't do one-night stands. Neither am I looking for a long-term commitment; in fact, the very thought of one sends me running scared. And there's not too much in between.'

NEATH PORT TALBOT LIBRARIES

'Why don't we stop being so analytical? Science and the abstract don't mix; never have, never will.'

'So where does that leave us?'

'With our instincts.'

'I'm not so sure I'm ready to trust mine again yet.'

'You haven't let yourself down, Joanne; others have done that.'

'That's so glib; how could you possibly know that?'

'Instinct … and I trust mine.'

'I've too much to lose, little to gain.'

'Thanks! Now it's my chance to say, *how glib*! and *how could you possibly know that*?'

'Instinct.'

'In which you have no faith.'

'I've a strong suspicion that all we really have in common is the riddle of Emily Dresden's death. When that's finally put to bed, we shall have lost the pillow on which our relationship rests.'

'I think you could be wrong.'

'*Could be* isn't the greatest vote of confidence I've ever heard.'

'Time will tell.'

'Exactly. And now it's time to go.'

'In opposite directions?'

'No, in different ways, which could be parallel paths.'

While waiting for taxis, they kissed outside the restaurant. Nothing sensational, but it was special. One tender, trembling kiss and a threshold was crossed. Then they squeezed hands, tightening their hold on one another, if only symbolically.

'Goodbye,' said Lowen.

'Goodnight,' said Sloane.

Nuances of the night always carried more weight than their face value.

CHAPTER 16

Sloane woke up alone.

So did Lowen.

Nothing unusual about that for either of them, but it might have been so different.

Perhaps it's for the best, thought Sloane ruefully, struggling for a positive spin and not really believing his own propaganda.

Lowen had no time for introspective considerations. No regrets. No recriminations. No emotional inquest. Work beckoned. The present had her full attention.

Before leaving home, Lowen called headquarters. 'What's the news on Parkes?' she asked one of her early-shift officers in the detectives' pool.

'No news.'

'Well, get me some. Call me back on my mobile. Pronto!'

The return call came five minutes later, like a slow-motion rebound.

'He's improving and had a comfortable night.'

'More than he deserves. Let's start making him uncomfortable again.'

Spontaneously, she phoned Sloane to update him.

'Thanks for the early-morning bulletin,' he said sleepily. 'What's your plan?'

'Not to wait the thirty-six hours for access. I'll negotiate with the hospital's chief executive – direct.'

'Do you want me along for company?'

It was only then that Lowen paused to question what the hell she was doing making Sloane a priority for shared information before she had even hit her office. She further challenged her own judgement when realizing she had been about to say, *Of course I'd like you along.*

So she was still chastizing herself when saying, 'Operationally unwise. He might be intimidated if we go in double-handed. Leave it to the gentle touch.'

'So *you* won't be going, either!'

'Ha! Ha! Catch up with you later.'

Ernst and Greta Lergen had been sleeping in separate bedrooms for many years. Ernst had moved out of the matrimonial bed when suffering from a chest infection. He had not wanted his rasping cough to keep Greta awake. After antibiotics had killed off the cough, Ernst saw no point in returning to the nocturnal battleground and long nights of dour struggles protecting one's territory. In any case, they were both sleeping better apart. All sexual activity between them had petered out several years ago, like a reservoir running dry and never being replenished. Nothing was ever articulated between them on the subject, but they had been jointly content with the new arrangement, which would have been of considerable interest to Lowen and Sloane if they had known. But, of course, they did not.

Greta worked out in their own private gym before joining Ernst for breakfast in the sun lounge, which could be kept artificially bright and warm year-round; just like Florida, but without a hurricane season and cold winter snaps. Greta, still glowing in her leotard, sipped freshly squeezed orange juice and nibbled brown-bread toast; no butter, but a light skim of marmalade. A silver coffee-pot dominated the circular table.

Ernst, still in his silk pyjamas and matching dressing-gown, decapitated a boiled egg, then poured coffee for himself, without offering to fill his wife's cup.

'You're heaping on the butter these days,' Greta remarked, disapproving eyes frowning on Ernst's toast.

'Please don't bother warning me it's bad for my health.'

'It's still important for you to take care of yourself.'

'Condemned men are allowed to eat anything they like.'

'Only for their last meal.'

'Which this could be.' He tapped the egg-shell with his spoon, like a physician checking for reflexes.

'Don't talk like that!' she berated him.

'Well, it's true.'

'It could be true for anyone.'

'But much more likely for someone who has already had the death sentence passed.'

Greta could not look her husband in the face. 'When do you have to see the specialist again?'

'What's the point?'

'That wasn't the question.'

'I should have gone a week ago.'

'You mean you skipped an appointment?'

'What can he do? Only up the dose of my medication, only re-measure the distance remaining between me and the black hole. My own GP can do all of that perfectly adequately. A specialist isn't needed for signing a prescription and speculating on departure dates.'

'How do you feel?'

'How do I look?'

'Fit – that's what makes it all the harder to accept.'

'That's life, in all it's irony, not to mention perversity.'

'At least you can still play golf.'

'I wouldn't go that far; let's say I can still make it to the nineteenth hole.'

It was mid-morning when Lowen learned of the call from Pauline Hayter, who would say only that she had information about the Corfe Castle murder. She had left a mobile number and her Christchurch address with a uniformed officer in the control-room.

Lowen, who had been bogged down with paperwork since, called Mrs Hayter from her office.

After a perfunctory introduction, she asked Mrs Hayter how she could help the investigation.

'Not over the phone,' she decreed pithily.

'I'm far too busy for a wild goose chase,' Lowen demurred.

'Me, too,' Mrs Hayter retorted tartly.

'Give me a taste. Whet my appetite.'

'How about a name and a motive?'

'Go on.'

'When you get here.'

'I'm on my way.'

Five minutes later, Lowen was on fast-forward to Christchurch, having already contacted Sloane to say, 'Meet me in an hour in Christchurch, outside the Boathouse restaurant on the quay. I'll explain then.'

The Reverend Simon Rowlands was not wearing his dog-collar when he entered the betting shop in Poole's High Street, a pedestrian-only shopping precinct. Poole was well outside his territory, though near enough to reach by car in under an hour, any time of day and even at the height of the summer season. Most importantly, there was little chance of his being recognized there.

Poole, part of an urban sprawl along the east Dorset coast of affluence and effluence, in roughly equal portions, was not the kind of place to which rustic Purbeck folk naturally gravitated. So whenever Rowlands fancied a punt on the horses, it was to the High Street of Poole that he headed; which was most days, Monday to Saturday. And since horseracing had been introduced on the Sabbath, it was not uncommon for him to make a round trip from Corfe Castle to the betting shop in Poole between morning family service and evensong. Sometimes his private morning prayers for a lucrative reward in the afternoon were answered. More often they were not. Consequently, the theme of many of his sermons cautioned against expecting too much from divine supplication. What one beseeched of the Lord and what He deemed desirable for one were not always compatible.

Rowlands was not a lucky punter. Hence his parlous financial situation.

'I wouldn't be seen dead there' was the most oft heard comment of Isle of Purbeck people about the Poole/Bournemouth blot on the landscape. All the more surprising, therefore, that Rowlands had seen Emily Dresden there just a few months ago, as he slunk shiftily from the betting shop one sleepy Sabbath.

Ever since, Rowlands had wondered querulously whether Emily had seen him. If she had, he could have been in trouble. Big trouble. But not any more. His secret was safe, at least for the time being.

*

Pauline Hayter was the kind of woman you could easily envisage banner-waving at the head of a protest lobby group. Sloane was later to describe her in a report as 'fired up'. Lowen immediately categorized her as an 'organizer', someone who would have been tagged 'bossy' during her schooldays.

'Come in … I'll have your coats … Please leave your shoes just inside the front door on the mat … I've made a pot of tea …We don't have coffee in the house; too much caffeine is bad for you … Tea suit you both?' (She did not wait for an answer before pouring.) 'Not a bad day for the time of year, is it?' (She showed no interest in the mumbled replies.) 'You sit there, Inspector … I'll move the newspapers … There! That's better; there you are. And you sit there, er …'

'I'm just plain Mister,' said Sloane.

'Oh, I see,' said Mrs Hayter, not seeing at all, but insufficiently concerned to pursue the matter.

'I'll come straight to the point,' she journeyed on, with no time for breathing. 'Have you heard of Dr Sefton Cameron?'

Responding to the empty house, lights-out expressions in front of her, Mrs Hayter answered her own question. 'Well, you jolly well should have done. His name is most certainly one for your notebook. He had every reason to harm Miss Dresden. And it wouldn't have been his first murder. Oh, dear, you must be thinking you've been lured to the lair of a madwoman.'

Lowen decided against answering honestly and instead said diplomatically, 'I'm just beginning to wonder where this is heading.'

'And well you might! Hopefully, you'll quickly see,' said Mrs Hayter, smoothing out her blue woollen skirt, not because there were any creases but to keep her hands occupied. She had a hawkish face, with spiky features, panicky eyes, a snappy mouth and hair that would have broken the spirit of any brush.

Lowen and Sloane were simultaneously guessing Mrs Hayter's age. Lowen would have gone for a safe forty-five, while Sloane would have shot higher; fifty maybe. Both would have been wrong. She was thirty-nine, but a hyper-active temperament and racing metabolism had done her no favours. She was being burned out prematurely by internal combustion.

'Doctor Cameron murdered my mother.'

Lowen looked at Sloane. Sloane looked at Lowen. The message was in the eyes. *Murders always bring out all the nutters.*

'I'm sure you're going to elaborate,' Lowen said drily.

'Oh, indeed,' Mrs Hayter trilled hastily. 'Doctor Cameron killed my mother with high doses of diamorphine. She had cancer and was in a lot of pain, I am the first to admit that. But Dr Cameron, her GP, wasn't interested in trying to cure her or extend her life. Oh, no! All he did was embark on a course of upping the diamorphine dose in ever-larger increments to hasten her death.'

'But why should he do that?'

'For her money. He cajoled her into changing her will, so he got his thieving hands on the lot, everything; had me and my family totally erased from it, as if we no longer existed. You're very welcome to a copy of the will. You'll see for yourselves then. It's all there in black and white. My mother wasn't his first and only victim, either. He's been up to the same trick for years all over his patch. I've made a complaint to the General Medical Council, but it's about time the police got involved, too.'

'But how does all this have anything to do with Miss Dresden?'

'Because I hired her to investigate, that's why. She was garnering evidence to make a case against Dr Cameron, to expose him. That's why she was killed. You can bet your last penny on that.'

The doctor in charge of Harry Parkes's care gave permission for his patient to be interviewed 'for no longer than ten minutes' at five o'clock that afternoon, some twenty-five hours after Lowen and Sloane had forced their way into Parkes's home.

Parkes had been moved into a general medical ward now that he was out of danger. Later that evening he was to be seen by a psychiatrist, who would conduct a risk-assessment.

Lowen had U-turned on her original decision that morning to keep Sloane and Parkes apart. Now she and Sloane took up seated positions at the bedside.

'Oh, no, not *you* two again!'

Unshaved and still with a tube clipped to his nose, Parkes had all the appearance of a cadaver-in-waiting.

'We won't be here long, I promise you,' Lowen said flatly.

'I'd rather you weren't here at all.' Parkes's voice was weak and hoarse, like an artless stage prompt.

'I must ask why you took those tablets?'

'What a ridiculous question!'

'It *was* intentional?'

Parkes rolled his head sideways on the soft bank of pillows, only to feel like a fox encircled by hounds. Closing his eyes gave him a few seconds of bogus escape.

'Of course I acted with intent. How could anyone swallow that quantity of tablets by accident?'

'Which leads me in a circle to my first question.'

'Remind me.'

'Why?'

They had a very long wait before Parkes whispered, almost in a death-rattle, the shutters of his eyes clamped down like visors.

'My business, not yours.'

'I don't want to distress you …'

'Then don't. Just leave.'

'Before I do, I must ask if your action was directly related to the crime outside the church where you are the verger?'

'You can get warrants to enter my house against my will and trash my home and invade my privacy, but there's no way into my head and soul without my invitation, which you're not getting now or ever.'

'And that's your final word?'

'I don't know about that, but it's the end of my conversation with you. If I'd been allowed my way, my last word would have been spoken yesterday. The fact that it wasn't is solely attributable to you and your *friend* here, for which I thank you not.'

'I hope you soon feel better, Mr Parkes.'

'I'm sure you do; as baleful as ever. I want to die and you want me to live. How do you propose bridging that gap?'

Neither Lowen nor Sloane had an answer.

CHAPTER 17

L owen caught an early train to London for a noon appointment with Professor Gordon Armitage of the British Medical Association. The subject: Dr Sefton Cameron.

Sloane, being a devotee of the principle that working in tandem tended to halve efficiency and output, rather than doubling it, exploited Lowen's absence to embark on some lone scouting.

Philip Darke, an accountant for more than thirty years, worked from a two-room office above the designer shops in Bournemouth's fashionable Westover Road. From his windows, he could usually see across the bay, where ferries, shuttling between Poole and France, had the iridescent Purbeck hills as a dominating backdrop. But not today. It was going to be one of those winter days when night did a double shift.

Darke greeted Sloane with wary fascination.

'I had a visit from a uniformed officer from the local constabulary; said he had instructions from the chief constable of the county, no less, to say it was in order for me to speak with you openly about Emily Dresden. Said you would be here in an official capacity, though it all seemed rather shrouded in mystery. I'm sure it's all bona fide. If there is anything I can help you with, I shall. Now that she's *gone*, I can't be accused of acting unprofessionally by discussing her financial affairs. It's not as if I'm a Catholic priest or a doctor.'

'Quite. And in return I promise not to misappropriate any information that comes from you.'

Darke – aptly named – nodded approvingly, as if saying, *I'm grateful for that.*

Sloane was already thinking that this was somebody with whom he could do business.

'How long had you been doing Miss Dresden's accounts?'

'Do you want me to be exact?'

'An estimate will do.'

Darke ran his puffy fingers through his bushy, raven hair as he reclined in his chair. He wore the conservative uniform of an accountant, though cigarette ash had speckled his black suit with a silver tint.

'Without referring to her file, I can't give you the year, but it was around the time she bought her cottage and started her business.'

'What business are we talking about?' Sloane tested him.

Darke straightened and eyed Sloane shrewdly.

'She declared two sources of income. One came from her civil service employment.'

Sloane smiled inwardly, while his face remained impassive. *So that's how she explained it.*

'And the other?'

'She ran her own little business.'

'How *little*?'

'She did quite well, actually.'

'For an accountant, so far you've been incredibly short on substance.'

Darke leaned forward to extract a buff folder from the top drawer of his desk. Even that small task left him breathless, triggering a smoker's cough. He opened the folder like a teacher about to mark a student's homework, flicking through pages irreverently as his wet eyes read selectively.

'I'm assuming you're aware of her line of work?' His paunch rose and receded with each laboured heartbeat.

'She spied on people.' Sloane played the shock card.

Darke choked a while, before saying somewhat reproachfully, as if correcting his visitor, 'She ran her own one-woman private detective agency.' Spittle washed every word. Clearly he was unaware of the truth of Sloane's stark statement.

'How much was she making from sleuthing?'

'Net or gross?'

At last Darke really did begin to sound the part.

'Gross will do.'

Darke, severely owlish, squinted through bifocals that had slipped halfway down his aquiline and empurpled nose.

'In the last financial year, she grossed forty-two thousand, one hundred and eighty-six pounds. Turnover ran to nearly double that. Expenses were considerable, but they were paid by clients, of course.'

'Did she have a mortgage on her home?'

'No. She bought the cottage outright.'

'For how much?'

'I couldn't tell you exactly.'

'It must have been a tidy sum, even then.'

'Oh, undoubtedly.'

'So where did the money come from?'

'Miss Dresden was quite forthcoming about that. It was paid for by a relative in Norway. A very wealthy gentleman.'

'You wouldn't happen to recall the name, would you?'

'No, but it's written down somewhere in her file. Just give me a few seconds to locate it.' His speech was as pedantic as his manner.

Darke thumbed through the paperwork, finally stopping towards the bottom of the pile. 'Here we are; yes, that's it, a Mr Ernst Lergen.'

'And you say he's a relative of hers?'

'That's my understanding.'

'That's what she told you?'

'She did.'

'Did she have other large assets?'

'She had shares.'

'In what?'

'A portfolio, but mainly in pharmaceuticals; drug research companies. Managed by the City brokers Carmichaels.'

'What's the current value of the stock?'

'Something in the region of half a million.'

'When were the shares purchased?'

'Not all at once; over a period.'

'What period?'

'Once again, from about the time she bought her cottage; that's when she acquired the bulk of her stock, about seventy-five thousand pounds-worth. Since then, she added to it and it rose in value. Her financial advisers, or she, knew what they were doing.'

'As her accountant, how did you square this with her income?'

'I didn't; it wasn't necessary. It came from the same source as the capital for the cottage. All the shares were donated to her.'

'From Mr Lergen?'

'Correct; Mr Moneybags.'

'What happens to the shares now?'

'They form part of the estate, to be distributed in accordance with her will, which will be dealt with by her solicitor, of course.'

'Well, thank you.'

'I hope I've been of some help.'

'You've been much more than that.'

Professor Armitage's pendulous features somehow accentuated his credibility in his role of policing his profession.

'Mrs Hayter has been threatening for some time to make allegations to the police, now she has done so and here you are, Inspector Lowen.'

A chain was looped between two pockets of his black waistcoat and a bulge marked the repository for his solid gold watch. He was tall and austere, with a military bearing, although slightly stooping.

'So what is the position?' Lowen asked neutrally.

The professor of medicine threaded his fingers and crunched white knuckles. 'We don't take accusations like these lightly. Neither do we rush in like stormtroopers. We begin gently, looking at the doctor's history, right back to his or her medical schooldays. We search records for any previous complaints. In other words, we do our homework first.'

'And what did your homework tell you in respect of Dr Cameron?'

'That he was well qualified and very popular with his patients. In fact, you could say he has almost a cult following.'

'That doesn't necessarily make him a good doctor.'

'Of course not and I didn't mean to imply that it did.'

'No previous complaints against him?'

'None whatsoever, not a blemish.' He stroked his bald head a few times before adjusting his unfashionable spectacles. 'After that, we became more focused on Mrs Hayter's specific allegations. We asked for the medical records of Mrs Hayter's mother and others.'

'*Others?*'

'Yes, Mrs Hayter named other patients of Dr Cameron. She believed there were grounds for investigating their deaths, too.'

'Was she able to provide *any* supportive evidence?'

'Not medical.'

'What then?'

'I'll come to that in a minute, if I may. Firstly, let me concentrate on the medical care of Mrs Lesley Mortimer, the mother of Mrs Hayter. She was diagnosed as having bone cancer some two years prior to her death. By the time she was referred to a specialist, her condition was terminal.'

'Do I detect a suggestion that there was a delay in referral?'

'Not at all. I'm sorry if that's the way it sounded. No, the timescale of events was within what I'd call the norm. Bone cancer can be very painful, excruciatingly so. As soon as the prognosis is hopeless, only one thing dictates treatment and that is pain-management. Diamorphine, a heroin derivative, is nearly always the drug of choice. The problem is that the dosage has to be stepped up incrementally as pain levels rise. Although controlling pain, diamorphine also suppresses respiration. To explain it in layman's language, a point is reached where the pain is killed, but so too the patient.'

'Is that what happened in the case of Mrs Mortimer?'

'Undoubtedly, I'd say. The death certificate cited pneumonia as the primary cause and bone cancer a secondary factor, which is consistent with the way the end comes for that category of patients. We have not been able to find anything faulty that sets alarm bells ringing over the medical care of any of Dr Cameron's patients. However ...'

'Do I detect the introduction of a scorpion's tail?' Lowen cut in.

'I don't know about a sting in the tail, but there's certainly a complication. Mrs Hayter's mother did change her will to leave everything to Dr Cameron, something we frown upon. Mrs Mortimer wasn't what you'd call rich, but she was a widow and owned her house outright. In today's inflated property market, her house would have been valued at almost three hundred thousand pounds.'

'Do you know if any of his other patients changed their wills in his favour?'

'We do and they did.'

'How many?'

'Eight in all.'

'Have all those patients died?'

'They have.'

Lowen shuffled her thoughts and dealt from the top.

'Were all the deaths predictable?'

'Certainly. They were all terminally ill with cancer and we cannot fault Dr Cameron's prescribing.'

'How were the drugs administered?'

'Good question. Mostly by mouth in tablet or medicine form, as opposed to intravenous injection.'

'Would those patients, in their condition, have been capable of taking the medication unaided?'

'Unlikely, but most of them were visited at least twice a day by a district nurse, who oversaw the drug-management.'

'You mean the nurse would have given the tablets or medicine?'

'Mostly, yes.'

'Were autopsies carried out on any of these patients?'

'No. They were due to die. Cause wasn't in doubt.'

'But it could be.'

'I don't follow.' His frown went deep into his conscience.

'Doctor Cameron's prescriptions were in accordance with your expectations, but it doesn't follow that the dosage given matched what was written.'

The professor's confused expression indicated he did not have a devious mind and his trust in human nature made him more suitable to his own chosen profession than to Lowen's.

'It's possible, isn't it, that someone could have returned after the nurse's last visit of the day to give the patient a further dose of the drug, perhaps by injection?' Lowen continued with her hypothesis.

'Well, put like that ... Yes, it's possible, but my gut feeling is that one of the district nurses would have noticed something not quite right and become suspicious.' And then, almost as if thinking aloud, he added, 'But in the case of Mrs Mortimer course, she may not have been visited by a district nurse.'

'Why not? Why should she have been an exception?'

'Because her daughter, Mrs Hayter, is a qualified nurse, who worked in a large hospital for many years. She would know all about pain-management.'

'And be capable of giving injections,' Lowen observed meaningfully.

CHAPTER 18

Professor Armitage had sown the seed. By the time Lowen was back on her patch, meeting Sloane for a sociable catching-up session in the convivial Baker's Arms, a pub dwarfed by the castle ruins, the seed was flowering out of control.

Was it really possible that Pauline Hayter had murdered her own mother?

'Quite possible,' speculated Sloane, inspired by the dangerously potent scrumpy cider he had decided to experiment with, like a teenager puffing on his first joint. 'She has been a nurse. She knows all about the delicate borderline between safe and potentially lethal doses of powerful drugs. We know absolutely nothing about her relationship with her mother, but let's surmise that it was a relatively normal, loving one. She could have been devastated by her mother's prolonged suffering. Her mother could have pleaded with her daughter to be put out of her misery.'

'You're suggesting a mercy killing?'

'It's happening all the time. Doctors and nurses deny it, but it goes on – and not always for the most altruistic reasons. Let's suppose she did hasten her mother's end, only to learn that she's been struck out of the will and everything went to an outsider, the GP.'

'A daughter scorned!'

'And her revenge is to point the finger at the doctor. Make him the villain and scapegoat. Make him pay. Make sure he doesn't benefit. If found guilty of murder, he won't be allowed to profit from his crime. The will would be revoked.'

'And Pauline Hayter would scoop the lot.'

'How about it?'

'There's a glitch.'

'Only one?' Sloane feigned amusement.

'The chances are there wasn't much of a relationship between mother and daughter, explaining why Pauline Hayter was expunged from the will. Also … if Mrs Hayter was out of the money, she'd be eager to prolong her mother's life, rather than to shorten it, giving her the chance to sweeten things between the two of them.'

'Much hinges on when Mrs Hayter first knew about the change of will. Maybe she had no wind of it until after her mother's death, which would explain her outrage, especially if she'd been caring for the old girl.'

'Why would Mrs Mortimer exclude her daughter from her will if there had been a conventional mother/daughter relationship?' Lowen directed the question as much to herself as to Sloane.

'Who knows what psychological and emotional pressures were exerted on Mrs Mortimer by Dr Cameron. Maybe she was delirious at the time and didn't fully realize what she was doing. Do you know who witnessed the signing of the new will?'

Lowen rotated her head with the rhythm of a nodding donkey. 'Nope.'

'When and where was it signed?'

'Can't tell you, which shows just how much work there's still to be done.'

Then it was Sloane's turn to report on his morning.

'Quite a day for both of us,' commented Lowen, after hearing about Sloane's meeting with Darke, the funding of Dresden's cottage and her portfolio of shares.

They both recognized the problem without the necessity for it to be articulated. Rather than crystallizing the case, the new leads further fragmented it, multiplying the possibilities instead of dividing them.

'How about applying for the exhumation of Mrs Mortimer's remains?' Sloane said in the manner of an indecent proposal. 'Would Mrs Hayter go for it?'

Lowen took her time. The wine was providing a soft cushion on which to rest the stress of the working day.

'Before going down that route, I want to be absolutely certain where it's taking us.'

'If all goes well, we find out the morphine levels in her body at the moment of death.'

'But does it help in any way to prove how – and by whom – it was administered?'

'It's a start, a foot on the ladder. Let's assume the pathologist establishes that death was due to an overdose of morphine, not pneumonia, and it was intravenously injected into the body. Now, we know for sure Mrs Mortimer couldn't have done it herself, so we confirm murder.'

'Not necessarily.'

'Pardon?'

'Not necessarily murder. For murder, we have to prove intent. The overdose – as opposed to the prescribed dose – could have been administered accidentally.'

'By a doctor or a trained nurse? Come on!'

'It happens. Often. Apart from that, there's no way I can see of proving, beyond all reasonable doubt, which of the two did it – if anybody.'

'Surely this is where you rely on that good old faithful friend – circumstantial evidence?'

'I think we first have to try to get some bearing on when Mrs Hayter initially learned she was out of the money. If it was before her mother's death, then she's relatively in the clear.'

'Even then it could still be either of them.' The alcohol was stimulating Sloane's brain, rather than stultifying it, for a change. 'A mercy-killing motive required no knowledge of the contents of the will.'

'But if Mrs Hayter did know about a major alteration – a rewrite, in fact – then she wouldn't have been inclined towards mercy,' Lowen observed bleakly. 'The worst thing about going round in circles is the dizziness.'

The rest of the evening was spent structuring their approach.

'Softly, softly, catchee monkey,' said Lowen, after a few more glasses of sparkling wine. 'I'll hit Mrs Hayter with an early morning call and you can bowl a few bouncers of your own at Ernst Lergen.'

Next morning, they woke up together, side by side.

Drink had played its part, but only as a facilitator. Something much more adhesive had bonded them.

When Sloane peered in the mirror in Lowen's bathroom, an image of blissful disbelief stared bleary-eyed at him. *Smug bastard!* he berated the reflection.

Lowen had always pinned great faith on her own judgement. Perhaps the time had come to review such a blanket endorsement in herself, she was thinking self-critically.

CHAPTER 19

'**O**f course I remember you.'

Sloane had spent half a minute reminding Ernst Lergen of the 'silent man' who had accompanied Detective Inspector Lowen to his house.

How could I possibly forget such a nonentity? Lergen might have said, if he had been less polite and more honest.

'I've just a couple of things I've been asked to run past you,' said Sloane, as disarmingly as possible, happily blending into the self-effacing role of a lackey. His whole life was one of playing character parts in low-budget government productions.

'How long will this take?' Impatience flickered.

Lergen sounded in a hurry. In a rush for the golf course, no doubt, thought Sloane, who was calling from Lowen's house phone.

'As long as your answers.'

'I'll be economic, then.'

'Not with the truth, I hope.'

They both chuckled insincerely.

Sloane prefaced his first question, couched as a statement, with a little affected cough. 'You didn't tell us that you paid for Miss Dresden's cottage.'

Sloane regretted not being able to see Lergen's face and to register the unspoken language.

Lergen caught his breath, then dropped it. Several seconds elapsed before he recovered sufficient composure to engineer a flinty response.

'Who told you that?'

'Miss Dresden's accountant. It's documented.'

'So what?'

'It's true, then?'

'*You've* just told *me* it is. As I also said, *so what?*'

No Mr Charmer now. All the veneer had been rubbed off to leave a rough, abrasive surface.

'Why didn't you mention it?'

'How could my giving money to an old flame – a very *old* flame – have any connection with her death so many years later?'

'She could have been blackmailing you.'

'That's offensive!'

It was, indeed, and Sloane was ashamed of himself, but provocation was always a useful tool for prising open reticence. On another level, he was beginning to wonder if he had really ever known Emily Dresden.

'By being secretive you arouse suspicion.'

'I was *not* secretive. I venture to suggest that most people in my position would have been far less forthcoming.'

Of course, he was right. Sloane and Lowen had underscored that very point to each other, but Sloane was not about to make such a concession now.

'It's not exactly every day that a house is bought for someone as a present.'

'Was that meant to be some kind of question?'

'I'm inviting an explanation.'

'What I do with my savings is my own affair. I'd paid income tax on the money I gave to Emily. It was clean cash. The transaction was lawful. That's all you need to know; nothing more.'

'The gift was completely voluntary?'

'The fact that you ask such a question demonstrates how little you know about me.' Every word from Lergen now was barbed.

'How about the shares?' *Hit him while he's hot,* Sloane urged himself on.

The pause was pained. 'You're not embarrassing me, if that's your objective. I'm simply bored. And disappointed.'

'Tell me about the disappointment.'

'What I did for Emily is sacred to me.'

A rogue thought flashed through Sloane's head like an electric charge.

'You weren't in business with Emily, were you, by any chance?'

'She wasn't laundering money for me, if that's what you're getting at.'

'I wasn't, but now I might be.'

'Well, you can forget it. Emily had her accountant: I have mine. All money that comes in and goes out is accounted for. That's how it has always been. Every transaction is transparent. I have one thing only left to say to you.'

'Which is?'

'Goodbye.'

Pauline Hayter had not been expecting to be contacted again by the police so soon after Lowen's visit. Her surprise was telegraphed, pleasing Lowen.

'You have given me plenty to think about,' Lowen began illusorily.

'I'm glad you're taking it seriously.' There was a tinge of admonishment in Hayter's rather shrill voice.

'Reflecting on what you told me, I realize there are many holes.'

'*Holes*?' Mrs Hayter challenged indignantly.

'Questions I should have put to you. Omissions by me. My fault, not yours.'

Mrs Hayter was placated. 'Anything to see that rat behind bars, where he belongs.'

'First things first. What was the date of your mother's death?'

That was the soft ball, which Mrs Hayter fielded effortlessly.

'Ninth of August, this year.'

'At home; her home?'

'Yes. She didn't want to die in hospital, surrounded by strangers. She wouldn't even consider going into a hospice, where patients are kept free from pain and allowed to die with dignity.'

'Your father died some years ago, so your mother was alone in her home?'

Mrs Hayter reacted as if threatened. 'I tried to persuade her to move in with us, but she didn't want to be a burden. You know how stubborn independent people can be as they age. I would pop around several times a day to prepare food for her and see that she had a drink and anything else she needed. She wasn't far away. Less than a mile. Sometimes I'd sleep at her house if she was particularly poorly.'

'You're a qualified nurse.'

'So?'

Her radar was over-active, as if warning of an impending attack.

Prickly, thought Lowen, before continuing with her gentle, though inexorable, probing. 'You would have been keeping an eye on the drugs she was taking.'

'There wasn't anything wrong with the drugs she was prescribed; that was perfectly in order. My worries were over the dosage, as I explained when you were here.'

'But you wouldn't have wanted your mother to suffer unnecessary severe pain, would you?'

'Of course not. What are you getting at?' Mrs Hayter could not follow the plot, though she was sure that there must be one.

'Did you ever give your mother painkillers?'

'Not when she was on high doses of morphine. You can't mess with that. Monitoring the interval between each intake is crucial; that was the job of the visiting nurses.'

'Didn't you discuss your reservations with them about your mother's treatment?'

'Towards the end, my mother's deterioration was tragically fast. While she was alive, my main concern was her comfort. It was only afterwards, with the benefit of hindsight and an overview, that I was able to piece it all together.'

'Plus the change of will factor?'

'But of course; it wasn't just one thing.'

'Was your mother bedridden?'

'She wouldn't go to bed. For the last two months of her life she was confined to an armchair in her living-room. She was wrapped in a blanket and had to be helped to and from the toilet. That was her life.'

'At what time of day did she die?'

'During the night. She was dead when a district nurse arrived at eight in the morning.'

'Dead in the armchair?'

'She'd rolled forward, head first on to the floor.'

'When had the pneumonia set in?'

'About three days previously.'

'And what treatment was she getting for that?'

'Antibiotics. But she was too ill; too weak. The nurses wanted her in hospital.'

'But she wouldn't go, even then?'

'She dreaded hospitals; she had a phobia about them going back to childhood.'

'Did you discuss her treatment with Dr Cameron?'

'Several times.'

'What did he say?'

'That he was doing the best he could for my mother and that she was content with the care.'

'Did you have an argument with him?'

'We argued, but we never had an argument; not while mother was alive. I was anxious to avoid her being caught in the cross-fire.'

'When did you first learn that she'd dumped you from her will?'

'A couple of days after her death, when I started to make the funeral arrangements. I had to find out if she'd made any special requests for the funeral service.'

'What would your attitude be if I made an application for your mother's body to be exhumed?'

'I'd advise you not to make a fool of yourself. My mother was cremated.'

'I see ...' What Lowen really meant was *damn it!* 'That was her wish, was it?'

'Always had been.'

'Incidentally, who witnessed her signature on the new will?'

'A Faye Mitchison, whoever she might be.'

Excitement induced an adrenaline-rush and a surge of blood to Lowen's head. 'Did Miss Dresden have this information?'

'Oh, yes, that was one line of enquiry she was following up.'

Well! Well! thought Lowen. Now we really have almost come full circle. Fancy that!

CHAPTER 20

Carrington had to be tackled. Clearly it made sense to leave this to Sloane. Accordingly, Sloane invited his cloak-and-dagger chum to a lunchtime drink in the pub he had used previously on the Swanage seafront. Sloane attacked a pint of muddy-brown cask ale. Carrington toyed with a gin and tonic. Two very different characters bound by a common professional purpose; so much in common, yet also so disparate; a Constable alongside a Lowrie, both masterpieces demanding to be taken seriously, but galleries and galaxies apart. The traditionalist Carrington hanging out with the iconoclastic Sloane; a pastiche of plural society if ever there was one.

'What progress, if any, is there to report on the Emily front?' The rather stilted enquiry inevitably came from Carrington, who was packaged true to his genus in a tweed jacket – leather pads protecting the elbows – and cavalry twill trousers. He was military to the core, but something melancholic in his eyes and voice implied that he was tiring of cat-and-mouse games. The straight kill in conflict, on the battlefield, had always been acceptable to him as an integral part of a soldier's high-risk life, but his Corinthian spirit for fair play and openness meant that the duplicity inherent in clandestine warfare went against the grain. Perhaps Emily's murder was a cat and mouse too many for him, a watershed of sorts, thought Sloane.

'We're on the threshold, I reckon,' said Sloane, his confidence emblazoned across his sanguine face.

Carrington brightened. 'I don't detect any equivocation.'

'Neither should you; there isn't any.'

Carrington peered into his glass as if consulting a crystal-ball over the future. 'Should I be prepared for repercussions my end?'

'I wouldn't have thought so.'

'Now that wasn't quite so unequivocal.' Carrington no longer fiddled with his drink. He drank it in one hit, as if taking nasty medicine.

'I had a specific reason for this meeting,' said Sloane, closing down on the maundering warm-up.

'I didn't think for one moment that you wanted an idle chat about my plans for Christmas.'

The tensility of the tension between them was being tested.

'How well do you *really* know your housekeeper?' Sloane probed affably.

Carrington stiffened, like a corpse reacting to rigor mortis. 'Now, now, Mike!' he began to remonstrate.

'I'll explain.'

'I *insist* that you do.'

This was proving tricky.

'But first deal with my questions, please.'

'I think I've told you something about her before,' Carrington retorted imperiously.

'Only in the most generic terms,' said Sloane, undaunted.

Carrington took his time and when eventually he replied, his response was measured. 'It's hard to say much more, now I start to think about it.'

'OK, let me lead you.'

'I wish you would; that might make it easier.'

'What do you know about her social life?'

'Well, Faye enjoys the theatre and going out for a meal; that I do know. But ...' He made an expansive gesture with his hands that said in sign language, *I can't believe we're having this conversation in the context of Emily's murder.*

'Just bear with me a little longer, Hugh. Has she been seeing anybody?'

'*Seeing anybody?*'

Sloane had lapsed into quaint old English for Carrington's benefit, but that appeared to have misfired, so he resumed normal-speak. 'Is there a man in her life?'

The lights came on in Carrington's eyes. 'As a matter of fact, there is.'

'Does she talk about him?'

'Not much. Faye is reserved. But most importantly of all, she's discreet, which goes with her breeding. It's her discretion that I find most appealing about her as an employee.'

Sloane ignored the commercial on behalf of the English middle-class.

'Do you know the identity of her lover?'

Carrington held up a halting hand, like a police officer directing traffic. 'Hold on a minute, Mike. I said there was a man in her life; I made no mention of a lover. It's just someone she goes out for meals with and to the theatre. I have no evidence of the relationship being anything other than platonic.'

'You don't have a name?'

'Grief, no! That's one line of intelligence-gathering I'm most certainly not into. However, there is one thing I *can* tell you about him.'

'Which is?'

'He's a doctor. That's something she's mentioned casually once or twice. So far she hasn't volunteered his name and I wouldn't be so rude as to ask for it.'

Ever the gent, thought Sloane, as much in admiration as in deprecation.

'How did the subject come up about his being a doctor?'

'Oh, just in passing. It was no big deal. I don't even know if he's a GP or hospital doctor. On one occasion she just happened to mention that she was going out to dinner with him, but feared the evening might be ruined because he was on call. It was around then that she told me he was a doctor.'

'So this relationship has been going on some time?'

'Over a year. Well over. Maybe two. Nearer three, perhaps. Time flies.'

'Maybe she used his first name on an occasion?'

Carrington pinched his pink chin with thumb and forefinger, drifting into reverie. 'If she did, for the life of me I can't recall it.'

'Might Sefton ring any bells?'

'*Sefton*,' Carrington repeated absently, eyes dimmed as they mirrored the mind stumbling in the dark. 'Do you know, I think it could have been! Don't hold me to it, mind you. Now, how about telling me what this is all about? Come on, spit it out. If she's involved in anything untoward, I have a right to know.

What's more germane, I have a *need* to know. You can see that, surely?'

'I'm sorry, Hugh, but I really am not at liberty to brief you on this one, save to say that it's totally unconnected with our line of work – that I promise you.'

'But it is connected with Emily?'

'Very much so, I'm afraid.'

'Shit!'

Sloane smiled whimsically, thinking to himself, He swears so eloquently, with such clear and rounded enunciation.

'How much do you *really* know about Faye's past?'

Carrington was visibly irked.

'Well, I didn't simply pluck her off the street. She wasn't sheltering from the rain and I invited her in for tea and, while eating scones said, "And how about taking a job with me? You needn't go back into the rain then. Instead, you can hang around with me for the next ten or twenty years." Come on, Mike, give me some credit! I made proper checks.'

'I'd expect nothing less.'

'I was able to delve deeper into he background than would be possible for most employers.'

'That's why I asked the question. Our trade is a way of life. We trust no one. We begin by assuming the worst of everyone; that the whole world's a fake, populated by pathological liars.'

'Intelligence is a profession, not a *trade*,' Carrington reprimanded Sloane haughtily. 'And, unlike contemporary operatives, secular cynics all, I have trust in the innate goodness of most people.'

Carrington liked and respected Sloane, without being fond of his fabled generation.

'We're straying,' said Sloane.

'We are, indeed.'

'The subject was Faye Mitchison.'

'Yes, dear Faye ...'

'You're obviously attached to her.'

'I'm *obviously* nothing!' Carrington's glare was withering.

'I stand corrected.'

'You're doing no such thing. You're sitting. Say what you mean, in precise English, for God's sake!'

Sloane felt like the apprentice rather than the master craftsman.

'Tell it your way.'

'I intend to. Well, for a start, she comes from good stock.'

He could be talking about a Fresian for sale at the cattle market, thought Sloane.

'Father was a colonel, in fact,' Carrington continued dreamily.

Ah! Now we have it; to be the daughter of a colonel must be the next thing to godliness in Carrington's estimation, Sloane teased himself.

'Went to prep school, then an all-girls grammar. Didn't go to university. Father posted overseas. She went with her parents. Doubled-up with her mother as housekeeper; you know how it can be with stiff-necked families.'

Carrington was as unpredictable as the English weather; that was his charm. Just as you had him typecast as a Colonel Blimp reactionary, so he would confound you with an opinion that revealed him on the side of the proletariat.

'Did she ever have a career?'

'She had jobs. She was nanny to a couple of Swiss families. More governess than nanny, I suspect. Excellent references.'

'Genuine?'

'But, of course. I verified them personally.'

'Nannying didn't last, I take it.'

'Her father had a stroke. Faye's mother couldn't cope. Faye did her filial duty and returned home to care for her father.'

'No marriage?'

'No time to nurse a relationship as well as her father.'

'Romances? Affairs?'

'Only one semi-affair that I know about. If anything, it would seem she gravitates towards men older than herself.'

'Looking for her father in someone else?'

'Possibly. I'm no Freud. Her father died about a year before she came to me.'

'And how *did she* come to you?'

'Replied to an advert. As she said when I interviewed her, she couldn't type, do shorthand, take blood, sell property, or stand up in court to defend or prosecute. What she could do, however, was manage a house, a job for which few were better qualified.'

'So she got the job?'

'And I've never had reason for regret ever since.'

Sloane's eyes narrowed into sly slits. 'What changes have you noticed?'

'*Changes?*' Carrington intoned.

'Over the years.'

Carrington pondered. 'None really. I suppose she's aged a little visually, but the increments have been so gradual that I haven't noticed.'

'I really meant in her ways and habits.'

'Well, she goes out more, that's all. She's free to come and go as she pleases, as long as she does her chores.'

'No evidence of her coming into money in recent years?'

'She's always dressed smartly, in a dignified fashion. She's never been exactly short of money. Her father left the family reasonably well off. Faye was an only child. She didn't take the job with me because she was desperate for cash.'

'So she hasn't suddenly become financially flush?'

'If she had, Faye isn't the kind of person to show it; her British reserve is worn with pride.'

'I'm sorry to be a bore about this, but on the Saturday night that Emily was killed, Faye definitely was indoors when you returned?'

Carrington exaggerated his sigh for impact. 'There's no doubt about that, something we've been over before. She couldn't have had anything to do with Emily's murder. I must warn you, before you go any further with this nonsense, I'll stand up for her. In my estimation, she's beyond reproach.' And then, as a ghastly, almost haunting, afterthought, 'You're not suggesting that Faye could be a plant, a sleeper?'

'No, this isn't political, I'm convinced of that.'

If Faye was a murderer, Carrington would be appalled; if she was a traitor, however, he would be mortified.

'Thank goodness for small mercies,' said Carrington. 'I couldn't bear the thought of the last English rose in my life being exposed as poison ivy. Faye may be prickly at times, but who's ever heard of a rose entirely without thorns?'

CHAPTER 21

Winter can spring pleasant surprises, just like any season.
The new day was born bathed in summer sunshine.
Weather forecasters predicted a 'rare respite to make the most of'
before normal service was resumed with a vengeance. Mary
Parmiter was echoing a similar sentiment, though slightly less
eloquently. 'We'll pay for this. A taste of the tropics today, an
Arctic slap in the face tomorrow; you see.'

Her husband, Tom, nodded sagely, not taking his eyes off the
road as he negotiated their ten-year-old Rover from the outside,
fast lane of the M3 to the inside, and then on to the slip road,
winding in a zigzag into the Winchester service station. Their 9-
year-old twins, Heather and Peter, were submerged in their own
banter in the back of the car. The state of the weather was irrelevant to them. In fact, if anything, snow would have been
preferred to sunshine. The twins had every intention of making
the most of their day off school, even though they were going to
their grandmother's funeral in London.

'Why are we stopping, Mum?' asked Peter, peering out of the
window, suddenly aware of the car slowing to a crawl.

'So we can have a drink, stretch our legs and use the toilet,'
their mother explained patiently.

'Boring!' the children chimed in unison, then cheering up as
they spied a playground.

'Can we play?' beseeched Heather, encouraged by her brother.

'We'll see,' said Mrs Parmiter, evasively.

'Oh, please!' Peter cajoled.

'Let's see how you behave and how much time we have to
spare,' Tom Parmiter joined the bartering.

After Mr Parmiter had parked the Rover as near as possible to the fenced-in playground, the children piled out and made a dash for the swings and slides, without waiting for permission.

'Come back here this minute!' shouted their mother, fruitlessly.

'Oh, leave them,' said Mr Parmiter, with the children out of range. 'It'll do them good to let off steam and it might work to our advantage.'

'How do you make that out?' his wife demanded, sceptically.

'By tiring them out. Then they might sleep for the remainder of the journey.'

'And pigs might fly! You're too soft with them by half, you really are. If they make themselves filthy, then it's your job to clean them up before we get to the church. I'm not going to take two mucky urchins to a funeral.'

'I'll have a word with them,' said Mr Parmiter. 'I'll also see if they want a drink and a bite to eat. You go in and I'll catch up with you.'

'You make sure now that you read them the riot act.'

'Leave it to me.'

'Like leaving foxes to take care of chickens!'

The Parmiters made use of the public toilets, bought a magazine and a newspaper, two takeaway coffees, and Cokes and muffins for the children, all of which took them no longer than fifteen minutes. They then headed straight for the playground, only to discover it empty. No sight nor sound of a child.

'I told them not to wander off,' said Mr Parmiter, more cross than concerned.

'Which just goes to show how much notice they take of you.'

There was a green knoll behind the playground, bordered on three sides by bushes, baby shrubs and young trees to shield the site from the motorway.

'Peter!' Mrs Parmiter called out.

'Heather!' cried Mr Parmiter.

Just as Mr Parmiter's irritation was transcending into worry, so the children emerged from the trees, not gambolling as they usually did when running free, but walking cautiously, as if threading their way through a minefield, heads down.

'What have you been up to?' their father bellowed, his anger now a catharsis for his relief.

'Look what we found,' Peter said, proudly.

He was holding a knife, the blade of which was about six inches long, with a considerable amount of mud and grass on it.

'Where did you find that?' Mrs Parmiter snapped, shrew-like, appalled by what could occur in such a short period of time.

'It was stuck in the grass at the foot of one of those trees,' Peter explained gleefully, pointing behind him in the direction from which they had trooped.

Heather held up a pair of latex gloves.

'These were over the handle,' said Heather, glumly. 'I wanted to bring the knife, but Peter said it was too dangerous for a girl. Pig!'

'Its too dangerous for either of you,' Mrs Parmiter stated, harshly. 'Give it to me – at once!' She held out a hand to her son. 'Not that way, silly boy! Do you want to stab me to death? Really! Handle first, the way you've been taught.'

Peter obeyed, remarking, 'It's in good nick. All it needs is a good clean up.'

Not all of the blade was covered with dirt. Most of the steel was stained with something else.

'What do you make of that?' Mrs Parmiter quizzed her husband, handing the knife to him.

Mr Parmiter held the knife gingerly, turning it around clockwise, then anti-clockwise, like a pawnbroker valuing an offered heirloom.

Finally, he answered, 'That looks like dried blood to me.'

'I *know* it is,' replied Mrs Parmiter, assertively.

The search for the weapon that had killed Emily Dresden was over.

CHAPTER 22

The first Lowen heard about the knife was three days later.

After the discovery at the service station, the Parmiters had continued their journey to London and the funeral of Mary Parmiter's mother. Late that afternoon, they had taken their find to Muswell Hill police station, where their fingerprints were recorded for elimination purposes and a report was filed. The next day, the knife and gloves were delivered by hand to the Hampshire Constabulary, which was responsible for policing the region where the Winchester service station was located. A computer search showed that neighbouring Dorset Police were looking for a knife that had been used to stab to death an elderly woman. The investigating officer was listed as Detective Inspector Joanne Lowen, who was contacted the next day. Buoyed, Lowen said she would collect the items personally, which she did without delay. Frustration set in, though, when another two days elapsed before she had the preliminary findings from forensics.

Blood on the blade was a perfect match with Miss Dresden's, but the only fingerprints on the knife belonged to members of the Parmiter family. Tests were continuing on the gloves, but Professor Charles Hunter, the notoriously pessimistic head of the western region Criminal Forensics Department, did not hold out much hope from that source. His exact words to Lowen over the telephone were, 'Don't hold your breath, Inspector.' And she did not, which was a big mistake, though fortunately of little consequence in the great scheme of things.

Sloane was as uplifted as Lowen. Neither of them was the least disheartened by the lack of direct clues on the weapon.

'It's *where* the knife was found that probably tells us more than anything else,' opined Lowen, bubbling.

'Roughly seventy miles from the murder,' Sloane calculated.

'Alongside the London-bound carriageway of the motorway.'

'The killer was driving eastbound away from the scene of the crime.'

'Mike, the killer was driving home. He wasn't going as far as London.'

'You're thinking of Ernst Lergen.'

'Who else? He would have left the M3 at one of the Basingstoke or Reading junctions, then cut across country to Henley; a doddle of a journey at that time of night. Neither Parkes nor Dr Cameron would have made the hundred and forty-mile round trip, when they could have disposed of the weapon much more effectively in the sea or one of the nearby rivers. The killer was almost certainly someone unfamiliar with the Corfe Castle area.'

'Unless the killer was laying a false trail.'

'Going to all that trouble to make me dismiss the possibility of a local connection?'

'A two-hour drive isn't much *trouble* when your freedom and future's at stake.' And then, 'Has the knife itself any distinguishing features?'

'No, unfortunately.' Some of Lowen's fizz had faded. 'It's a common kitchen utensil. A million like it. One in every household.'

'Part of a set?'

'Might be, but that won't help us.'

'What next?'

'I'm going to the golf club where Lergen claims to have been at a birthday celebration. We've rather neglected putting that particular alibi to the sword.'

'It's hardly an *alibi*. It doesn't cover the all-important, material time. If it stands up, which it will – I bet you – so what? It neither eliminates nor incriminates him. So, what's the point?'

'It puts the veracity of his testimony to the test.'

'Which will still be meaningless. He could be having an affair and needed an excuse to be away from his wife. That doesn't make him a killer.'

Lowen sighed, ruefully acknowledging Sloane's logic.

'But I might hear something that touches a nerve,' Lowen said, wishfully. 'If I don't go, I'll never know.'

'True. It's worth a shot ... if you've nothing better to do.'
They were back to rainbow-chasing.

It took Harry Parkes barely five minutes to pack a suitcase. He threw in shirts, socks, underwear, electric shaver and a tooth-brush, not bothering about a change of suit or a spare pair of shoes. The future held no interest for him. He had no idea where he was going – except away from Corfe Castle, away from Dorset, away from persecution, away from the nightmare, away from his own haunting shadows. Not even death would befriend him. The whole world, and beyond, was against him, he felt. Not good enough for God; not bad enough for the Devil. The ultimate in universal rejection.

He would not confide in Father Rowlands about his intentions. How could he? He did not have a plan. Even when he had dialled for a taxi, he had no notion where he was going.

'I want to go to the station?' he had blurted.

'Which station?'

Which station? Which station? Does it matter? Who cares? Not me!

After much anguish, he had given instructions to be driven to Wareham railway station, where he boarded a train for London, travelling on a one-way ticket.

Around the same time, Father Rowlands and his wife, Sandra, were having a familiar row.

'You just can't give it up, can you?' Sandra trilled, her normally pallid cheeks roseate with rage.

'You have no right opening my letter.' Her husband tried to recede behind a smokescreen.

'I wouldn't need to if you were honest with me.' Sandra's voice mounted the scale, as if at choir practice. The decibel level was now shrill. 'You've got another county court judgement against you from yet another credit card company. If you default on this, they're going to send in the bailiffs. Can't you see where this is going to end? We'll lose our home. We'll be on the streets. Just imagine the shame and what it'll do to the kids. Haven't you thought of that? No, of course you haven't! All you care about is what's running in the two thirty, or whatever, at Kempton Park, or wherever, and how much of *our* money you can blow. Instead of trying to pay off your debts, you squander more on gambling.'

'I don't try to lose,' he said plaintively.

'You're a loser, Simon, full stop; always have been, always will be. If you'd only accept that fact, we might have a chance.'

'I'm in too deep. I have to win my way out; plot my own salvation.'

'Grow up! When has chasing losses ever saved anyone?' There was more pity in her voice now than hostility. 'It was the same in the army. If it ever comes out that you stole money, the Church will wash its hands of you.'

'The Church was founded for sinners; to forgive and to redeem.'

'Don't bet on it, Simon – it'll only be another losing gamble for you.'

'I had every intention of paying back that money.'

'That's what all thieves say.'

'I'm not a thief.'

'Don't kid yourself, Simon. You pinched that money from mess funds not only to pay off some debts, but to finance more gambling. You were the luckiest man alive not to be court martialled. It was only to protect the army from scandal and embarrassment that you were allowed to resign.'

'That's history.'

'Modern history, though; not ancient. If anyone starts digging into your past, it'll surface, rest assured. You're sick, Simon.'

'What do you mean?' he challenged indignantly.

'You're addicted. It's a sickness. You need professional help – if it's not already too late.'

'I can't possibly go to Gamblers' Anonymous.'

'And why not?'

'It would leak out. Someone would recognize me and tip off the newspapers or my bishop – or both. I'd be finished.'

'And what makes you think you're not already?'

'Believe in me, please.'

'You'll never know to what lengths I've already gone for you, to preserve your reputation, for us, for the children.'

'What does that mean?'

'Never you mind. But never lose sight of this fact: whatever

I've done that I'm immensely ashamed of – and there's plenty – is all your fault. Father Rowlands, man of the cloth, man of God, forgiver of sins, messenger of the Almighty, is the root of all evil in this parish.'

'That's enough of that!'

'No, I've had *enough* of you.'

'We have to stick together.'

'We parted years ago, spiritually. We've stayed together this long only because the glue that holds us makes a mess when tampered with. But now I'm at the end of my tether and I've no intention of hanging around here to be pilloried by the public, for our children to be humiliated and taunted at school. No fear!'

'Are you threatening to leave me?'

'No threat, Simon.'

Ernst Lergen's golfing friends could not remember much about the Saturday afternoon bash Lowen wanted to talk to them about.

Club secretary Major Hugh Fanshawe chortled, 'If you can remember too much about a do like that, then it must have been a flop. And it wasn't. It was a damn good legs up, I can tell you. Now what can I get you to drink? You look like a champagne girl to me. How about it, eh?'

They were in the clubhouse bar. The hands of the clock were on noon. The major tweaked his moustache.

'Time to wet the whistle. A rule of mine, to demonstrate self-control, is that I never drink before noon – well, not doubles! Did you say yes to champagne, young lady?'

'No, I didn't.'

'Shame on you! What will it be, then? G and T? Biggie, eh?'

'Make it a tomato juice, with ice and Worcester sauce.'

'Bloody Mary, eh? Good strategy for lunchtime. Lateral thinking. Smart girl.'

'Without the vodka.'

'No vodka! It's bloody undrinkable, bloody unthinkable!'

Lowen indulged him.

'What's the country coming to? Conquered by the Temperance Society! Brought to our knees by the League Against Liquor!'

Lowen allowed him to play to the gallery without spoiling his fun, but only because it was to her advantage.

There were about seven men lounging at the bar, all of them in Oxford-blue blazers and white golfing shoes. Two of them sported cravats. The others wore old school or college ties. Faces were florid. Waistlines bulged. They were caricatures of caricatures, *Punch* characters brought to life by a shot of gin. Conversations were driven by personal reminiscences of wars that were being taught in schools as military history. A couple of women sat at a distant table, but, in truth, they were scarcely distinguishable from the men. For Lowen, this was an unnerving time-warp, as if she had unwittingly stepped into God's waiting-room and was anxious that He would spot the mistake before tapping her on the shoulder and ushering her over the threshold.

'Let's go somewhere a little more private, shall we?' the major said rhetorically. 'How about in the corner by the window?' He led the way, not waiting for Lowen's assent. 'Here to talk about that shindig the other Saturday, eh? That was what I call a good thrash, a premier league do. Don't get many like that any more. The country's gone soft. We've become an orange squash nation. You people are to blame, of course, breathalyzing anything with a mouth.'

Lowen refused the bait.

'You have a lovely view from here.' The observation was deliberately anodyne in order to defuse any alcohol-fuelled confrontation.

From where they were sitting, they had an unimpeded, panoramic view of the eighteenth green and its undulating, immaculately manicured fairway, part of an idyllic course, framed by the River Thames.

'This is my home,' Major Fanshawe said, rather dolefully. 'I'm a widower, you see. Son's in Australia. Daughter ran off with a loafing layabout hippie when those sort of dolts and lifestyles were fashionable. Never seen her since. Could be dead, for all I know, like her mother.' A tear froze in each rheumy eye. 'What family I have, relevant to my current life, is here.'

Lowen experienced a sudden pang of pity for him and guilt for her own premature judgement.

'And Ernst Lergen is part of that family?' Lowen seized the opportunity to refocus.

'Nice chap, for a foreigner. Hasn't been a member long. Quite new to this country, but a good sort. Could do with more like him. You'd never guess he wasn't a true Brit from the way he speaks the Queen's English. His wife's charming, too ... even though she doesn't play. She often comes with him on Sundays, when they lunch here.'

'But she wasn't with him at the party?'

'Hell, no! It was a stag do, you know. Lots of barrack-room jokes and ribbing. Not suitable for ladies.'

'What time did it end?'

'Hard to say. You don't clock-watch when you're partying, do you? These days people reserve that for the work-place.'

'Approximately?'

'Well, I suppose it started to break up at about seven-thirty to eight.'

'Was Mr Lergen one of the first or last to go?'

The major retreated into a private conference with himself. 'I've no recollection of his leaving,' he said, on emerging. 'Nor of anyone else, for that matter. We just had a damned good time – all of us. Look, I do hope Ernst isn't in any kind of trouble. I appreciate you said on the phone it wouldn't be possible for you to explain everything and I'd have to take you on trust. That sort of thing was common in the army – nudge and a wink, hush-hush operations, don't say a word to the next fellow, and all that cloak-and-dagger stuff, but I'd hate to think I was dropping the poor chap in the proverbial. He didn't drive away from here and have an accident, did he? I should have kept my mouth clamped. I really can't tell you how much he had to drink. He was just enjoying himself; as high-spirited as anyone. Please assure me I haven't sold him down the Swanee.'

'I can, indeed, assure you of that. If anything, you've proved yourself his staunch ally.'

'Well, that is good news,' he beamed. 'I suppose you're going to ask me to keep our little conversation to myself.'

'Do you think you're capable of that, Major?'

His fresh flush was not induced by the gin. 'I doubt it,' he answered candidly.

'So do I.'

'You're a shrewd judge of character, Inspector.'

'I need to be. Mr Lergen would be surprised if I hadn't been here, asking you these questions.'

The major was soon his old self. 'Doesn't sound like a hanging job, to me, thank goodness. If you won't spill the beans, maybe he'll tell me what he's been up to.'

'Maybe he will,' Lowen said non-commitally.

'Now, how about a spot of lunch? The bar food here is mouth-watering. I can recommend the steak and kidney pie. Just the ticket for a rubbish day like this. Be my guest. It'll give you the chance to have a chat with a couple more chaps who were here *that* day, such as Jack Fairweather. It was his Big Sixty-Five.'

'Put that way, how could I possibly refuse?'

'You can't!' the major agreed triumphantly.

By the time Lowen departed, replete, she was in no doubt that Lergen had been truthful about his attendance in the golf club for the celebration. Nevertheless, her journey had been far from wasted. No one could recall what Lergen had been drinking that evening and at what speed. He could have been knocking back nothing more potent than lemonade, which is easily mistaken for gin and tonic, and then feigned being legless in order to blend in with the uninhibited conviviality. A local taxi firm had indeed despatched a cab to the golf club for Lergen, who was driven straight home. The driver had been unable to throw much light on Lergen's condition that evening. 'He hardly spoke,' the cabbie had told detectives. 'I assumed he was worse for wear, but I couldn't swear to it.' Lergen could have deliberately created an illusion of probability to underpin his account of that Saturday evening, Lowen was thinking.

While Lowen was in Henley, Sloane busied himself reading the four volumes of the Shipman Inquiry, which had been presented to Parliament by the Secretary of State for the Home Department and the Secretary of State for Health. Doctor Harold Shipman, a GP in the north of England, was convicted of murdering fifteen of his patients. However, it was recognized that the total number of people he killed deliberately far exceeded those for which he stood trial and it was not long before he was acknowledged as the most prolific serial killer in the history of British crime. Since then, he had committed suicide in prison.

Sloane was particularly drawn to the third volume, prepared by Dame Janet Smith, who chaired the inquiry. In the Foreword, she wrote of people trying to persuade her that 'there would never be another Shipman'. But she resisted such complacency, writing:

It seems to me that there are two reasons why those arguments should not prevail. The first is that we do not know that Shipman is unique. We know that he has killed more people than any other serial killer yet identified, but we do not know how many others may remain hidden. If Shipman was able to kill for almost twenty-four years before he was discovered, who can say with confidence that there are not other doctors, still unknown, who have killed in the past? Who can say there will be none in the future? If there is a risk that a doctor might kill in the future and if, as is now clear, the present system would neither deter nor detect such conduct, surely the system must be changed.

Then came the Summary, which began:

Following my first report, which set out my findings that Shipman had killed at least 215 of his patients (this figure has since risen to well over 300) over a period of twenty-four years, it was clear that the arrangements for death and cremation certification and the coronial system, which are intended to protect the public against the concealment of homicides, had failed to fulfil that purpose.

Buzzing in Sloane's head were the phrases, ...*we do not know that Shipman is unique. We know that he has killed more people than any other serial killer, yet identified, but we do not know how many others may remain hidden ... who can say with confidence that there are not other doctors, still unknown, who have killed in the past? Who can say there will be none in the future?*

When Sloane eventually closed the volumes, he was not thinking so much of Harold Shipman, but more of Doctor Sefton Cameron.

CHAPTER 23

Sloane put to one side the volumes of the Shipman report, stacking them like bricks. He had been reading them, hundreds of pages, cover to cover, in his hotel bedroom in Lulworth Cove. Now it was time for serious contemplation, an overview. Doodling, he listed names thrown by Pauline Hayter into the melting-pot. These were patients of Dr Cameron who, in addition to Mrs Hayter's mother, had supposedly died in suspicious circumstances. The Shipman report was a wake-up call not to be dismissed as a one-off, tragic phenomenon. Historically, doctors had enjoyed saintly status, their dedication to sustaining life beyond question. Shipman, single-handedly, had murdered that myth.

Out of the names submitted by Mrs Hayter, there must be at least one who had not been cremated, Sloane reasoned to himself. He would recommend that Lowen detail one of her team to look into that and see where it led them. One exhumation ought to be enough to establish whether the investigation in that direction should be extended.

He stood schoolteacher-style at one of the windows, hands clasped behind his back, watching winter tighten its grip, like a remorseless strangler, squeezing the life out of everything in sight. The spring-like weather of three days ago had been frozen out by icy blasts from Siberia. The rain-clouds had been chased off, true, but the sun carried little weight and was not to be trusted. It offered the warm-hand of friendship, but its heart was cold. Even through the glass, Sloane could feel its spiteful bite. Nature was a master of the optical illusion. The water in the cove appeared to have been stirred into a bubbling cauldron. The reality was that the foam was closer to ice-cubes than boiling water.

A couple, hurrying hand-in-hand down the narrow lane that sloped to the sea, turned his thoughts painfully, like a thumbscrew, to Lowen and their relationship. They had slept together only the once, after which Lowen had applied the brakes. 'Not so fast,' she had said. He acknowledged a certain validity in her contention that the investigation was the vehicle for their relationship and journey's end might leave them without anywhere further to go. 'Let's just see where it takes us,' she had said. Sloane had agreed to take his foot off the juice. Cruise control was an acceptable compromise for them both.

After a bar lunch in the hotel, he drove into Bournemouth. He had not even begun his Christmas shopping and it was about time he made a start. He also wanted to stop at the Carlton Hotel, on Bournemouth's East Cliff, to see what they were offering in their Christmas programme, which, he was hoping, might appeal to Lowen.

Sloane had just collected a brochure from the reception desk of the Carlton Hotel, when his mobile, which he had switched to discreet mode, vibrated in his overcoat pocket. It was Lowen.

'Where are you?' she asked.

He told her.

'I'm only ten minutes away, on my way back from Henley,' she said. 'Stay where you are and I'll join you for afternoon tea. Let's spoil ourselves.'

And that was how they came to be tucking into finger-licking sandwiches, cakes and biscuits in front of a roaring fire, discussing their respective day's work.

Lowen had not even finished her account of her visit to Lergen's golf club in Oxfordshire when a text message enjoined her to call Professor Hunter in forensics 'urgently'.

A look of electric expectancy crackled between them. They had the lounge to themselves, so Lowen made the call from her sumptuous leather armchair, without leaving the room.

'Something's turned up,' the professor began, in his tantalizing and pedestrian fashion.

'From the knife?' said Lowen, eagerly. She could hear her own heart beating. Her hands and feet were damp. The suspense spurred her pulse.

'No, from the gloves, actually, against all expectations.'

'The gloves!'

'A couple of things of interest.'

'How *interesting*?'

'Crucial, I suspect.'

Get on with it, man! she screamed to herself. Professor Hunter was a life-long devotee of amateur dramatics. Melodrama was made for him.

'Sweat, Inspector; tacky sweat.'

'You're losing me, Professor.'

'Sweat – you know, what you do on a hot summer's day, or when you run for a bus or train, or when you have an adrenaline surge.'

'Just what has this to do with the investigation, Professor?'

'Oh, everything. Sweat can dry and stain or freeze, but it doesn't disappear until washed away.'

'Are you saying you've found the remains of sweat inside the gloves?'

'Of course that's what I'm saying! Wasn't that obvious?'

Always histrionics! Always a song-and-dance routine. Never a straightforward report. Always we have to sit through a show.

But patience prevailed.

'Go on,' Lowen urged.

'The reason for the killer sweating is immaterial, though it's unlikely to have been due to overheating, considering the weather and temperature on the night of the crime.'

'And I doubt very much that he'd have run from the scene,' opined Lowen. 'He wouldn't have chanced drawing attention to himself at such a quiet time of night. True, he wouldn't have hung around, but there was no reason to run. No one else was out and about in that road or we'd have heard from them, I'm sure of that. House-to-house enquiries have been unproductive on that score. So we're left with an adrenaline surge.'

'Precisely, though, as I've stressed, the cause is inconsequential. The point is that, through DNA analysis, we should be able to isolate the killer from the rest of the world's population. We have retrieved enough DNA data to build a complete chemical profile. Match a suspect to that DNA photokit and bingo! Case closed! Good night, Vienna! Pop the champagne corks.' And then, almost as if he had forgotten something, he said with acrid nonchalance, 'None of the suspects – that's assuming you have some – owns a dog, by any chance?'

'A dog? Why?'

'Oh, there were a couple of fibres, virtually invisible to the naked eye, that we came across when one of the gloves was examined under the microscope. Further tests confirmed that the fibres are dog hairs. I'm going to send them off to Joy Halverston at Sacramento University in California. She's the world's number one animal DNA specialist.'

'Are you suggesting that it might be possible to match those hairs to the exact dog they've come from?'

'Not *suggesting*; it's entirely possible.'

'Has DNA dog profiling ever resulted in a successful criminal prosecution?'

'Absolutely.'

'In Britain?'

'Oh, yes. Four men in Yorkshire were convicted of murder in January 2004 with Joy Halverston's assistance. Her team matched fibres to a bull mastiff, making the vital connection with the killers. This was the first time such evidence was used in a criminal case in Britain. The odds of a possible mistake were calculated scientifically at five hundred million to one. All you'll need to do is add a modicum of circumstantial evidence to the science and you'll be home and dry.'

'It's always possible that the hairs could have come from a dog sniffing around after the gloves had been discarded, isn't it?' Lowen acted as devil's advocate.

'That's why it's fortunate there were human sweat stains to analyse from inside the gloves, so that the scientific evidence is overwhelming and without a flaw.'

'I'm out of breath just listening to you.'

'All in a day's work,' the professor added, with exaggerated casualness. 'Oh, before you go, one last thing about the killer the DNA indicates …'

'What's that?'

'I suggest you strike off all the men on your list of possibles.'

'What!'

'Oh, yes, your killer is a woman.' And then with a twinkle in eye and voice, 'Don't tell me you didn't know that already, Inspector.'

CHAPTER 24

The following day, Assistant Chief Constable Helen Cusack was chairing a mid-morning council-of-war meeting in her office at police headquarters. Present were Lowen, the two next senior members of her team, a representative from forensics, a superintendent from the uniform branch and the head of the external communications unit. Only one item was on the agenda: how to proceed in the wake of Professor Hunter's revelations. The meeting was also a chance for the top administrators of the force and the different branches to be briefed on the latest developments.

They sat at the round, mahogany table, reserved predominantly for mini-conferences of this nature and shut off from the main section of Cusack's office when not in use. Jugs of coffee and milk, plus a plate of biscuits, had already been delivered by the catering staff. A glass and a small bottle of sparkling water were provided at each place at the table, alongside yellow writing pads.

After opening the meeting and briefly explaining why she had called it, Cusack handed over to Lowen, who was mindful of the fact that she was the only person in the room conversant with the big picture. Consequently, she took a full hour to tell her story, even synoptically. No one interrupted her. When she had finished, there was at least a minute's silence while everything was absorbed and sorted in their heads.

Cusack kicked off the discussion. 'The detective work seems to have been solid and sound. It's apparent there have been many opportunities to go astray, but blunders have been avoided. The investigation has been far from straightforward, with numerous tangents and threads. Lines of inquiry have oscillated between suspects. From the outset, it was never going to be a one-dimensional case and it was further complicated by a national security issue that remains to be resolved definitively, but isn't a matter for us today. As with most complex murder inquiries these days, the breakthrough seems to have come through forensic science. My first question to DI Lowen is this: are you confident that we have the killer in the system?'

Twenty-four hours ago, Lowen would have answered unequivocally. Now she was not quite so adamant.

'I must admit that the DNA evidence, pointing to a woman, has rather thrown me,' she admitted.

'Are you saying that you don't have a woman among the possibles?' Cusack began her evaluation.

'No, I'm not saying that, but they weren't among the *probables*.'

'So it's quite likely that it could transpire you're well off target?'

'Not *likely*, but always possible, of course, but my gut tells me we're on the right track.'

'I'd prefer to hear about what your brain tells you.'

The tone was set. Cusack opened up the discussion to the others. No one's sensitivity was spared. The cut-and-thrust of the exchanges was healthy. Lowen always responded well to this kind of free-for-all, in which the meek were mauled.

The consensus was that Lowen should proceed with caution, gathering all the scientific evidence before rushing into the next positive move. Lowen was in general agreement with the strategy, though this did not mean she was prepared to 'sit, twiddling my thumbs, waiting for the killer to come knocking on my door'.

Samantha Knight, head of the external communications unit, wanted a steer on the spin that should be fed to the media.

'I still get calls every day about this case, especially from the local Press and regional TV,' she told them.

'It's your show,' said Cusack, motioning towards Lowen.

'I don't want it known, under any circumstances, that the murder weapon has been found,' Lowen said, peremptorily. 'If that became public knowledge, we'd have to move quicker than planned or desirable. The same applies to the DNA clues. A complete blackout is imperative for the time being.'

Heads nodded around the table in affirmation.

As the meeting dissolved, Cusack indicated that she wanted Lowen to stay behind for a few words in private.

'I'm glad you stayed with the case,' said Cusack, as soon as they were alone.

'Me, too,' Lowen confessed.

'Quite a change of heart.'

'I've come to realize I was being too hasty. There were bad vibes and mixed messages. I feared losing control and being used as a puppet, unsure of what really was going on around me, and possibly ending up as a scapegoat.'

'But it hasn't been like that?'

'It was a bit like that for a while.'

'Not now, though?'

'No, not at all.'

'And how are you getting along these days with your shadow, Mr Sloane?'

'Very well, in fact.'

'He's not getting in the way?'

'On the contrary, he's proving a useful ally.'

'It's my understanding he's been speaking most highly of you, too ... and in all the right places. All of a sudden we have quite a thriving mutual admiration society in our midst. My, my, who'd have thought it!'

Cusack's smile, just like a graphic photograph, was worth a thousand words.

CHAPTER 25

A condition of Harry Parkes's bail was that he continued to live at his home address and that he reported to the police twice a day. He was now in breach of that undertaking and magistrates issued a warrant for his arrest. The story of his disappearance appeared on the front page of the local evening newspaper, the *Daily Echo*, which told the facts straight. A couple of national tabloids, although devoting considerably fewer column inches to the narrative, spiced it up, congruous to the genre, both newspapers linking Parkes to Miss Dresden's violent death. 'Murder Suspect on the Run' was one of the sensational headlines.

By lunchtime of the day that the story appeared in the *Daily Echo*, the police had been contacted by the taxi driver who had driven Parkes to the railway station. Staff at the station vaguely recalled Parkes, but could not remember to which destination he bought a ticket. However, records of the ticket machine in the booking office revealed that twelve tickets were sold around the time Parkes had been dropped off at the station. Three of those tickets were for children at reduced fares. Five were returns to London, two were singles to Weymouth, and the remaining two were singles to Southampton and London respectively.

From this skeleton information, Lowen was able to make a plausible deduction, as opposed to an educated guess.

'I think we can exclude the people who travelled on return tickets,' Lowen said to Sloane, as they warmed themselves drinking cappuccinos in the Café Francais patisserie in Bournemouth town centre, while the rapidly approaching season of goodwill to all spat at them from the other side of the windows. 'If I'm right, what are we left with? He could have gone a few miles westward to Weymouth.'

'Which I somehow doubt,' Sloane chipped in.

'Alternatively, he went eastwards along the coast to Southampton, a sea port, a cosmopolitan social mix.'

'A better bet.'

'Or, finally, he went all the way to London.'

'The best bet of all.'

'That's my reckoning, too.'

'A big place, London.'

'If you want to find a needle, look in a haystack.'

After they had finished guffawing at Lowen's flawed, home-spun philosophy, Lowen remarked stoically, 'Not much more we can do about Parkes for now, except post him on the network as missing and wanted. He'll surface, one way or another, in the good old passage of time.'

As a result of the DNA profile, Lowen had subconsciously booted Parkes to the back-burner. Somewhat reluctantly, Lowen accepted that Parkes had become a non-runner in the murder stakes. Of course, his offences were still serious, but tracking him down was now not the priority it would have been without Professor Hunter's contribution. Parkes's file could descend the chain of command to be managed by a detective sergeant or even a detective constable.

After their coffee stop, Lowen and Sloane continued towards Christchurch for a little surreptitious snooping on Dr Cameron, well aware, though, that they must avoid anything too proactive that would breach the decision of the council-of-war meeting, chaired by Cusack. They knew from Carrington that Faye Mitchison did not own a dog. 'I like dogs,' Carrington had told Sloane. 'To be more accurate, I like *other people's* dogs, but I'd never allow one in my house. They're a nightmare in winter, padding through homes with muddy paws and shaking off the rain all over furniture and food. One canine blighter can knock off fifty grand from the value of a decent property, I kid you not. Dogs, as far as I'm concerned, are the last taboo.'

Now Lowen was pursuing the possibility that Cameron might own a dog and Faye Mitchison could have come into contact with it. The dog hairs were white, the reason why they would easily have been missed by the naked eye. The fibres, according to

Professor Hunter, were short and coarse. A large, long-haired dog was not indicated.

'Every doctor owns at least one pair of latex surgical gloves,' commented Lowen, adding meat to the bone of the burgeoning case against Cameron and his mistress.

'And the point you made about the hairs possibly having originated from a dog roaming around the service station site is a very cogent one, probably the most likely explanation.'

'So today's mission could be nothing more than an academic exercise; going through the motions and catching only pneumonia.'

'Without doing it, we'll never know.'

Sloane was right, of course, and Lowen acknowledged the fact by staying silent.

'What troubles me more is the inescapable fact that if Faye Mitchison did it, for whatever reason, then somehow Carrington is implicated, which I just can't take on board,' Sloane poured out his soul-searching. 'She couldn't have been in Corfe Castle killing Emily and taking Carrington his bedtime drink in Swanage at around the same time. If she's our woman, then Carrington's a liar. He's her alibi. There's a nasty smell that's finding its way to my nose.'

'He could be confused about the timescale, especially if he was tired and had had a few drinks at the bridge club.'

'Carrington doesn't make those kind of mistakes. Accuracy is part and parcel of his trade; *my* trade. If his account to me of events that evening is wrong, then it's deliberately so. It's not something I like thinking about.'

'Then don't, until you have to. It might not be necessary.'

They took the coastal route, a drive of only six miles through the upmarket, urban sprawl. Glimpses of the ocean qualified the cliff-top road for scenic status, though today the glimpses were fewer than usual because of the ugly weather. Even the Isle of Wight's jagged, white rocks – the unmistakable Needles – had been eclipsed in the poor visibility. The Channel was in such a rage that it gave a good impression of banging its head against the sea-wall, splitting itself open.

Cameron's house, close to the Priory and the quay, was built in the style of a miniature yacht club, with white flagpole, though no flag. Any fluttering ensign would have been blown away in seconds. A balcony facing seawards resembled the bridge of a galleon, while the front patio was constructed in the configuration of a sailing ship's deck, with rigging. All the houses in the crescent-shaped road were individually designed; none was more than thirty years old. Here was a cosy nesting ground of the local *nouveau riche*; property speculators, entrepreneurs and those who had come into money through inheritance or more dubious means.

'Not too many folk around here living on welfare,' Lowen made a social comment, as they drove past Cameron's luxurious refuge.

The wipers were as hypnotic as metronomes, flip-flapping in front of their eyes with mesmerizing monotony.

Lowen waited until they had rounded a bend and the Camerons' house was out of sight before pulling up and making a tight, slow U-turn. No gnashing gears. No rubber friction.

'You're going to get soaked,' said Lowen, with the concern of a love partner rather than a work colleague, as Sloane prepared to vacate the car.

'Got to be done,' he said.

Sloane burrowed as deeply as he could into his overcoat. Even so, within just a few strides, water from puddles had sloshed into his shoes, soaking his socks and freezing his feet. Rivulets of rain streamed down his face from his drenched hair, blurring his vision.

The script, a collaborative effort, was easy to follow.

Sloane rang the bell at the last house before the Camerons' residence. A woman, probably in her late fifties, opened the front door a few inches, not releasing the safety-chain.

'Yes?' she demanded shrilly, in a haughty manner that suggested tradesmen should use the side door and, even then, by appointment only.

'I'm sorry to disturb you,' Sloane began disingenuously.

'Then don't,' retorted the woman, in a ricochet reflex.

'I won't keep you a minute.'

'You won't keep me another second.'

The door would have been slammed in Sloane's face if he had not already prevented its closure with a well-trained foot that had taken considerable punishment in its time.

'I live down the road—'

'What number?' she cut him short. 'I've never seen you before. I know everyone who lives in this road.'

'I'm in the next road, to be accurate—'

'Which road?'

None of this catechism was legislated for in the script. The antidote had to be attack instead of defence.

'Look, I'm not here to exchange addresses, I've lost my dog and I'm desperate to find it. When I say it's my dog, it's really my daughter's. She'll be heartbroken if I don't have it back by the time she comes home.'

'What sort of dog is it?' The sharpness was only marginally blunted.

'A white poodle. I understand they have a white dog next door and I was wondering if ours had followed theirs, if you see what I mean.'

'No, I *don't* see what you mean. No one owns a dog either side of me. In fact, I don't know anyone around here with a dog. Is that all?'

'Yes. Thank you for your help.'

The door finally went where the woman had intended it to go a couple of minutes earlier.

Sloane then repeated the ruse at the house the other side of the Camerons' home. The outcome was similar, but without the verbal acid in his face.

With the rain cascading from him like a fountain, Sloane returned as quickly as possible to the shelter of the car.

'No dog,' he reported.

'But we do have a drowned rat.'

An hour later, Sloane was drying out in front of Lowen's fire as they browsed through Christmas hotel brochures.

'How about it?' he said.

'Not now,' she replied, mischievously misinterpreting the *double entendre*.

Jenny serviced the last customer of her shift. He was a pensioner and into domination and humiliation. She relieved him of a hundred pounds and excused herself while she deposited the money with the manageress of the massage parlour, a euphemism for sex emporium or brothel. Then she returned to the depressing little room to fasten a dog choke-chain around the customer's wrinkly neck. For the next ten minutes she led the naked client around the threadbare carpet like a panting dog on all fours, lashing him sporadically with a riding crop, for which he thanked her with grunts and groans of pleasure. Jenny was down to her underwear, which made her just about the most overdressed person in the building. After he had come – and then gone – she dressed, collected her cut of the earnings from her shift, and departed for home, saying, 'See you tomorrow, same time.'

As she slipped furtively through the side door that led into a dim, sleazy alley, she almost tripped over the manageress's white poodle, aptly named Dickhead.

Jenny was not her real name, of course. All the girls at the massage parlour had a working name. Sandra Rowlands, wife of the Reverend Simon Rowlands, was no exception.

What I've done and sacrificed for that bastard! she was thinking bitterly as cars splashed her stockings and fawn over-coat while she queued for the bus home. Now I'm working for one person only – myself. Everything for myself. He can go to hell, for all I care, which would be poetic justice for a clergyman!

Harry Parkes had an attic room in a bed-and-breakfast place in London's Pimlico. The room comprised a single bed, wardrobe, ceiling light without a shade, a bedside lamp that had blown, a cracked basin and a small black and white TV. All the furniture looked as if it had been bought secondhand, probably from bankrupt stock. A bathroom on the floor below had to be shared with the occupants of five other rooms. Breakfast – one frazzled egg, one cremated rasher of bacon and one deformed sausage – was served between 7.30 and 8.00. Burnt toast was the house speciality. Coffee and tea had the appearance and taste of a Victorian remedy for constipation. For these luxuries, he was paying sixty-five pounds a night – in advance; no cheques nor credit cards, which suited Parkes because he could use any name and there was no paper, plastic or electronic trails. The proprietor did not even smirk when he signed the register as Smith, giving a Northampton address.

Each day, he bought every national newspaper and assiduously scanned them for stories about himself. The text in two tabloids that reported his flight was accompanied by a photograph of himself, but in each case it was too small and distorted for him to feel in danger of being recognized at the boarding-house. At national level, he was stale news within twenty-four hours. He was safe now until his cash ran out.

Three times in one week Parkes used a bank card to draw out a total of £600 cash. Lowen soon heard about this from Parkes's bank.

'So I was right,' she commented to Sloane, alluding to her wager that Parkes had headed for London.

'What else have you learned?' asked Sloane.

'The withdrawals were made from different machines, but all within the Bloomsbury area.'

'So he's holed-up in one of the myriad private guest houses peppered throughout Bloomsbury or a B&B around Russell Square or King's Cross; that area's a forest of those kind of places. He's drawing out the cash to pay for his accommodation so we can't pinpoint his exact location.'

'I've already had copies of his photo wired to the Met and now it's just a question of waiting for him to make a mistake. If we can persuade the London *Evening Standard* to run a piece, he may be shopped by a public-spirited landlady, especially if he owes her money.'

Both Lowen and Sloane were underestimating their quarry, who had taken into account that the police would quickly hear about his withdrawals and would be charting the transactions on a map of London. They'll draw a circle and conclude that I must be somewhere within it, he said to himself with a confident smile, at least deriving pleasure from the game of hide-and-seek.

Whenever he needed cash, Parkes deliberately travelled outside of Pimlico in order to throw Lowen off his scent. He changed accommodation at least every two days. The battle of wits gave him a new reason for living, but it was not destined to last.

Christmas came. Lowen was seduced by the proposition of Christmas Day and Boxing Day at the Carlton Hotel. 'Only another murder or a confession to Miss Dresden's killing will keep me away,' she told Sloane. 'However, there's one important condition.'

'Which is?'

'We go Dutch.'

'No, this is my treat. It was my idea; my invitation.'

'No Dutch, no deal.'

'Put that way, I relent.'

It was a good Christmas for them both. They exchanged cards and presents in bed on Christmas morning; a lucky charm bracelet for Lowen, a gold pen for Sloane, inscribed with his initials. Both avoided cloying sentimentality in the choice of cards, playing safe with inoffensive humour.

They joined in the pagan festivities, pulling crackers at dinner and wearing paper hats. They dozed by a log fire in the lounge, went for bracing walks along the wind-swept cliff top, and took part in an all-morning treasure-hunt on Boxing Day. Many ghosts of past Christmases were exorcized in those two escapist days. For more years than Sloane cared to remember, he had been intimidated by the approach of Christmas. His memory was his worst enemy, having tortured him mercilessly with mental videos of Christmases in the halcyon days of his marriage. There had been no hiding place, except in the bottle. So his recent Christmases had been blind spots, marked only by the extent of the hangover. In contrast, Lowen had always volunteered for duty over the holiday period.

There was an element of trepidation for them both, like a couple embarking on their first flight, worried about how they would cope with any turbulence and the claustrophobic, sardine-tin ride. Knowing they could eject at any moment was no comfort. Resorting to a parachute-exit from this relationship would represent failure, not a lucky escape. Neither had room in their lives for any more negative milestones. But it was a success and they emerged from Christmas as survivors, refreshed and mentally invigorated, winners from a season responsible for more suicides and marriage break-ups than any other time of year. The ratchet of their relationship had turned a couple more notches, tightening it and bringing them inexorably closer.

*

Parkes was not so fortunate. Nearly all the small and cheap private guest-houses were closed for Christmas. After much tramping in the rain, he managed to find accommodation in the Tavistock Hotel for two nights. Eating Christmas dinner alone was no joy. The dances and carol concerts held no appeal for him, so for most of the time he locked himself in his room and watched TV, the cheerfulness of which, paradoxically, only magnified his depression. With his money rapidly running out and penury looming, he left the Tavistock Hotel on 27 December without checking-out, leaving behind his few meagre belongings. Purposefully, and with a sense of nemesis in his doomed step, he walked to Covent Garden tube station, where he threw himself in front of a Piccadilly Line train. No one had a chance to spoil his plan this time. Death was instantaneous and his bloody mess was someone else's problem.

Lowen heard about Parkes's suicide on the 28th. There was no suicide note. No one would ever know now if he had seen the lipstick insult on Miss Dresden's face. Awkward to the last gasp. Journalists had one collective question: 'Is the Emily Dresden investigation closed?' Lowen volunteered only a one-word answer: 'No.'

Midnight Mass on Christmas Eve and the Christmas morning family communion are traditionally the best attended services of the Christian calendar, rivalled only by Easter Sunday. Father Rowlands's sermon on Christmas Day was as traditional as the season itself – and almost a repeat of his homily the previous Christmas and the one before that.

'We are here to commemorate a very special birth,' he began in a sing-song monotone. 'When Jesus was born, so was our faith. And because we are celebrating that child in a manger in a humble stable, inevitably our thoughts focus on children and the family. Christmas is for the family, for togetherness, for sharing, for forgiving and starting afresh, wiping clean the slate and embarking on a new year with a Christian commitment to renewing one's faith. The Christian faith is founded on optimism and the belief that it is never too late to find God and to return to go, like in the popular board game of Monopoly; to have more throws of the dice and to make amends for previous follies and poor judgement.'

The one person the sermon was most aimed at – his own wife – was missing from the congregation. He had implored her to be there, in the front pew, as had always been her custom. 'After all, if the vicar's wife can't be bothered to listen to him, why should anyone else?' he had said, early in their marriage.

But this Christmas morning, she had told him, 'I've heard enough of your sanctimonious crap. You've got a bloody nerve to climb into that pulpit in front of those good people and preach to them, when God wouldn't give you houseroom, not even if he was looking for a janitor.'

Nevertheless, he had hoped she might change her mind.

'People will gossip if your pew is empty,' he had added, trying to pressure her.

'They certainly will if I get to talk to them first!' she had replied meaningfully.

While Simon Rowlands peddled his hypocrisy in the pulpit, his wife was imbibing the brandy that had been intended for the Christmas pudding. And, as the collection plates were being passed around in church, she was upstairs at home counting her secret cache of immoral earnings that would go towards feather-bedding the rebirth of her own life; seasonally topical, if outrageously irreverent.

No worse than her husband's duplicitous double life, she would have contended. And who could have argued with that? Only a hypocrite!

The Lergens put on a show of unity over the festive season for the benefit of their family and friends, who joined them for Christmas Eve drinks, lunch on Christmas Day and a noon cock-tail party at the golf club on Boxing Day. No one, not even their grown-up children, would have considered them any other than a mature married couple growing old happily and gracefully. During that period, to sustain appearances, Ernst and Greta slept together once again in the master bedroom, an experience that did not do anything towards bringing them closer together.

'Thank goodness that's over,' sighed Greta, after their children had departed on the 27th and all pretence could be stored away. 'Now the cold war can recommence.'

And before Ernst set off alone for the golf club that morning,

Greta said balefully, 'Did you get around to telling the children you're dying?'

'Dammit, woman! Don't you have a sinew of sensitivity in your ageing body?'

Unmoved, she replied clinically, 'You're the one who's insisted on no mawkish sentimentality about the prognosis. I've tried to encourage you to seek more opinions; to try anything; to go to America; to give alternative techniques in Switzerland a chance, but no, you've resigned yourself to a fate that maybe is of your own making. In short, you've given up. You've decided unilaterally you haven't anything worth living for. That's fine; that's your right. I get the message. But don't you think our children deserve to be enlightened, to avoid a death-bed shock for them?'

'I'm not going to burden them. They have their own lives to manage, without forever watching their father's clock, wondering at what time it will stop.'

'They'll never forgive me for not telling them.'

'Then tell. You don't respect any of my other wishes these days, so how come this one's sacrosanct?'

'Because it's probably your last.'

CHAPTER 26

The two hairs from a white dog were sufficient for Joy Halverston to complete a full DNA profile. Her report was e-mailed to Lowen on January 12th. This report subsequently became an appendage to Professor Hunter's analysis of the dried sweat extracted from the interior of the gloves.

Lowen was convinced the time had come for a return to a more proactive approach. 'We have to make things happen,' she said to Sloane that evening in the Dog and Duck, an attractive pub that was not frequented by other police officers from headquarters and there-fore the reason Lowen had chosen it for a rendezvous. 'This isn't going to be solved by information from a member of the public.'

'I agree,' said Sloane.

'So we have to prise open the case ourselves. We have to be the architects and engineers of the denouement.'

'One question. How?'

'For a start, the days of softly, softly catchee monkey are over.'

'But where's the monkey?'

'Already in the net.'

'You really think so?'

'I know so. We're missing something. No, I'll rephrase: *we've* missed something.'

'Fine, but what?'

'The motive.'

'Which is?'

Lowen threw up her arms. 'If it's not money, then more likely it was fear of being exposed over something.'

'Must have been a serious transgression.'

'Such as murder; mass murder.'

'Dr Cameron?'

'If he's done a fraction of what Mrs Hayter alleges, he must have the most compelling motive of all. Any observations?'

'Only repeats. We've no proof Cameron was aware Mrs Hayter had engaged a PI to investigate him.'

'She made enough threats. He'd have been expecting it. Having been alerted, he'd have been on his guard.'

'I pray you're wrong.'

'Because of the Carrington connection?'

Sloane nodded miserably.

'I guess there'll be waves in Whitehall.'

'A chain-reaction no less than a tidal wave.'

'I hope you won't be included in any washed-up flotsam.'

'Who knows. It's always hard to foresee the extent of damage in advance of cyclones. It's too late to even contemplate damage-limitation. Just run it, Joanne. Are you going for the exhumation of one of his recently buried patients?'

'I've thought about that and, firstly, I'd rather go at it through the back door.'

'How?'

'I want a surreptitious DNA test on Faye Mitchison. That's where you come in. Visit Carrington, ostensibly on your own cloak-and-dagger business, then bring me something back.'

'Such as?'

'A few locks of Mitchison's hair; that'll suffice.'

'And how the blazes do I manage that *surreptitiously*?'

'You use your ingenuity. Do your spook stuff; prove your worth. She must have a hairbrush. Knotted fibres will be tangled in it. Just lift a few tufts and hotfoot it back to me with them.'

'Just charge into her bedroom, saying, "It's OK, don't be alarmed, I'm only here to steal a little of your unwanted hair; that's the kind of freak I am. I'm into women's hair, though only the sort that's already parted company with the head. Don't be afraid, I'm harmless." '

Lowen waved away the sarcasm.

'You'll need to enlist Carrington's assistance.'

'Bad idea, Joanne, if he's involved in any way. How could I be sure he was giving me something of Mitchison's? He might palm me off with strands of his own hair, saying he'd pulled them from her hairbrush.'

'You'll have to organize it so that you do it.'

'And how do you propose I go about that?'

'You're supposed to be the Machiavellian one. You'll come up with something.'

Sloane drove to Carrington's house in Swanage that same afternoon, arriving just before four o'clock.

Carrington's expression was a facsimile of his thoughts: *what brings you here unannounced?*

The fact that Carrington had answered the door himself was a good indication that Mitchison was out.

'I'll detain you no longer than five or ten minutes,' Sloane promised.

'I'm not going anywhere,' said Carrington. 'Come in. Faye's gone into Bournemouth for lunch and then some shopping, but I can rustle up tea and biscuits.'

'Don't go to any trouble, Hugh, I won't be stopping. As I said, I'll be on my way in a few minutes.'

By now they were inside the house with the front door closed and Carrington about to guide Sloane towards the sitting-room.

'I'm glad your housekeeper's not in because it's going to make life much easier than if she'd been here.'

Carrington stopped and wheeled with such military precision and sharp click of heels that he might still have been in the army, leading by example on the parade ground.

'You're up to something, Mike, and I don't like the smell of it.'

Sloane went for the jugular. There was no other way. Deviousness was not an option.

'I want you to take me to your housekeeper's bedroom.'

With the speed of a camera's shutters, Carrington's face changed from friend to foe.

'Damned if I will!'

'I want you to show me her bedroom dressing-table,' Sloane continued unchecked, hating himself.

'For what reason?' Carrington's voice was now overflowing with disgust.

'She'll have a hairbrush and I want to take from it.'

'Take what?' Carrington demanded incredulously. 'Strands of her hair?'

'Nothing more.'

'This is absurd.'

'It's preferable to the alternative.'

'Which is?'

'Inspector Lowen will arrest her.'

'*Arrest!* This is getting out of hand, Mike. Sheer desperation, I'd say. I'm sure this cannot be justified.'

'If your housekeeper is arrested, the Press will soon get a whiff of it and she'll be subjected to considerable stress. This way, she can be eliminated without her and the Press ever knowing that she's been put under the microscope.'

'This whole business is becoming uglier by the day.'

'Let's get it over with, Hugh, it's a *fait accompli.*'

'It's nothing of the sort and you know it. For a start, I don't have to co-operate. Secondly, you don't have police powers. I'm the last person in this world you can take liberties with. I could force your Inspector Lowen to obtain a search-warrant and make her do it by the book.'

Carrington's reference to *your Inspector Lowen* was heavy with innuendo.

'Just who's side are you on, Hugh?'

'The side of rectitude.'

'Crap! You're no different from me, from any of us; you're on the side that pays you. Most of all, you're on the side that it pays you to be on.'

'That's insulting.'

'It's the truth.'

'Your class-complex is betraying you, Mike.'

'Class plays no part in my life; it's your hang-up.'

Carrington sighed wearily, resigning to attrition.

'This is the last personal favour I do for you, Mike.'

'Ernest, this *isn't* personal.'

'Excuse me if I don't take your word for that. Wait here. I'll see what I can do.'

Carrington prepared to mount the stairs, leaving Sloane in the inadequately lit hallway.

'I'll come with you,' Sloane said hastily. 'This is something I must do myself.'

A look of distaste distorted Carrington's imperious features, as if he had a mouthful of poison.

'You don't trust me, do you?' said Carrington, beyond belief.

'It's not that, Hugh. We have to be able to demonstrate that all evidence is free from contamination and that the chain of collection was unbroken. Everything must be transparent.'

'Waffle!'

'Please!'

Carrington shook his head disdainfully, then surrendered.

Five minutes later, Sloane was leaving the house with hairs of the suspect wrapped in tissue.

The manner in which the front door closed behind him was a statement in itself.

As Sloane gunned his car away from the house, so a Vauxhall Astra growled towards him up the steep drive from the main coastal road. As the cars passed each other, so the eyes of the drivers exchanged frosty recognition. If Faye Mitchison had returned just a few minutes earlier, the hair-poacher would have been caught picking the locks!

They had to wait another five days before Professor Hunter and his detective scientists had concluded beyond all doubt that the sweat stains in the white latex surgical gloves, discarded with the murder weapon, were *not* compatible with Faye Mitchison's DNA.

'My God, another deadend!' droned Lowen.

'The world's full of them, so don't start getting paranoid about it,' Sloane commiserated.

Lowen admitted, but only to Sloane, 'This has to be my lowest ebb.'

Sloane tried to console her with the cajoling thought, 'Every tide has its turn; a high always follows a low.'

Lowen's spirits were not immediately lifted. She had begun, unwisely, to pin most of her hopes on a scenario that embraced Faye Mitchison and Dr Sefton Cameron in a murderous liaison. Now that theory appeared in tatters, though fragments of it were still worthy of further examination, but the possibility of tying

Mitchison to the actual stabbing now seemed remote, if not hopeless. Carrington's indignation appeared justified and, in that respect, there was considerable fence-mending ahead for Sloane, with little prospect of returning their relationship to its previous dignified status.

Sloane's glib talk of ebbing and flowing tides of fortune was just a salve and dismissed by Lowen as nothing more than a slick sales pitch.

Yet within twenty-four hours, the tide *had* indeed turned.

And the investigation was back in full flow, with Lowen and Sloane carried along on a strong, new current of clues.

CHAPTER 27

L owen handed Sloane a single white sheet of A4 copier paper. It had been folded neatly three times and posted to Lowen the previous day in a white, self-sticking envelope. There were thirteen words on the piece of paper: *Did you know that Ernst Lergen is dying of cancer? Think about it.* There was no name nor address of the sender; no moniker of any kind. The postmark on the envelope evinced that the letter – if it qualified for such status – had been posted the previous day in the city of Oxford. The envelope had been addressed in capital letters with a ballpoint pen, while the message had been written on a word processor or computer.

'What do you make of this, Mike?'

Sloane read the note twice, then turned it over, like a ceramics expert checking the all-important manufacturer's backstamp of a piece of fine china, then casting his eyes over the envelope, as if hoovering it for evidence.

'How far's Oxford from Henley, would you say?'

'Twenty miles, thereabouts.'

'This tells us two things,' said Sloane, waving the letter as if it was an identity pennant. 'It has come from someone who knows the Lergens intimately. Even more importantly, it's from someone who is also privy to the connection between Ernst Lergen and the murder of Emily Dresden, or there's no point sending this. That really limits the field.'

'I didn't even confide in the secretary of the golf club the reasons for my questions,' said Lowen. 'Can it be true?'

'What?'

'That Lergen's dying.'

'He looked fit enough to me.'

'To me, too, though that doesn't mean much. I've seen some fit corpses in my time. What if he *is* dying, Mike? What relevance can it have to us? If he knows he's dying, surely he had even less reason to kill Dresden. There's nothing for him to gain.'

'*Less* than what? We haven't been able to establish any real motive for him to kill Emily.'

'Except the possibility that she was blackmailing him.'

'That's all it's ever been – a *possibility*; a hypothesis built on very shaky foundations. How can Lergen's medical condition conceivably help us? We both agreed – do you remember? – that we must have missed something of quintessential importance.'

'So?'

'Let's think about this: what *is* the consequence of Lergen dying?'

'I suppose his estate goes to his wife. The kids will get a slice.'

'But we don't *really* know, do we? We've only been looking at who stood to benefit from Emily's death. Maybe *that's* the mistake we've been making; looking down the wrong end of the tele-scope, so to speak, and not getting the proper picture; being concerned with the wrong last will and testament.'

'I'm not sure that I follow,' said Lowen, her frown sculpted from manic soul-searching.

'I'll explain on the way to Henley,' said Sloane, like someone who has just stumbled from the darkness into the light.

CHAPTER 28

Greta Lergen was not pleased to receive unexpected visitors, especially in the shape of Lowen and Sloane.

Conversely, Ernst Lergen greeted them as if they were old friends of the family.

The snappy, white-haired West Highland terrier, snarling at the feet of Mrs Lergen, accurately mirrored the likes and dislikes of its mistress.

'I didn't know you had a dog,' Lowen remarked casually, as she scuffed the soles of her shoes on the doormat.

'That's Charlie,' Ernst said cheerfully. 'He belongs to my wife. He's getting on a bit now; the old fella must be nine or ten.'

'He certainly knows how to make himself heard, but I don't recall hearing or seeing him when we were here before,' said Sloane, as if just making small-talk.

'He sleeps most of the day in his favourite snug spot at the rear of the house and his hearing's not what it used to be,' Ernst explained. 'He probably didn't hear you when you came calling last time.'

'I'm sure they haven't come all this way just to talk about Charlie and his senility,' said Greta, displaying disbelief in the apparent banality of the conversation. She had both hands on her hips in a pose of pained impatience, her persona one of hostility, shrouding her in an aura of cold inhospitality.

'They have less time to waste than we do, so it's up to them to set the tempo,' said Ernst, content for a public contest with his wife.

'In that case, I'll leave you three to it,' said Greta, preparing to walk away in a huff.

'I'd be obliged if you'd stay,' Lowen said, severely.

'And why?' Greta's piercing eyes drilled through Lowen's head with laser intensity.

'Because my questions mainly concern you.'

'*Me*! I don't see—'

'If you listen to the questions, you'll find out soon enough,' Ernst joined in icily.

'Of course, we don't have to do it here,' said Lowen, her meaning transparent.

'Let's all sit down and be civilized about this,' said Ernst, fluently taking charge. 'Leave your coats here.' He pointed to a coat and hat stand. 'Then we'll go into the lounge, sit down, have a coffee, and you two can fire away.'

Greta shot her husband a glance that symbolically killed him with a bullet to the brain that she doubted existed.

No point was reached when they were all settled. Lowen and Sloane declined drinks. Greta declined to sit, instead posturing at the white marble fireplace, lighting a cigarette with a bulky, coffee-table lighter. She puffed like a steam engine, without inhaling. Her free hand was as jumpy as a toad.

'If I may start with you, Mr Lergen, would you kindly tell me who benefits in your will in the event of your death?'

'That's a rather impertinent question,' Greta interjected, abrasively. Then to her husband, 'If I were you, I'd tell her to mind her own damned business.'

'But you're *not* me, dear.' The *dear* was uttered with the cut of a whiplash, rather than a caressing term of endearment. Relaxed and congenial – the antithesis of his wife – Ernst turned to Lowen to address the question. 'I'm happy to discuss the contents of my will with you. It's quite a simple one, really. I leave my estate – that is this house, my stock investments and money – to my wife. The boys get the business. In a nutshell, that's it.'

Greta drew more slowly on her cigarette now. Sloane noticed how composed she had suddenly become with her husband's answer.

'This is a very personal question, Mr Lergen, and, of course, you don't have to answer it,' Lowen continued pleasantly.

'Then don't,' decreed Mrs Lergen, pulling up the drawbridge again.

'What is the question?' Ernst once again overrode his wife.

'How is your health?'

'How do I look?'

'Fit, but looks, just like words, can lie.'

Ernst laughed heartily, while Greta scowled.

'Very true, so it might not surprise you too much to hear that I'm a dead man walking, as the Death Row saying goes.'

'We're all dying from the day we're born,' snapped Greta. 'Some more quickly than others; that's the only difference.'

'My wife is a very private person,' Ernst said apologetically. 'She prefers to keep our affairs within the four walls of the Lergen fortress. I'm dying of cancer. All escape routes have been exhausted. God willing, my exit isn't imminent, but it's not far off; there will be an acceleration in the deterioration process very soon.'

'I can't believe you're talking like this to strangers,' Greta gasped, exasperated. 'You might as well take out an advert in the announcements columns of *The Times*. Tell the whole frigging world!'

Charlie, the West Highland terrier, jumped into Lowen's lap, having decided that this was not an invasion. Animal instincts could not always be relied upon.

'His hair's coming out all over the place at the moment, just push him down,' said Ernst solicitously.

'I love animals,' replied Lowen. 'I don't mind a few dog hairs on me. They'll brush off easily enough.'

Sloane smiled slyly, thinking, *Nice one, Joanne!*

'You've told me about your will, as it stands,' Lowen went on quickly, not wanting to lose the momentum. 'Has this been a long-standing document?'

'In its present form?'

'Yes.'

'No.'

'When was it redrawn?'

'Only since Christmas.'

'Were there codicils, or was it completely done anew?'

'The latter.'

'Would you care to elaborate.'

'I think not,' Greta snapped.

'As my will stood before Christmas, my wife got sweet F.A.' said Ernst, flagrantly ignoring Greta's appeals.

'Shut up!' Greta now resorted to trenchant orders.

But Ernst was beyond the Rubicon. 'The business still went to my sons.'

'But not your estate and other assets?'

'No.'

'So who would have benefited, instead of your wife, before the post-Christmas version?'

'Emily Dresden.' Ernst did not even blink. Did not miss a beat. Triumph shone in his eyes. Now he was dead man taunting.

For a few seconds, not another word was spoken. The scene mimicked that of a theatre drama when all the actors on stage have forgotten their lines simultaneously. However, rather than embarrassed, Ernst was buoyed with belligerence.

'Bastard! You bastard!' Greta shattered the silence with such ferocity that Sloane prepared to spring into action, fearing that Mrs Lergen was about to attack her husband physically.

'Did your wife know about the content of the earlier will?' Somehow Lowen managed tunnel focus, blocking out Greta.

'She found out about it, didn't you, *dear*?' He turned his head to meet the cold steel of his wife's stare.

'I came across a copy.' Some of Greta's outrage had subsided.

'Yes, *dear*, you were going through my things while I was out, if I recall correctly.'

'Damned lucky for me I did, too, or I'd never have known about your treachery.'

'Did you confront your husband about it?' Now Lowen targeted Greta.

'What do you think?'

'Is that a yes?'

'Talk with my husband. I want no part of this.' Greta stubbed out her cigarette in a pique, as if squashing three maggots. As she made for the door haughtily, so Lowen blocked her path, having tipped the dog from her lap.

'Out of my way,' Greta exhorted, with spume around her mouth like a rabid dog.

'Not so fast,' Lowen warned, levelly, continuing to obstruct physically. 'While Emily Dresden was alive, you stood to lose everything and you were fully aware of that.'

'Let me out of here, you're imprisoning me in my own home.'

And then to her husband, 'Do something for me for once in your rotten life.'

Ernst remained muted and motionless.

'Miss Dresden had to die before your husband. You knew he was dying, so something had to be done quickly. If your husband died first, all his estate would go to Miss Dresden and you had no way of knowing what provision she had made in her will – or, indeed, if she had made one at all. In all probability, the money and property of your husband would be lost to you forever. That was a prospect you couldn't live with. Nor could you allow Emily Dresden to live with it.'

A suffusion of evil-serenity had suddenly settled over Greta.

'It's flawed,' she stated, with a certainty born out of innate arrogance.

'What is?'

'Your summation. You know as well as I do that I would have mounted a successful challenge to the will. A husband can't in law get away with cheating on his wife like that these days. I've been a good and faithful wife. I've given him the support to build his business and I've managed the home and reared the children. I would win my entitlement.'

'It's not that straightforward, and you know it. Your husband is of sound mind.'

'That's *your* opinion!'

'A last will and testament is a legally binding document and is taken seriously by the courts. It is not easily revoked and even if it was, it might be on ice for years while the legal battle raged.'

'I'd win in the end.'

'But you couldn't wait. However, there was more to it than that.'

'Oh, yes?'

'Yes. You couldn't abide the prospect of having to plead in public for your share of your husband's wealth, of having your family's dirty linen aired in the courts and then in the newspapers. You couldn't allow your friends to discover that, despite all the veneer, your marriage was a sham and your husband regretted not having married the sweetheart from his past; a woman's shadow has stalked you every step of your shallow marriage. That, more than anything, was the reason you murdered Emily Dresden.'

Greta Lergen rocked on her heels as she laughed and guffawed; a roar straight out of the special effects department.

'You really think I'd stoop so low as to bother killing that whore?'

Lowen and Sloane exchanged a telepathic message that read, *Use of word whore noted!*

'We shall prove it.'

'You're forgetting that I was in London at the theatre.'

'How did you purchase your theatre ticket?'

'By credit card. American Express. It's itemized on my account.'

'Did you carry out the transaction at the box-office?'

'No, by phone.'

'On *the* Saturday?'

'No, about a couple of weeks earlier.'

Premeditation. Lowen filed the thought.

'I collected the ticket from the box-office about half an hour before curtain-up, proof that I was there.'

'But not proof that you stayed for the show. After picking up the ticket, you had plenty of time to drive to Dorset, reaching Corfe Castle well before midnight.'

'And how did I know about *that woman's* routine?'

'You probably did some dummy runs.'

'*Probably*! Is that what you're basing this slanderous allegation on, sheer speculation?'

'*Speculation* will not come into it.'

'What will, then?'

'You'll find out soon enough.'

'You're bluffing. I can tell you everything about the show.'

'I don't doubt you've seen it, but not on the evening that Miss Dresden died. You knew your husband would have plenty to drink at the golf club party and would go to bed early, therefore not being aware of the time you returned. You also guessed, perfectly correctly, that we would be interested only in your husband's alibi and trying to verify his movements; that was sound psychology on your behalf.'

'Am I supposed to be flattered?'

'Have you ever stopped at the Winchester service station?'

Greta was a competent actress, but not in the Hollywood

class, and her eyes gave her away as surely as a traitor's testimony.

'I might have done,' she said hesitantly. Recovering, she added, 'I don't know when. Not recently.'

'Do you own a pair of white latex gloves?'

'No.'

Too quick, too desperate.

'Did you kill Miss Dresden?'

'Of course not!'

Lowen acted on impulse. 'I'm going to arrest you.'

'Arrest *me*! What for?'

'On suspicion of murder.'

'You're barmy! You'll lose your job for this.'

'That's my risk.'

'You can count on that!'

Sloane looked almost as astonished as Greta Lergen.

Paradoxically, the most unfazed person in the room was Ernst.

'Ernst!' Greta summoned dictatorially. 'Get our solicitor Joseph Reichert. Get him here immediately. He'll sort out these cowboys.' The heat from her mouth burned like a branding-iron.

'Your husband's perfectly at liberty to call your solicitor, but it's pointless to have him come here.'

'And why is that?' There was something jeering about Greta's question.

'Because you won't be here.'

'You think you're going to snatch me from my own home, just like *that*, like a kidnapper?' Greta snapped her fingers.

'Yes, just like *that*!' Lowen's reply was toneless but uncompromising.

'Are you just going to sit there and allow these imbeciles to cart me off, as if they're dealing with a working-class halfwit?' Now she played the *grande châtelaine*, trying snobbery as a weapon.

'You're old and big enough to look after yourself,' Ernst responded, with a mixture of irony and derision.

Ernst did not even condescend to leave his chair when his wife was led away.

'Greta will show you the way out,' he said, symbolically leaving it to his wife to close the door on her future, while his own life's door remained barely ajar.

As an afterthought, Lowen returned to the sitting-room to scoop up Charlie.

'Mustn't forget the star witness,' she said.

CHAPTER 29

Sloane and Lowen did not speak to one another throughout the stormy, two-hour drive to Dorset.

Greta Lergen, sitting alongside Sloane in the back of the car, was allowed to cuddle her dog.

'What are they doing to us, my pet?' Greta kept murmuring woefully to her pooch. 'I won't let them hurt you. They'll pay for this. My God, we're going to make some money out of this for wrongful arrest.'

Just before they approached the periphery of the Bournemouth/Poole conurbation, Charlie leapt from his mistress on to Sloane, promptly peeing all over him.

'Good boy!' Greta praised her dog enthusiastically, clapping with delight. 'You certainly know where to do it. If you feel the urge for something messier, feel free. No need to wait for walkies.'

Lowen smiled into the driving-mirror. 'Perfect timing,' she said, bewildering Greta yet again. 'You *really are* a good boy, Charlie.' Continuing to address the dog, Lowen said, 'As soon as we reach Poole police station we'll get my colleague's pee-soaked clothes to the forensic lab and we'll reward you with a drink – and a haircut!'

Greta was really beginning to fear that she had been abducted by a pair of psychos.

'You're both as loony as one another!' Greta exclaimed, seething.

The talk about Charlie and forensics did not alert Greta to danger. On the contrary, it served only to enhance her belief that the police were whistling in the wind.

Before setting off from Henley, Lowen had spoken with her

chief constable, when it was agreed that Mrs Lergen should be processed at Poole police station.

Greta, true to form, made a scene when she was separated from her dog. By the time she had been booked-in and locked alone in a cell, where she continued screaming abuse in the argot of the *demi-monde*, a betrayal of her breeding, Sloane's clothes had dried.

Detectives in the pool held their noses as Lowen and Sloane entered, Sloane sheepishly.

'Will someone take off his trousers for my friend!' Lowen said playfully. 'He's in need.'

One of the detectives, who was about the same size as Sloane, fetched a pair of tracksuit bottoms from his locker. Giving them to Sloane, he said, 'Next time you get caught short, give another nick the pleasure of your company, OK.'

The laughs all round were in the spirit of locker-room humour, devoid of malice.

Lowen then took Sloane for a drink and a sandwich in the canteen, their first opportunity for a private powwow since the arrest was made.

'Wasn't that a shade impulsive?' said Sloane, more in admiration than criticism. 'I didn't expect such a positive strike today.'

'Neither did I. You're right, I did act on impulse. I decided, because of the way it went – her answers, attitude and the appearance, like a rabbit out of a hat, of a white dog with short, coarse hair – to push it; to push my luck, if you like, and, most of all, to maintain the momentum. A calculated gamble. In for a penny, in for a pound. But I tell you this, we've got her, Mike. She's going down as surely as if she'd been christened *Titanic*.'

'I'm sure you're right, but why the rush?'

'I wanted her in custody before applying for a search-warrant, something I've already set in motion. It was imperative to prevent her from doing a runner.'

'Do you really think she would have?'

'I wasn't prepared to take the chance, but, yes, I think she'd have taken off. She has the money to give us the run-around if she's on the loose. Of course we'd get her in the end, but it might be a long haul. There were good reasons for an immediate arrest and also to delay. The scales were evenly balanced, so I trusted my instinct. You pays your money and takes your choice. Now for the confrontation and pyrotechnics.'

During the formal interview that followed, in the presence of the Lergens' lawyer, Joseph Reichert, Greta said, her voice now almost caressing rather than barbed, 'Are you really intimating that I drove all the way to Corfe Castle to stab that woman? Would not someone in my position, if so inclined, be much more likely to pay someone else to do the dirty work? You know, a hired gun; I think that's the common term.'

'I doubt whether you'd know such people,' Lowen replied equably. 'Certainly I don't believe you'd trust a stranger with such a task that would forever give him a stranglehold over you. You're a control freak.'

'I'm no such thing!' Even in this situation, her whole being was perfumed with affluence.

'I suggest you don't hire home help because you couldn't entrust even the most basic domestic chore to someone else?'

'I don't employ staff because I'm prudent.'

'But the main reason for killing Emily Dresden personally was your raw hatred for the woman whom you considered had cast a long shadow over your entire marriage. You wanted to see her face. You wanted to look into her terrified eyes and stare into her soul at the moment of pitiless retribution. It was worth all the risks you were taking, which weren't many. You're not known in Corfe Castle; there was almost zero chance of your being seen at that time of night, in winter, at such a remote spot; even if seen, no one would have recognized you. No doubt you parked your car well away from the church. On the way home, you stopped at the Winchester service station to dispose of the weapon and the gloves you'd worn. You surmised correctly that it would be your husband's alibi that we'd be testing. By providing him with an alibi, giving the time of your return from the theatre at about twelve-thirty, you were, in fact, absolving yourself, not him. Clever.'

Reichert, who until now had remained silent, tapped a silver pen on the table and held up a podgy hand adorned with ornate rings.

'As a story-teller – or should I say fabulist? – you have few peers, Inspector,' he began owlishly, the lenses of his glasses so large that he appeared to be looking through portholes. 'But I'm a busy man. My client is a busy lady. We have no space for daytime entertainment. Could we please have some facts. Have you anything – *anything at all* – that places my client at the scene of the crime at the material time; clues that connect her to the killing?'

'We shall have.'

'You mean you've arrested Mrs Lergen while you're still trawling?'

'No, I mean we already have the evidence. I'm confident the lab reports on DNA profiling will close the case for us. Perhaps your client would care to assist by agreeing to provide blood or urine samples?'

Reichert and Greta Lergen eyeballed one another. For the first time since her arrest, Greta appeared unnerved. Reichert whispered in her ear. She nodded. He then said, 'OK, Inspector, level with me. What have you got?' At a stroke, he had gone in style from City trader to secondhand car dealer.

'We have sweat stains from inside gloves found abandoned with the bloodstained murder weapon and white dog hairs, also from the gloves. The stains have been sufficient for forensics to produce a perfect DNA profile. The blood on the knife has been matched to the victim.'

Lowen then explained about Joy Halverston's work in California, adding, 'Your dog, Mrs Lergen, obliged by urinating all over my colleague, much to your amusement. Charlie also left hairs on me and the dog is in our possession for further tests. We are in the process of applying for a search-warrant so that we can take away such belongings of yours as a hairbrush that will enable our scientists to compare your DNA with the sweat stains. In the meantime, we're going to hold on to you because I have a feeling you won't be going anywhere except to gaol.'

'Don't say another word,' Reichert instructed his client. 'Don't make their job any easier for them. They're the ones who have to do all the proving.'

Everyone in that room recognized the shift in the balance of power.

CHAPTER 30

Next morning, Ernst Lergen welcomed Lowen and her team, plus Sloane, as if greeting his golfing chums.

After Lowen had produced the search-warrant, Ernst said agreeably, 'I understand. Take all the time you need. I'll give you the grand tour. It's probably going to be thirsty work for you, so I'll go to the kitchen first to prepare some hospitality.'

The search lasted most of the day. During a coffee-break, Sloane asked Ernst how much he was aware of Emily's professional career in recent years.

Uncomfortably, he replied, 'She told me more than she should have, I guess, though she never went into specific cases she was working on, but, yes, I did know she had some kind of minor role with the spooks: I believe that's the argot for it. She was an honourable lady and achieved a lot from a very hard introduction into this world. She had a brutal beginning and a violent end. She deserved better; much better. And it could have been so different.' He watched birds winging past the window as faintly as his fluttering memories.

'Did you ever discuss her work with your wife?'

'Good gracious me, no!'

'Was there any way she could have learned about Emily's clandestine activity?'

Ernst pondered over this with a faraway expression. 'Emily was once or twice a shade indiscreet in letters to me, although she often used semi-code when mentioning delicate matters and they went to my office. That was before we moved to England. You didn't need to be a professional code-breaker to get the message. Greta could have read those letters. She had a free run of my publishing house.'

Just before they withdrew from the Lergens' residence, Sloane said to Ernst casually, 'We're grateful to you for the note. Without that, we would never have seen the light.' It was a shot in the dark.

Ernst blushed, shame-faced.

'It *was* you who sent me an anonymous letter, wasn't it?' asked Lowen, catching on and catching up.

Ernst thought hard for a moment, before answering, 'I suspected she'd done it, though I have no proof; none whatsoever. I couldn't allow her to get away with it, now could I? I let down Emily once before. I couldn't do it again. I owed her, big-time. I owe Greta nothing.'

The repressed anger in his voice was matched by the savagery in his eyes.

Lowen was interested in the reason for Sloane's questions to Ernst Lergen about Emily Dresden's Intelligence career and she raised it with him during the return journey.

'It answers the riddle of the lipstick graffiti daubed on Emily's forehead – MOTHER WHORE! All the time we've been thinking it doesn't fit because Emily never had children, but we've been thrown off kilter by thoughts of the wrong kind of mother. Lateral thinking was called for: *M for Mother* as in British Secret Service parlance, the world of James Bond and John Le Carre's Smiley – another diversion.'

'Well put together, Batman!'

Professor Hunter and his forensic scientists worked day and night on objects removed from the Lergens' residence, particularly Greta's hairbrush and lipstick. Through molecular biology and the known double helix structure of DNA, the chemical of which genes are made, genetic fingerprinting linked Greta Lergen conclusively to the crime.

Meanwhile, samples of Charlie's hair and the trousers on which the dog had urinated were despatched by air courier to Joy Halverston in California. Even before Halverston's positive findings were relayed to Lowen in England, Greta Lergen was charged with murder. She entered a formal plea of 'Not Guilty' and was held in custody awaiting trial at Winchester Crown Court.

Inquiries continued into the conduct of Dr Sefton Cameron.

Two weeks after Mrs Lergen's arraignment, the remains of a Margaret Porter were exhumed. Mrs Porter had been a patient of Dr Cameron for ten years. She had died ostensibly of pneumonia, three months after codicils to her will made her doctor a substantial beneficiary. She was eighty-eight years of age at death. After diagnosing pneumonia, Dr Cameron prescribed antibiotics and also Roxanol, liquid morphine to alleviate the severe chest pain. No inquest had been deemed necessary.

After exhumation, the post-mortem examination was performed by Home Office pathologist Professor Martin Tremaine. The outcome? Margaret Porter had died from natural causes. There had been acute congestion of her lungs and the samples of morphine in her body at the time of death were consistent with a safe dose. Lowen, after consulting her chief constable and the Crown Prosecution Service, decided that there were no grounds for further police inquiries.

The General Medical Council, however, charged Dr Cameron with serious professional misconduct and, after lengthy hearings, he was struck off.

Cameron's wife sued for divorce. The disgraced doctor and his mistress, Faye Mitchison, set up home together in Brighton. Sloane and Carrington never spoke to one another again.

Sandra Rowlands left her husband, Simon, after he gambled once too often, this time stealing much of the money collected from the bumper Easter Sunday congregations. Ironically, Father Rowlands was exposed by his new church verger, who had replaced the late Harry Parkes, whose perversion might never have been uncovered without that fateful November night when Miss Dresden caught the last bus to the grave.

Sandra Rowlands took their children with her to Manchester, capital of the north, where she rented a one-bedroomed basement flat in which cockroaches were asserting squatters' rights. Within days, she was advertising her visiting massage and escort service. Six months later, she moved with her children into a luxury apartment in a newly, custom-built block of flats. By then, the children were pupils at a private school that boasted not only of its academic excellence, but of its tradition for 'turning out young ladies and gentlemen'. Blasphemously, Sandra marvelled at God's mysterious ways of working.

As for Greta Lergen, she maintained her innocence throughout her trial, which proved a platform for highlighting the continuing scandal of Norway's 'whore children', putting on a performance that even Lowen had to agree grudgingly was worthy of an Oscar for Best Actress. The jurors were enthralled by the entertainment and spent five days deliberating over their verdict. Ultimately, science won over theatre. A ten-two majority guilty verdict was returned and Greta Lergen was taken away in handcuffs to begin a life sentence, beaten by her own sweat and the dog over which she had doted. The hair of the dog would be her lasting hangover, instead of its cure.

Ernst Lergen was not there to witness his wife's nadir. By then, he had already joined Emily Dresden.

After Mrs Lergen had been charged, Sloane was recalled to London. Everyone in high places had breathed a sigh of relief. There was much verbal back-slapping, though Sloane and Lowen were the last to feel the reverberations of relief.

Sloane had delayed his return by twenty-four hours so that he and Lowen could dine together in a private celebration. This was the night they had both been secretly dreading for days. Hanging in the air throughout the evening was a threatening black cloud, not giving a clue as to which way it would be blown.

It was Sloane who had finally articulated the question gnawing away in both their heads, and then only after two bottles of wine. 'Is this the end or merely the end of the beginning?'

'I resented your presence,' admitted Lowen, with all the forthrightness that is generated by a good grape. 'That changed and I appreciated your contribution and companionship. And now ...'

'Yes?'

'I regret that you have to go.'

'But at least it doesn't have to be a final farewell.'

'Then let's not make it one.'

They kept in touch by phone and text every day after that – and were together in Winchester for the seven-week trial.

One outstanding mystery concerned the fate of Miss Dresden's mobile phone.

'I doubt whether we'll ever know for certain,' Lowen opined to Sloane during the lunch-break on the first day of the trial. 'My guess is that Mrs Lergen stole the mobile and made the call to her husband's cell phone, without speaking, simply allowing the call to be logged with the network supplier. She probably discarded the phone in a place where it would be found quite quickly.'

'Intending to incriminate her husband,' Sloane followed Lowen's drift. 'What a sweetheart!'

'The scaring thing is that it could so easily have worked. You see, I'm sure it was picked up – but by someone who decided to pocket it, possibly to trade it on the black market. Recycling stolen cell phones is big business. Mrs Lergen's luck ran out.'

'And her husband turned the scales of justice with that note to you.'

'And poetic justice was done!'

The morning after the verdict, they woke up alongside one another in a Winchester hotel, their heads throbbing.

'Only one thing for it,' said Sloane.

'What's that?' groaned Lowen.

'The hair of the dog, of course!'

NEATH PORT TALBOT

WITHDRAWN

FROM

CIRCULATION

LIBRARIES